THE TWO SIDE...

The weapons could ..., blackmail, bribery, betrayal. It didn't matter. All that mattered was the destruction of your enemy and the survival of yourself.

That was the way Russell Thurston, FBI district chief, played the game.

That was the way Anthony Gardella, Mafia *capo*, played it, too.

Caught between them was an honest cop named Christopher Wade.

And as both men sank their hooks deeper and deeper into him, using every weapon at their command, while the murder count mounted and the chances of keeping clean went down, Wade knew he had to make a choice before he was torn apart....

SWEETHEART

SWEETHEART

A Novel of Revenge

Andrew Coburn

AN ONYX BOOK

NEW AMERICAN LIBRARY

PUBLISHER'S NOTE

This novel is a work of fiction. Names, characters, places, and incidents either are the product of the author's imagination or are used fictitiously, and any resemblance to actual persons, living or dead, events, or locales is entirely coincidental.

NAL BOOKS ARE AVAILABLE AT QUANTITY DISCOUNTS
WHEN USED TO PROMOTE PRODUCTS OR SERVICES.
FOR INFORMATION PLEASE WRITE TO PREMIUM MARKETING DIVISION,
NEW AMERICAN LIBRARY, 1633 BROADWAY,
NEW YORK, NEW YORK 10019.

Copyright © 1985 by Andrew Coburn

This is an authorized reprint of a hardcover edition published by Macmillan Publishing Company.

SIGNET, SIGNET CLASSIC, MENTOR, ONYX, PLUME, MERIDIAN AND NAL BOOKS are published by New American Library, 1633 Broadway, New York, New York 10019

First Onyx Printing, November, 1986

1 2 3 4 5 6 7 8 9

PRINTED IN THE UNITED STATES OF AMERICA

For my wife,
Casey Coburn, and our brood,
Cathleen, Krista, Lisa,
and Heather

Acknowledgments

Ignatius Piscitello, the late Carl Velecca and Don Kiley, Mary Ellen Evans, Captain Joe Fitzpatrick, Norma Nathan, Ned Chase, Rosemary Ford, Peter Grose, Rose Moudis, and Peter Skolnik, for help past and present.

1

I⟨T WAS⟩ the heart of the winter in the western part of Massachusetts when two ski-masked youths, smelling of the hide and dung of cows, funneled through the bitter night and invaded the farmhouse of Santo and Rosalie Gardella. They were a proud and handsome couple in their eighties, with a youthful vigor that belied their age. Santo Gardella still had a wave in his white fluff of hair, and his wife was almost as trim as she had been as a young woman. Three nights ago, under a comforter of warm colors, they had made love. Now they stood threatened.

"That's all we have," Santo Gardella said, spreading fifty-three dollars on the table. He had come to the United States at age eight and spoke English without an accent. His wife, who had a slight one, said in an honest voice, "We swear to you."

The youths sweated in their masks. The wood stove in the next room pounded heat into the kitchen, and the heat clawed at their clothes, melted the mess on their boots. They were brothers, and the sockets of their identical blue eyes were punched deep. They were quick of hand if not of mind, their weapons the raw knuckles of their fists. The bigger brother said, "Where's it hid?"

"Don't make us ask twice," the shorter one said, his nose leaking through his mask.

Everyone in the rural town believed, correctly, that the Gardellas had money. The brothers believed, incorrectly, that it was squirreled away in the house. "Liar!" the bigger brother said when Santo Gardella tried to convince them of the truth, and the smaller brother spewed obscenities, mostly ethnic. The old man shot an arm around his wife and turned his face to hers with a helplessness that seemed to mock every year of his life, all but twenty married to her.

"They're going to hurt us," he murmured, but she already knew that. Her eyes stretched up to his. Each wanted to protect the other.

"Her first," the bigger brother said, instantly pleased with his decision. " 'Less you say quick where it's at."

The other one, breathing through his mouth, said, "That old stove in there must be plenty hot."

"Do it!"

The old man lunged. He never had a chance. The bigger brother had the kick of a horse in each fist. The old woman had no chance either. The smaller brother tore at her hair and spun her toward the stove.

Neighbors heard nothing, there was no way they could. The nearest of them lived a half-mile away. Some thirty minutes later, however, a man named Silas Rogers chugged along in his pickup truck and saw fire clutching an upper window. In the moonlit night he also saw two youths scrambling into a Thunderbird, rusted and shattered at the edges.

———

Chunks of cloud filled the early morning sky, and the wind whistled over the small farmhouse, which stood shattered from the fire. The black remains of the roof gave off wisps of smoke. The cold air was acrid. A crowd had arrived, mostly in pickups and vans, but they kept a respectful distance, faces sharp with a mixture of curiosity and fear. An hour earlier an ambulance had taken away the bodies. Victims of a murderous assault, mostly fists and feet, according to the quick eye of the medical examiner.

Detective Lieutenant Christopher Wade of the state police had been summoned in from a day off. He arrived in an unmarked car and was greeted by a trooper named Denton and a local cop named Hunkins. Placing his back to the wind, Lieutenant Wade said, "Was the motive robbery?"

"Seems that way. Place was ransacked." Trooper Denton tightened his fur-lined gloves. "We've got what you might call a witness."

Officer Hunkins, wearing a fur cap and a mackinaw, interrupted. "They sat the old woman on the wood stove and fried her ass. Can you imagine that?"

Lieutenant Wade hiked the collar of his dark overcoat. He had a lean and faintly handsome face, deepset greenish-gray eyes of a somewhat somber cast, and a rangy hard-muscled frame, which the quick cut of his coat accentuated. His terse yet unhurried manner made him seem controlled at all times, though at the moment he was wincing inside. Homicides of the savage sort never ceased to sicken him, and more so when a woman was a victim. It seemed a direct threat to his own wife and daughters. He said to Trooper Denton, "What witness?"

"Man named Rogers."

"Silas Rogers," Hunkins butted in. "He was driving by and saw the fire and two guys running to a car. Too dark to see their faces. This was like ten o'clock."

"There was a moon," Wade said. "He must've made out the car."

"Says he didn't." Hunkins lowered the earflaps of

his cap. His face was bluntly shaped, like the badge pinned to his mackinaw.

"He still might've recognized them," Wade said. "Maybe by their clothes."

"He was more interested in sounding the alarm. Good thing he did, otherwise there wouldn't be a house standing there now." Branches creaked in the wind, as if the nearby trees were full of doors. "Those suckers, you know, were stupid. They started the fire upstairs, and it never did get down. I found the Gardellas the way they left them. Turned my stomach!"

Wade shifted his eyes, as if from a disturbing glimpse of himself in some inner mirror. His last murder case, three towns away, involved the rape and strangulation of a child. There were no witnesses and not enough evidence to convict the man Wade knew was responsible, and he had watched the man walk.

With a swift glance at Trooper Denton, he said, "Where's the witness?"

Hunkins answered. "Home. I told him to stay there."

"What's he like?"

"Old Yankee, tight-mouthed, you know the type."

"The type that keeps to himself?"

Hunkins shrugged. "What are you thinking?"

"I'm thinking he might've seen more than he let on. Possible, isn't it?"

Hunkins shrugged again. "Hell, I don't know. That's hard to tell. Hey!" he said suddenly as some of the curious began venturing onto the gray frozen ground of the front yard, bare except for a few fierce patches of ice. "What the hell do they think they're doing!" With the flourish of an arm, he stomped toward them.

"Takes over, doesn't he?" Wade said from the side of his mouth and moved toward the house, Trooper Denton following. The smell of the damage was rank. Fire fighters had battered back the storm door nearly off its hinges. The inner door stood open a crack. Wade paused on the middle step and shivered. "I don't like winter, do you, Denton?"

"I try not to think about it, sir."

"Most murders are in warm weather. Suicides are for the cold. Nothing growing, nothing coming. More nosebleeds in the winter than the summer, did you know that?"

"No, sir, I didn't."

"Statistical fact. What did *you* think of the witness?"

"Scared out of his wits," the trooper said. "He wouldn't talk to me, only to Hunkins."

"Why waste time?" Wade said, stepping up and reaching for the door. "We'll give him a polygraph."

"Sir, if you go in there you're going to ruin your shoes and freeze your feet. The floors are soaked."

"Tell me about it," Wade said and went in, nearly slipping where the water had iced over near the threshold. There was blood in the water that puddled the kitchen and traces of more in the next room, where furniture was broken. The wood stove was hot, still pumping heat.

Lieutenant Wade could not take his eyes off the stove.

————

Rita Gardella O'Dea came out of the ocean complaining of tar balls and tugging at her bathing suit. The Florida sun had baked and burnished her wide-boned face and nearly charred her shoulders. She had beautiful black eyes and was robustly overweight. Her feet left deep dents in the sand.

"They were looking for you," the towel attendant

said as she approached her chair. Her drink, an exotic emerald-green concoction, quivered in its holder staked into the sand.

"Who's looking for me, Alvaro?"

Alvaro, the towel attendant, was a youngish Cuban, perhaps thirty, with a close beard that lay hot against his handsome face. His neon-red swim trunks bore the logo of the hotel. Ignoring the stares of other guests, she placed her back to him, and he toweled it.

"You had a telephone call," he said. "There's a number for you to call back."

"Must be my brother," she said with small interest. "He's the only one knows where I am."

"They said it was important."

She freed her fancy drink from the holder and took a slow sip. Then she said quickly, "Help me on with my robe."

She shared the elevator with three elderly women who, as if threatened by her size, shied away from her. She glanced at their soft, privileged faces and then ignored them. Knowing she could probably buy and sell them all gave her a sharp feeling of comfort, and when the elevator hummed to a stop she elbowed them out of the way. "This is my floor," she explained, though it was theirs too.

In her room, sitting on the edge of the bright bed, she talked with her brother, who, without giving a reason, wanted her to catch the next flight to Boston. Her hand tightened on the receiver. She knew by his tone that something was terribly wrong, something to do with family. "Is it Ma? Has something happened to her?" Her voice quivered. "Is it Pa? Tell me, Tony!"

"It's both of them," he said.

She was no longer on the phone, though still sitting on the bed, inert, pale through her tan, eyes snapped shut, when someone slipped surreptitiously into the room and marked time with even breaths. Her eyes fluttered open, worked to focus, and saw the slim, straight waist of Alvaro. Sensing tragedy, he sat quietly beside her.

She said, "Pack my bags."

"Why? Where are you going?"

"Do as I say," she said and pushed him aside as though he were a child.

"Rita, be good."

She reached out and pretended to shoot a gun. "Someone's going to pay."

———

Anthony Gardella lived in a high brick house in Boston's Hyde Park, well away from his businesses. His first wife had died four years before, and his second wife, considerably younger than he, was vacationing in the Caribbean with her mother. His children, two sons, no longer lived at home. The younger one was a senior at Holy Cross and the older was in the Marine Corps. Gardella stood in the front room with a small glass of Saint Raphael in his hand, several of his people hovering near him. They were ready to weep for him, wait on him, and do for him in other ways. In his tailored charcoal-gray suit he was a courtly presence among them and an object of respect. At age twenty-one, down in Providence, he had received a pat on the head and a kiss on the cheek from Raymond Patriarca, and when he had turned forty, Don Peppino, better known as Bananas, had honored him with a birthday card from Tucson. Here in Boston, four or five times a year, he broke bread with Gennaro Angello, whose blessings meant more than a priest's.

Abruptly he laughed. The sound was low and ugly.

"I still can't believe it," he said, and the others fidgeted. His grief, bound inside him, expressed itself only in the tight set of his jaw. "Names," he said in an undertone. "I want names."

His close friend and right-hand man, Victor Scandura, said, "You'll get them."

Murmurs of support rose up.

Scandura eased forward, a slight figure with vanishing hair and gold-rimmed spectacles that seemed screwed into the gray flesh of his face. He could smile and repel people. "Do you want me to handle it personally?"

"Yes," Gardella said, the ice faintly rattling in his drink. "Don't disappoint me."

"Have I ever, Anthony?"

2

It was a Monday morning, a freezing day with a glaring sun; snow was predicted for Boston by night-fall, which did not bother Russell Thurston at all. He took things as they came and, when possible, capitalized on them. He was situated in a remote space in the Kennedy Building in the heart of Government Square, his office a comfortable cubicle overlooking several desks jammed into a narrow room. He was tall and sober-looking, with faded brown hair combed flat to one side and with neutral gray eyes buttoned into a parched face that rarely revealed his deeper feelings, not even now when an excitement was building in him.

He shouted for his assistant, Blodgett, but was answered by a man named Blue, the only black on a special team of agents under his supervision. He was occasionally civil to Blue but more often glib. Blue appeared in the doorway, slender, quite dark, meticulously groomed, as if his field were international banking, not investigation.

"Where's Blodgett?" Thurston demanded.

"He'll be back in a minute."

"That's not what I asked."

"He's in the head."

"Get him." Thurston watched Blue turn away and

take two steps. On the third step, Thurston said, "Blue!"

Blue returned to the doorway and placed a foot back inside the cubicle. "What is it?" he asked, and Thurston smiled cryptically.

"You take a lot of crap from me. Ever ask yourself why?"

"Never."

"Ever wonder why I picked you specially for this unit?"

"Because I'm smart."

"That goes without saying. What's the big reason?"

"I figure you'll tell me sometime."

"I'll probably let you figure it out yourself."

"I'll get Blodgett," Blue said.

"Do that."

Alone, Thurston swiveled in his chair to stare through the single window at Boston's frigid sky. He had never regretted his assignment here. He relished the charms and contradictions of the city, the sedateness of much of its architecture and the eccentricity of its streets, the incestuousness of its neighborhoods and the corruptness of its politics, and he found a challenge in the anarchy of its traffic. He delighted in occasionally breakfasting at the Ritz and lunching at Maison Robert in a city small enough to rub elbows with venerables like Archibald Cox, rumpled Brahmins like William Homans, and vulnerable beauties like Joan Kennedy. His biggest wish was for them to recognize him.

For many minutes his mind had been dwelling on the possible means to make that happen.

He turned back to his desk, rummaged in a drawer, and came up with a pair of shears. Carefully he scissored a double-column story out of the Boston *Globe* and laid the cutting in front of him. He had read it before, and now he read it again, slowly, savoring each sentence and pausing after each paragraph to reflect. Then his eyes returned to the headline. ELDERLY GREENWOOD COUPLE SLAIN. He could scarcely believe his luck.

"Where's Greenwood?" he asked when Blodgett appeared. Blodgett ruminated.

"Western part of the state, I think. Somewhere near Lenox and Lee. God's country."

"Your geography's good. Read this."

Blodgett sat in a chair to read the article. He was stocky and square-shouldered and had a businessman's close-cropped haircut. The hair was blond, the face bland. His head tilted. He was a deliberate reader, which soon taxed Thurston's patience.

"Skip down to the end. The survivors. Son, Anthony. Daughter, Rita O'Dea."

"Jesus Christ," Blodgett said, his eyes absorbing print. "Tony Gardella's mother and father."

"You've got it. What else do you get?" Thurston's voice was sharp. "Think, man, *think!*"

Blodgett thought hard. His smooth forehead dominated his face, and his mouth pressed in on itself. He was slow to lift his gaze. "It means Gardella's going to want the blood of the bastards who did it."

"Keep going."

"Give me a second."

Thurston's smile was smug and fixed. He had his elbows on the desk and his unusually long hands fisted together under his chin. "Take your time on this one."

"We make it easy for him?"

"That's only the beginning. That's how we sucker him in." Thurston moistened his lips as if he had the special spit of a snake. "I'm going to make opera out

of this. A big cast of villains. A grand production.
You keeping up with me?"

"You're going too fast."

"I'm thinking big. That's what you've got to do if
you ever want my job." Thurston's mind raced on.
"Who's Wade? Do you know him?" Blodgett didn't,
and he began to read the cutting again. Thurston
said, "Get me a rundown on him. Says there he's a
lieutenant, so he probably took the course at Quantico,
which gives us a hook. I want to know all about him.
Personal stuff. A complete profile."

Blodgett was nonplussed. "Why him?"

"Because I've got a hundred thoughts buzzing in
my head right this minute, and that's the best of
them. Get working on it. Blue can help you."

Blodgett heaved himself out of the chair and returned the cutting, which bore a damp spot from his
thumb. Before he turned to leave, he murmured
confidentially, "I suppose the less said to Blue the
better."

"You suppose right."

Thurston dropped back deeply into his swivel chair
and stared at two framed photographs on the side
wall. One was of Ronald Reagan, and the other,
which he peered at the longest, was of himself receiving an award from J. Edgar Hoover a year before the director's death. He remembered priding
himself on looking, a little at least, like Efrem Zimba-
list, Jr. He also remembered his awe of Hoover, as if
the man were more powerful than God, with dos-
siers listing everybody's peccadilloes.

———

Brother and sister traveled across the state in a
chauffeured Cadillac Eldorado to Greenwood Re-
gional Hospital, where they satisfied legal obligations
by identifying the bodies of their mother and father.

Anthony Gardella had not wanted his sister to make the trip, but she had insisted. In the gleaming basement of the morgue, near the almost soothing drone of a refrigeration unit, she viewed the still and brutalized faces and gagged. She did not cry. The medical examiner led her to a metal chair, which she would not stay in. She rose up and looked enormous. She had on a storm coat and knee boots that would not zip up all the way because of the heft of her calves. "I want to know every injury that was done to them," she said in a tone that disconcerted the doctor.

"I don't know everything yet," he said delicately.

Anthony Gardella said, "We know enough."

Rita O'Dea raised a fist and clenched it. "You know what I want." Her face, lacquered with a hard makeup, was, for the moment, fierce. Her brother gave a quick glance at the doctor.

"Leave us alone," he said, and the doctor did. The droning in the room seemed to intensify. Gardella, very quietly, said, "Get hold of yourself."

"I want to know what you're doing about this," Rita O'Dea said in a voice now unsteady. "Let's discuss it."

"Wait till they're buried."

"You should be on it now."

"Don't worry about it."

"You don't do something, *I will.*"

"You'll do nothing," Gardella said evenly. "Everything's being taken care of."

Rita O'Dea fixed her eyes upon him, her concentration intense and almost morbid. She stumbled in place, and her brother swiftly gripped the sleeve of her coat. The doctor returned. There were papers to sign in his office. On the way he said, "If I were you I wouldn't delay the trip back. It's starting to snow."

The mournful winter sky was already benighted,

and the snow fell fast, sticking to the rural road. The headlights picked up a rabbit darting in a jagged direction before the left front wheel killed it in its tracks. In the opulence of the Cadillac, Rita O'Dea pushed her hair back. "I want to drive by the house."

"No," said Gardella. "There's nothing to see."

"There might be some things we want."

"There's nothing we want."

"Speak for yourself."

"I speak for both of us," he said, his voice dropping. A glass panel sealed their words from the driver, who doubled as a bodyguard. A sign showed the way to the highway, which was reached within minutes, a smooth ride. Rita O'Dea tugged at the collar of her coat. The car was warm, but she shivered. Gardella opened a compartment in the back of the front seat and removed a flask and a tumbler. He poured for her.

She took a taste. "I remember a time you only bought wop wine."

"That's an aperitif."

"I know what it is. I'd prefer a shot of gin."

"Show a little class, Rita."

"I got all that money can buy."

Anthony Gardella studied his hands. His wedding band was a half-inch wide. His nails were manicured. With deliberate cruelty he said, "Why'd you bring that spic up here?"

For a heavy moment it seemed she would not respond. Her dark head sagged. She was tired. "Does it bother you?" she asked, her large face softened by shadow.

"Yes, it bothers me."

"It's none of your business."

"It's an insult," he said bitterly, and she sighed.

"What should I do, Tony? Be lonely?"

"You can do better than him."

She smiled with hard irony. "No, Tony. I can't."

Twice Silas Rogers avoided them, the first time by pretending that he wasn't home, though it was obvious he was, and the next time by shouting that he was too sick to talk, which in a faint way was true. One of his mongrels was ailing, and he suffered for it. He had five dogs, and during the winter he kept them inside because their bodies breathed heat for the house and life into his solitude. He was a widower. Now, for the third time, the dogs alerted him that the two men were back. He let them knock several times before opening the door just enough to show his crag of a face. "You don't need to talk to me," he said with false bravado. "I told everything to Hunkins."

Trooper Denton stuck his foot in the door. Lieutenant Wade said, "You've been ducking us. What are you afraid of?"

"Nothing." The dogs pressed against him from behind, their paws scratching the floor. The dogs were odd sizes and colors, nervous, anxious for air. "You're upsetting my animals."

Lieutenant Wade said, "Do you want to talk here or take a ride to the barracks? We can do that."

"You threatening me?"

"Yes."

"I saw what I saw and nothing more."

"Let us in, we'll talk about it."

"You think I know more than I do. I don't!"

"We'll see."

They got nothing from him. They sat at his bare table, the dogs milling beneath, and interrogated him, the trooper rephrasing questions the lieutenant had already posed. It was a ploy to trip him up, but he was too smart for that. He kept his hands in his lap and his head high and gave out flat answers either negative or neutral. Once he got up to wipe piddle from one of the dogs off the floor. Lieutenant Wade shifted the substance of the questions to the Gardellas themselves.

"What did you think of them?"

"They didn't mean nothing to me."

"They lived in the town twenty-five years, I'm told."

"We didn't mix."

"Why not?"

"I don't mix with nobody."

"Especially Italians?"

"You said that. I didn't."

"You don't say much of anything, Mr. Rogers. Two good people were sadistically murdered, and you sit there blowing smoke up my ass."

Silas Rogers reddened. "And you come in here threatening a man. It ain't right!"

The lieutenant got to his feet. So did Trooper Denton, a young giant of a man who had played football for UMass. Together they stared down at Silas Rogers, who nervously patted a dog. In a stage whisper the lieutenant said, "He's only making it worse for himself."

The trooper agreed. "He doesn't give us a choice."

"There's only one way out of this, Mr. Rogers. Put you to a lie detector."

For a second Silas Rogers went sick inside, and his face wrinkled up like a baby's. When he rose out of the chair, he did not seem entirely lucid. Then he stiffened himself. "I know my rights," he said and stood on them.

———

"You scared?"

"Shit, no. You?"

"I keep thinkin'. S'pose he saw?"

"We'd've been arrested."

"Fifty-three fuckin' dollars."

They spoke in the dark, their faces pinched from the cold, and passed a Seagram's bottle back and forth. One was hiccuping. The Seagram's and the nearness of the cows inside the barn kept them from freezing. Outside it was snowing.

"Be a blizzard by the time it's through."

"Who cares?"

They huddled in hay, their knees drawn up. The cows were restless, and some were ailing, mostly from neglect. "Hate it here," the younger brother said, though he was used to the smells and sounds of the barn and never noticed them.

"Quit hiccuping."

"Can't. Christ, it's cold. Let's go in the house."

"No way. The old man knows something's up, and we ain't gonna let 'im guess what."

"We'll give 'im the bottle. That'll put' im to sleep."

"Shake it, you damn fool. There ain't none left."

One of the ailing cows let out a low moan of discomfort and then a screech of pain that sounded more human than animal. Snow blew in under the double doors.

"Leroy."

"What?"

"We had the chance to go back there and do it again, would you still do it?"

"I'd do it better."

A wind shot through the doors and cut into their mackinaws. They squirmed deeper into the sour hay. "Still and all," the younger brother said, "we oughta make sure."

" 'Bout what?"

" 'Bout Rogers."

A foot of snow fell through the night and much of
the morning. It was midafternoon when Lieutenant
Wade turned in his chair and peered out the window. His office inside the state police barracks was
small, his desk occupying most of it. The building
was just off the highway and surrounded by birch
and pine. Snow cuddled branches of the pine and
clung to the birch. Chickadees made twitchy and
brief appearances. Wade saw nothing but the stark
snow and blades of ice flashing in the cold sunlight,
which increased his dissatisfaction with the remoteness of the area. He disliked country winters, which
billowed with the fiercest of winds and the deepest
of drifts, as if the other seasons there had misspent
themselves, as he seemed to have done with the
years of his marriage. His sense of aloneness, dull
during the day, worsened at night when the only
sound might be a dog's barking in the dark.

A noise made him swivel around. A man he had
never seen before stood unannounced at his desk.
The man's outer coat was draped over his arm. His
suit was dark and tailored to accommodate the small
burden of a revolver. The man said, "You don't
know me."

"Sure I do," Wade said. "You've got government
written all over you. Let me guess. FBI."

"You're quick."

"Show me something."

Russell Thurston produced identification. Wade
read it and returned it. A metal chair was available,
but Thurston remained erect. "I understand you
went through Quantico."

"Hasn't everybody?"

"Nice to know you, brother," Thurston said and
extended a hand. The handshake was neither warm

nor cold. It was professional and bone dry, like the man himself. Each studied the other and hid his judgment. Wade had little liking for the FBI, which had never broken its habit of aiding local police and then taking full credit if the results were favorable. Thurston said, "You can guess why I'm here."

"More or less."

Thurston draped his coat over the back of the chair. "For me it's a break. Can you understand why?" There was no comment from Wade, no admission of any sort, and Thurston took another tack. "I wasn't always Bureau, you know. For a short time I was with the CIA. Good years, let me tell you, but I was a budget casualty. Saddest day of my life."

"You seem to have landed on your feet."

"I have that facility. I used to fight Communists, and now I fight scum of another kind."

"Sounds like an obsession."

"Everybody moves to his own music, Lieutenant. I imagine you move very nicely to yours—given the chance, that is. Out here, I suspect you march to a bored drummer."

Wade placed his hands on his desk, one covering the other, no wedding band, only an emerald, his birthstone. In a low and knowing voice, he said, "You want Tony Gardella."

"I've got his picture in my wallet. You want to see it?"

"I know what he looks like."

"I know you do."

"He's in Boston, but you come all the way here to get him."

"This is where the action's going to be, wouldn't you say?"

Wade preferred not to say. "Why don't you sit down, Thurston? You make me nervous. You're working on some kind of scam, aren't you? You want to squeeze Gardella."

"Wouldn't you if you were in my shoes?"

"I'm not in your shoes. Mine have been reheeled three times."

"Are you afraid to get involved?" Thurston's stance was the stillest, and his voice gave Wade an image of a spider climbing its silk.

"I wouldn't want a fed calling my shots."

"Get your coat."

"What?"

Thurston bared his teeth in what did not in the least look like a smile but was meant to be one. "I'm going to buy you a drink."

———

They went to a place called the Hunter's Cove, drank dark beer, and stayed for dinner. The huge stone fireplace blazed, igniting faces. The waitresses wore buckskin vests and skirts, and the music was country. Wade, who was known there, had steak. Thurston had soup, annoying Wade by the deliberate and almost mannered way in which he ate. They discussed the lack of immediate evidence in the double homicide—no workable fingerprints, merely a long list of area toughs thought capable of such violence and an uncooperative witness surrounded by dogs. Thurston said, "The witness intrigues me. What did you say his name is?"

"Rogers."

"You think he's holding back?"

"It's a feeling, nothing substantial to base it on."

"Law enforcement people have special feelings. Insights. I've always maintained that."

The waitress, pale and petite, made an unnecessary trip to the table and fussed over Wade, who had a solid, half-handsome face and usually a gentle voice.

He had once taken the waitress to a movie and later would have brought her back to his place had she not mentioned she was married. Thurston watched with amusement and afterward asked, "Are you a ladies' man?"

Wade did not trouble himself to answer.

"I didn't think so," Thurston said and for a number of moments gazed at other diners, sizing up men by the women with them. The light of the fire flattered many of the faces. Gradually he returned his gaze to Wade. "I'm curious. How the hell did you manage to get yourself assigned way out here?"

"I go where I'm told."

"Translated, that means you don't have the right people in your corner. Too bad. Your family's back in the Boston area, I understand. Wellesley, is it?"

"My wife and I have separated."

"I know that. You have two daughters going to BU. The tuition must be killing you."

"While you're at it, why don't you tell me my bank balance?"

"Two hundred and three dollars in your checking and not a dime in your savings. Account closed. How about an after-dinner drink? I like Bailey's Irish." Thurston beckoned, and the waitress came immediately.

A bit later Wade said, "You're smooth."

"No," said Thurston. "Just smooth enough."

"This all going on your expense account?"

"Of course."

"I'm an item."

"I'd like you to be an even bigger item," Thurston said in a tone meant to convey opportunity and promise. The waitress served their drinks, giving all her attention now to Thurston, who ignored her.

Wade bided his time. "Go ahead," he said restively. "I'm waiting for your pitch."

"First, let's put something down for the record. Tony Gardella is garbage, no better than the goons who killed his folks. Sixteen years old, he bit a kid's ear off in a street fight. That's a savage, not a civilized member of society. Eighteen, he made his first hit working for a loan shark. Used an ice pick. Boston police picked him up right away, beat the crap out of him, but he never said a word. Impressed the hell out of the Providence people."

"I'm relatively familiar with his file," Wade said. "Plenty of arrests in those days, but no convictions."

"You're wrong, there was one. He was fined for peddling pornography a couple of weeks after he came out of the army. He moved up fast in the organization. A smart boy. He knew who to crush and who to suck up to. At the same time he was developing a taste for custom shirts and clean fingernails."

Wade gave an ironic shrug. "Nothing wrong with a little polish."

"He's got polish like a snake's got glitter. Over the years he's mellowed a little, but that doesn't make him any less a killer."

"I still don't know what you want from me," Wade said tightly.

"I want you to do Gardella a favor he can't forget."

Wade laughed. "That has a nice ring to it, like 'an offer you can't refuse.' What does it mean?"

Thurston paused. A small group was leaving. He viewed the women and then, cynically, the men, as if censuring them. "It means as soon as Gardella gets done burying his parents he'll approach you. Either him or one of his people. You can count on it. For him, this goes to the gut. He can't eat or sleep right till it's settled. His brain's on hold because he's all emotion. You help him, you become special. You do it right, you become his brother. Am I getting through to you?"

"I can brief him on the investigation," Wade said with distaste. "What more can I do?"

"You can give him the witness."

Wade looked blank, then upset. "What the hell are you getting at?"

"You've heard the expression you can't get blood from a stone. Gardella can."

"I don't want to talk about this anymore."

But they did. For a good half hour, with much argument and no agreement. Twice Wade placed a hand to his brow as though his thoughts were slipping away. Frequently Thurston's voice dipped dramatically, which suggested theater had been his first love. "This guy's got friends at City Hall, the State House, the Union Bank of Boston. Imagine how sweet it'd be to strip him bare."

"There's got to be a cleaner way," Wade said. "Your way the witness could get crippled."

"You cut a deal with Gardella. No blood. Scare tactics only." Thurston scooped up the check. He scrutinized it and then paid it with bills he had to peel apart, drawn that morning from a special fund. "We wouldn't expect you to go into this for nothing. We're generous to a fault when it comes to people who help us."

"What are you going to do, buy me a new car?"

"No. But we'd pay for your children's education." Thurston's lips curved into a quiet smile as he shoved back his chair. "Two terrific daughters, I'm told. A lot of girls up and get married as soon as they graduate. We'd even pay for their weddings. Every penny of their happiness."

In the rest room they stood at opposite ends of the bank of urinals. Wade stared at pink tiles, his long legs wide apart, a hand on his hip. Thurston tossed him a glance. "Too much for you? If it is, say so."

Wade was silent for a long moment. He was remembering a trooper with whom he'd gone through the academy, a red-haired young guy who for a couple of years took bribes from a lower-echelon mafioso from East Boston. Then, to prove he was still his own man, he busted his benefactor on a petty charge. Two weeks later his decapitated body was found in a portable dumpster in the town of Wakefield, a thousand dollars in bloodstained bills bulging a pocket of his uniform. His head was never found.

"Yes, I could do it," Wade said. "The question is whether I want to."

They moved to the sinks and then to the dryer on the wall, where they hung their hands under hot drafts. It looked as though they were about to dance. "There's something else I can do for you," Thurston said with casual authority. "I can get you back to Boston."

"What makes you think I want to go back?"

Thurston played his trump. "That's where your wife is."

Silas Rogers, who worked odd jobs, loaded his pickup truck with bone-dry kindling from the lumber yard and, in a lonely drive over twisting winter roads, hauled it across town to the Gillenwaters'. It was dark by the time he got rid of the load, every stick stacked neatly in the makeshift shed beside the sagging frame house supported on two sides by drifts of snow. Old Mrs. Gillenwater, wearing three sweaters, poked her thin head out the door and gave him money. She wanted him to come in to warm himself,

but he declined with a quick mumble. He knew that
what she wanted most was to talk about the killings.

"Silas, wait!"

He wouldn't.

He drove into the lighted center of town and parked
in front of Ned's Superette to pick up Gravy Train
for the dogs. He pushed the truck door open, but
some sudden presentiment rooted him to the seat.
The cold crawled in and chilled him. As if paralyzed,
he watched two stolid figures break from a web of
shadows and approach him with boots crunching the
packed snow. They were the Bass brothers, Leroy
and Wally. Beyond them he saw the Thunderbird.

"How you doin', Mr. Rogers?"

The voice chilled him more than the cold did. It
came from the older one, Leroy, who was also the
taller one by six inches. Despite the cold, each held a
punctured beer can in bare hands that were studded
with bitten-open knuckles. They had squiggles in
their young foreheads and pouches under their fer-
ret eyes, as if they hadn't been sleeping much, and
they reeked of the cows their father owned, none of
which gave fit milk.

"Just fine," Silas Rogers answered in a small burst,
wishing someone would come along, anyone. Customers bobbed about inside the superette, but none
came out.

"Wanna beer? We got an extra in the Bird."

He shook his head and shivered. They were strain-
ing to read him, he could tell. The younger one
smiled out of a pale face raw and red at the nose and
swigged from a Budweiser can. He had known them
since their raucous years at Greenwood Grammar
School, where he had been the janitor and they
stay-backs, truants, vandals, and bullies. Remembering their cruelties, he feared them more than ever.

"What you want in the store, Mr. Rogers? Wally here will get it, won't you, Wally?"

The younger brother muscled his face nearer and loomed like a Hun. "What's he after?"

"He ain't said yet."

"What's he waitin' for?"

"He's thinkin'."

Silas Rogers wanted only to drive away. At home he had a hunting rifle, but it was unoiled, uncleaned, and he wasn't sure he had shells. Probably not, which made him want to weep. "Dog food."

"Give 'im money, Mr. Rogers. He can't go in there without money."

Reluctantly Silas Rogers pulled bills from his pants pocket and skinned off more than enough. Wally Bass raised a hand, one of the fingers mashed from an old injury. Silas Rogers fed it, which made the older brother frown.

"Will that do it, Wally?"

"Don't think so."

"Prices are high in there, Mr. Rogers."

Without hesitation he surrendered all that Mrs. Gillenwater had given him, overly willing to do anything to satisfy them. Their smiles showed they were pleased. Wally Bass crushed his Budweiser can and strutted toward the store. The older brother threw his empty into the dark.

"Bad thing about the Gardellas. I heard you were there."

"No." His voice rose in pitch, and his confusion was intense, almost violent. "I was only driving by."

"That's what I mean."

"I didn't see anything."

"No?"

"My eyes can see, but not far."

Leroy Bass smiled and spoke with chilling certainty. "I thought your eyes were good."

"They're bad," he insisted.

"My grandmother had cataracts. You got those?"

"Yes."

"Maybe that's good. Good they're bad, I mean."

The younger brother came out of the superette with a small bag, which he tossed into the back of the pickup, a light thump, scarcely enough for one dog. Silas Rogers started to close the door, but Leroy Bass stopped him. Their eyes locked. Leroy Bass's broad face was all meat.

"You oughta give Wally somethin' for goin', Mr. Rogers."

———

Later, ensconced in the idling Thunderbird, the heater going, the younger brother counted money and surrendered half to the older one. In an uneasy and tenuous voice he said, "You think he's lying?"

"Don't matter," Leroy Bass said.

"Matters if he saw us, matters a whole hell of a lot."

"No, it don't," Leroy Bass said with supreme confidence. "Like it was back in school, he's still scared of us—now even more." There was a smile. "We got nothin' to worry about."

Wally Bass loosened his coat, producing an odor exactly like unaired bedding. Now he smiled. "Remember the time down in the basement I told him I was goin' to shove his head in the furnace?"

"No, *I* told him. All you did was hold his arms."

"But I'd've done it," Wally Bass said.

3

THE DAY after the autopsies were completed, the medical examiner released the bodies of Santo and Rosalie Gardella, which were then delivered in a hearse across state to Boston, to Ferlito's Funeral Home in the North End. Sammy Ferlito and his nephew worked diligently in an attempt to ready the charred remains for viewing, but the task was staggering, the results dismal. "Tony, I don't advise it," Ferlito said apologetically and miserably to Anthony Gardella. They stood in Ferlito's dark-paneled office, where ficus trees sprang out of ornate pots and were kept healthy by a special blue light. Gardella nodded with understanding.

"It's Rita who wants the caskets open."

"Do you want me to explain to her?"

"I'll do it."

"Tony, I'm sorry."

"It's not your fault."

"Augie feels bad too," Ferlito said, referring to his nephew.

"Tell him not to worry."

"Maybe sometime you can use him. He's a good boy."

"You say he's a good boy, I believe it," Gardella said and reached for his overcoat, which was dark and glossy, with a midnight-blue lining. Ferlito, who was short, went up on tiptoes to help him on with it.

"Cashmere, huh? Feels like a million bucks."

"A thousand is all."

"Could've fooled me."

"I hope not," Gardella said. "I hope you don't fool easy."

Later in the day Gardella walked up the plowed drive of his sister's house. It was next door to his, nearly its twin, built by the same contractor. Hers was smaller, with less security, no alarm system, no peephole in the front door, no metal mesh shielding the windows that faced the street. Gardella entered without ringing and came face to face with the slender, bearded Cuban his sister had brought up from Florida. Galled at the sight of him, Gardella at first ignored him, then said, "Where's Rita?"

The Cuban pointed upward. "Taking a nap. She couldn't sleep last night."

Gardella regarded him aloofly. They faced each other in the small foyer, where the floor was stone. Twin mirrors captured their images. "Making yourself at home, Juan?"

"The name's Alvaro."

"What are you sucking around my sister for? You like fat women or something?"

Alvaro's brown eyes flared. He had on a crinkly saffron shirt and seersucker pants suitable for Miami, not for the Massachusetts winter. "I don't think Rita would like you asking me these things. She told me what she does is none of your business."

"Pretty sure of yourself, aren't you?" Gardella said, and Alvaro shrugged, undaunted. "You speak English okay. Where'd you learn it?"

"Harvard."

Gardella flushed. "You're a wise little prick."

"I learned it like you did. I was a baby when I came to the States."

"What are you, Puerto Rican? Mexican?"

"I'm Cuban, like you didn't know."

Gardella's eyes veered up. His sister came halfway down the stairs and clutched the rail, hovering in a robe that didn't fit her, her face sour from sleep and her eyes feeble from too little of it. He viewed her with momentary disgust. With effort, she came down the rest of the way and said, "You haven't asked him what he does for a living. Tell him, Alvaro."

"I'm a towel attendant at the Sonesta."

"You're what?"

"You heard him."

Gardella frowned with an air of sadness. He remembered when she was less large and more secure, though never reasonable, always self-indulgent in her rash choices of companions and self-destructive to a degree that never ceased to disturb him. At the same time, because she was of his blood, she was the only person in the world he totally trusted.

Alvaro made as if to leave them alone, and she said, "Stay!"

Gardella said, "Go. I want to talk to my sister."

Alvaro vanished, with a small fatalistic smile. Gardella led his sister into her living room, where they remained standing, facing each other in a solemn way, all disagreements cast aside. With care and delicacy he briefed her on the funeral arrangements and added that the caskets would be closed. Her eyes filled as she confronted feelings mostly buried until now.

"That means I don't even get to say good-bye to them."

"You say good-bye at the church," he murmured. "That's where we all say it."

"I'm going to miss them so much," she said hopelessly. "I was Pa's angel."

"You broke his heart a hundred times."

"Don't be tough with me, Tony."

He didn't mean to be and didn't want to be, not at this time, and he placed an arm over her shoulders. He was fourteen years older than she. She had been his angel too, and he her hero. His voice dipping, he said, "Is it forever, Rita, this way you feel about the spic?"

"Nothing's forever, Tony. I'm smart enough to know that."

"Good," he said. "Then I can live with it."

———

Deputy Superintendent Scatamacchia of the Boston Police Department personally directed traffic, and four white-helmeted officers manned motorcycles to lead the procession of more than fifty cars. The cars wormed their way through constricted North End streets from Ferlito's Funeral Home to St. Leonard's Church on Hanover Street, which had been scraped of snow. It was a cold, brittle day, which did not prevent a crowd from gathering. In the forefront, conspicuously displaying themselves, were Supervisor Russell Thurston and special agents Blodgett and Blue. Thurston was nettled. "Look at those cops on bikes. Like an honor guard." Blodgett agreed with an epithet. Blue said nothing. He scanned the crowd, his the only black face in a neighborhood that tolerated none.

"Who's the coon?" Rita O'Dea whispered as she struggled out of a limousine. She was wearing mink and stood voluminous in it. "He's cute."

"He's a fed," her brother said harshly, shading his eyes. "Feds you expect, a spade you don't. It's an insult."

Victor Scandura sidled up. "The tall one's Thurston. I had him pointed out to me once."

"I'd like to squeeze his throat."

"One thing at a time," Scandura advised.

A seemingly endless line of mourners filed into the church for the solemn high mass, family members sinking into front pews. Gardella's older son, the marine, was there in full dress uniform, his hair barbered close and his shoulders squared. The other boy, the Holy Cross student, sat less rigidly, with his head bowed. His grief was deep. Rita O'Dea sat next to him and pressed his hand. The church filled and overfilled. Out of respect for Anthony Gardella, Carlo Maestrotauro from Worcester was there, as was Francesco Scibelli from Springfield, both aging but still active, still in control. Raymond Patriarca, ailing, had sent a representative from Providence, and Joe Bonomo had dispatched a lieutenant from the Coast. Local respect was embodied in the presence of Gennaro Angello and Antonio Zanigari. In the back of the church, the last to enter, was Special Agent Blue.

Outside, Russell Thurston and Agent Blodgett loitered near the Caffè Pompei, which had a CLOSED sign on the door, though some people had gathered inside. Through the window Thurston spied the high-level police officer who had directed traffic. The officer had made himself at home. He had his cap off and was drinking coffee at a small table, one foot up on a chair. "What's his name?" Thurston asked.

"Scatamacchia. They call him Scat."

"We got a file on him?"

"A little one."

"Let's make it bigger," Thurston said and didn't take his eyes off the man. Scatamacchia had a virile head of steel-gray hair and a nose like the curved powerful bill of a parrot. The eyes were slits and the mouth compressed. When he finally came out of the Caffè Pompei with his cap planted hard on his head, Thurston said in a voice that carried, "While he's at it, he ought to run in the church and kiss Gardella's ass."

Scatamacchia stopped dead. At that moment, had they been alone together on a dark street he might have killed him. Instead he merely shrugged, as if he didn't trust himself to speak. He knew Blodgett by sight and guessed at once who Thurston was. Thurston he knew by reputation, that of a zealot, unyielding and overbearing, with never a good word for the Boston Police Department.

Blodgett said, "Hello, Scat. Met my boss?"

He tugged at his cap, the visor filigreed in gold, and said in a savage undertone, "Keep him to yourself."

"What's that, Scat? I didn't hear you."

"I'll let this pass, but I won't forget it."

Thurston said, "That's what we're counting on."

With satisfaction they watched him stalk off. Thurston's eyes flashed with excitement, as if he could see into the future, nothing but successes in it, big achievements, private rewards. Then slowly he scowled. Though the service was not yet half over, Agent Blue had left the church and was joining them. Thurston said, "I told you to stay to the end."

"Don't use me to bait them," Blue said after seconds of silence. "I don't like it."

"You don't have a say in the matter, Thurston said carelessly, a small smile forming. "If you've got a problem, take it up with the Civil Rights Commission. Otherwise get back in that church."

"Is that an order?"

"Blodgett, tell him."

"It's an order."

Inside the church the monsignor swung a censer over one casket and then over the other, and a sharp fragrance wafted into the front pews. For a wild moment Rita O'Dea looked as though she might sob. Instead she silently mouthed prayers, including a special one that may have been to the devil.

Deputy Superintendent Scatamacchia entered the church on surprisingly gentle feet and, slipping into a back pew, sat next to a large, baggy-faced man named Ralph Roselli. After a few moments Scatamacchia leaned against him and whispered, "Too bad you guys don't whack feds."

The day after Santo and Rosalie Gardella were laid to rest in Boston, Lieutenant Christopher Wade, always an early riser, drove to a coffee shop in downtown Lee. He was the morning's first customer, a regular, a place already set for him. His order seldom varied: dropped eggs on toast. Other customers arrived, and he nodded to most. He was on his second cup of coffee when a stranger entered and glanced casually about. With continued nonchalance the man hung his hat, scarf, and coat next to Wade's things and said, "May I?"

"Plenty of other tables," Wade said, but the man, who had an easy way of moving, every gesture timed, joined him anyway. He had scant, coarse hair, like a coconut, and wore a vested suit and gold-rimmed glasses that seemed bolted into his face. He could have passed for a lawyer or a broker of sorts.

"I was told you eat here."

"You must've got up early to get here."

"That's a fact. The name's Victor Scandura."

"I know what it is. I used to study pictures, a whole book of them." Wade, who had quit smoking and was starting up again, opened a green-and-white pack of Merit Menthols. "I never got close to you, but I busted up a booking operation a cousin of yours was running."

"You didn't bust it up. You made it difficult for a day."

Wade smiled pleasantly. "You're probably right."

Scandura removed his glasses, diminishing his eyes to specks, and breathed on the lenses. He polished them with a silk handkerchief. The waitress brought him coffee. It was all he wanted, as if the thought of food so early sickened him.

"Ulcer?" Wade asked.

"If I had an ulcer I wouldn't take the coffee." He returned the glasses to his face, carefully fitting them on. "I'm here on behalf of Anthony Gardella."

"I figured."

"You can understand what he's going through. His mother and father were wonderful people. Twenty-five years ago he bought the farmhouse for them. They wanted the country, he gave it to them. He wanted them to have a mansion, but the little house was all they wanted. The old man, you know, was never involved in anything. A straight arrow. Look where it got him."

Wade drew on his cigarette. The waitress freshened his coffee. "What can I tell you?" he said with a shrug.

Scandura spoke low. "How close are you to grabbing the bastards who did this thing? Anthony wants to know."

"You want an honest answer, I'll give it to you. There are plenty of local yokels around here capable, but we've got no solid lead. Maybe something will develop."

"That's not good. These yokels you talk about,

there must be some in your mind stand out bigger than others. You must've picked up something."

"Nothing." Wade sat back, his chin pulled in, his thoughts on his wife. The last time he had seen her, a hurried but sincere attempt at reconciliation, he had kissed her soundly, instantly, after which she had eased away from him with the words that there were no fresh starts in life, no erasures, no rolling back of a decade or even a year or two. All a person could do, she had said, was swerve. He said to Scandura, "The only thing I've got is an old guy who drove by the house in his pickup. You probably read his name in the paper. Maybe he's telling God's truth when he says he didn't see much, I don't know for sure. I've put as much pressure on him as I'm allowed . . . by law."

Victor Scandura instantly caught and read the inflection. "I like what you're saying."

"I'm not saying anything," Wade shot back. "You and Tony Gardella don't interest me. I'm bothered that two homicidal morons are walking the streets."

"Not too many streets out here. This is another world. How the hell do you stand it?"

"I'm trying to get back to Boston. Maybe it'll happen."

"Maybe we can help," Scandura said casually, and Wade looked at him severely.

"You don't do anything."

"I think we owe you something."

"You owe me nothing," Wade said. He had snuffed his cigarette, but it still fumed in the ashtray.

"How can you smoke those things?"

"I don't know. I hate 'em."

They left the coffee shop together, an icy wind stabbing them. Soiled snow that looked as hard as rock barricaded each side of the downtown street.

Wade saw the long dark car that Scandura had driven up in. He saw two men sitting in the front.

"You can scare the old guy, but you don't lay a finger on him. Understood?"

Scandura said, "You have my word."

———

Victor Scandura, who would not go into any house with dogs in it, stayed in the car. The two men in front got out and trudged through the cold to the front door. They looked like bill collectors, the sort a finance company might send out. One was Ralph Roselli, whose large, baggy face reddened in the wind. His eyebrows were bushy, and his eyes seemed deceptively unalert. He was in his forties and burly. The other man was Sammy Ferlito's young nephew, Augie, who was doing his first piece of work for Anthony Gardella, which made him a little nervous. He was angular and furtive and had little eyes and no chin. They rapped on the door, and when no one answered, Ralph Roselli put his shoulder to it.

Victor Scandura hunched his shoulders as the wind gusted against the car and tried to get in. He hated winter. Thirty years ago in Korea he had nearly lost his feet to frostbite, and twenty years ago during the Boston gang wars his older brother had been garroted and the body dumped in the path of a snowplow, which had buried it. Narrowing his eyes, he peered out at boundless snowscape and naked trees, and then he consulted his watch. He had given them ten minutes, which he considered only slightly unreasonable.

Inside the house Ralph Roselli wrenched the old rifle out of Silas Rogers's hand and, looking at it bemusedly, asked, "What the hell were you going to do with this?" The dogs began to yap. "Shut 'em up," he said, and Silas Rogers did. Roselli's approach was oddly phlegmatic. After searching the depths of his coat, one inner pocket and then another, he produced a nickel-plated .32-caliber revolver and pushed the tip of the barrel against Silas Rogers's forehead. Then abruptly he wrinkled his nose. "He's unloading."

Augie nodded. "I'm used to it. We get bodies do it all the time."

Lowering the revolver, Ralph Roselli grimaced with disgust and purposely hooded his eyes as if the old man were no longer worth looking at. "I'm going to ask you some questions. I don't get the right answers, I'll shoot a dog. That doesn't work, I'll shoot you."

The questions were asked.

Silas Rogers spoke with his whole face, everything moving, lines jiggling, cracks deepening, watery eyes rolling over the dry and frantic pull of his mouth. He answered everything.

Outside, Victor Scandura sounded the horn. The ten minutes were up.

4

MOTHER AND DAUGHTER returned from the Caribbean, and Anthony Gardella met them at the door. The mother, Mrs. Denig, said with an edge, "I'd have brought her back right away if you'd gotten in touch," and the daughter, his wife, said beseechingly, "Why *didn't* you, Tony?" He could have given several answers, but he let one suffice.

"I wanted to spare you."

"Spare her? She's your wife."

He tolerated the mother because he adored the daughter, whose eyes reached out to him. She stepped toward him on long, lively legs. Jane Denig Gardella, a conspicuous beauty from the day she was born, was tall and fair, long-necked and tight-waisted, with sea-blue eyes that focused wistfully on her husband. She was half his age. "Didn't you need me?" she whispered.

"Yes," he said, and she clung to him.

"It's so horrible."

"Yes."

Mrs. Denig said, "We should've at least been here for the funeral."

"I wasn't thinking," he said with perfect control and watched his mother-in-law rearrange the collar of her coat. She wore expensive clothes, confined her brindled hair in combs, and bore vestiges of a beauty that age and certain disappointments had coarsened and roughened. A deep disappointment was her daughter's marriage to a man who was not only Mediterranean but a reputed criminal, with looks too smooth and manners too obvious. She readily accepted the monthly allowance he provided her but felt within her rights to be distant. She backed away from her daughter's luggage and opened the door. "Where are you going?" her son-in-law asked.

"Where do you think? Home. I want to be in my own bed tonight."

"I'll arrange a ride."

"You don't have to," Mrs. Denig said stoutly. "The taxi's waiting. Kiss your wife."

When the door closed behind her, Anthony Gardella kissed his wife long and lovingly and then held her at arm's length to stare at her oval face and blond hair. "I'm so in love with you," she whispered, and he drew her near again, savoring her scent. "I should have been beside you," she murmured. "What did people say?"

"They didn't say anything."

"But you should have told me. It's like I'm not really a part of your life."

He spoke close to her ear. "That's not true."

"Take me upstairs, Tony. Carry me up." His reaction was slow, and she sensed the reason. "We're not alone, are we?"

"My sister and Victor are in the front room. It's business. It won't take long."

She separated from him and smiled weakly over the bow of her blouse. "Should I pop in and say hello?"

"No. Wait for me upstairs."

They looked up when he entered the room. His sister was ensconced on a sofa and drinking Saint Raphael. Victor Scandura sat woodenly across from her. He did not look happy. Gardella dropped into a deep chair and said, "What's the matter, Victor?"

"I've been trying to convince your sister, but she won't listen either."

"If this had happened to your mother and father," Gardella said with gravity, "would you wait?"

Scandura spoke with a long face. "Anthony, listen to me. One of the reasons you're where you are is you're a patient man. 'A patient man avoids mistakes.' I'm quoting you, Anthony, and I'm saying we should handle this like always. Six months at least to let things cool down. A year would be better. Let those punks think they got away with it. Makes it even sweeter when the time comes."

"No," said Rita O'Dea. "Six months, a year, a train might hit them, and they get off easy."

"Rita's right," Gardella said and made a fist. "I want them to die hard, and I want to be there. I want to see it happen."

"No, you don't, Anthony." Scandura was upset. "I don't advise it."

"I'm entitled."

"We'll both be there," said Rita O'Dea.

Scandura adjusted his glasses. He made one final plea. "I only met this Wade guy once, that's all. Maybe he's got something up his sleeve. He seems okay, but I can't guarantee it."

"So we'll be careful," Gardella said, undeterred. "Any other problems?"

"Anthony, I'm going to need time. A little time at least to set it up."

Rita O'Dea finished her drink. "Then get working on it," she said in a tone that never failed to offend Scandura.

———

With the blinds drawn against the stark winter daylight, Jane Gardella made room for her husband on the warm bed. She lay extended, her toes stretched to enhance her feet, her waist incredibly slim. His eyes absorbed her, and his hand traced over her. He said, "I missed you."

"You were supposed to," she said, bathing in his attention.

"Who did you meet on those white beaches?"

"Are you jealous?"

"Have you ever known me not to be?"

She rolled partly over him, digging in a gentle knee, and grinned into his face. "You'd have loved the Europeans. The women, even the husky ones, wore bikinis and took off the tops."

"How did that sit with your mother?"

"Not well."

"And with you?"

"I'd have done it too if you'd been there. We'd have swum in the buff. Some did."

"We wouldn't have."

"Oh, yes," she said confidently. "I'd have shown you off."

"You still don't know me."

"You're wrong, Tony. So wrong." She spoke slowly, working her eyes into his while she let her blond hair tumble down. Her fingers glanced over him. "My turn," she whispered. "My turn to touch."

Eventually, exuberantly, he embraced her, his voice stumbling out of his mouth. The words were heated and intimate, the sort he had never uttered to his first wife. She had been deeply devout, a clay Christ above her bed and saints beside it, a trace of martyrdom in her heart each time he had touched her, which he had stopped doing long before her death, though he had certainly still cherished her, more than she ever could have guessed. His second wife was from a different generation, another world. Legs bowed over him, she panted, "Yes, Tony, yes."

Later, wearing matching silk robes, they made their way downstairs, the whole house to themselves, which was rare. She settled on the sofa his sister had earlier occupied and watched him pour Saint Raphael into two glasses. He added soda and a twist to hers and then tasted it to make sure it was right. It always was. He joined her on the sofa; for the time being he was concerned only with immediate reality, grateful that she was back. He would have been content to sit there in silence with her, an arm around her, but she brought up the tragedy of his parents.

"What are you doing about it, Tony?"

He loved her passionately, but not blindly. Some things he would never tell her.

———

Lieutenant Christopher Wade had misgivings. In a small way he hated himself. Toying with pencils on his desk, all in need of points, he said to Trooper Denton, "What if I told you I'm a piece of shit?" Trooper Denton thought he was joking and smiled. "When I ask a question, why don't you answer?"

Denton said, "What's the matter, Lieutenant?"

"Nothing Jack Daniel's wouldn't cure. Run out and get me a bottle."

"You don't drink."

"I don't smoke either, but what am I doing with this?" Wade plucked out a Merit and lit it. "I have a riddle for you, Denton. What talks in the toilet and makes an offer you could've refused? You don't know, I'll tell you. A fed."

The trooper was uncertain whether to respond. He had much admiration for Wade, not a little of which was hero worsip. "You into something heavy, Lieutenant?" he asked, and Wade grimaced.

"Nothing you want to know about. I'm running off at the mouth, something I'd advise you never to do."

"Want me to leave you alone?"

"I think that's a good idea."

As soon as Denton closed the door behind him, Wade picked up the phone and punched out a Boston number. Eventually Russell Thurston came on the line, official-sounding, high-toned. Wade, without introduction, said, "What if I told you I'm having second thoughts?"

"Who is this?"

"Wade."

There was a tiny pause. "I'd say it's too late, since you've already tipped off Scandura about Rogers. What the hell's your problem, Lieutenant?"

"Maybe it's moral. Does that surprise you? I feel like I'm sinking to Gardella's level, and there's a good possibility you're already there."

"Come on, Wade, cops aren't expected to be saints. We do what we have to do. Otherwise society wouldn't be fit to live in. Christ, do I have to give you a lecture?"

"I'm a state cop, you're a fed. Maybe we play by different rules."

"The rules depend on what's at stake. They always have, always will. Do you doubt that?"

"I doubt what we're doing."

This time Thurston made his pause significant. "Do you love your wife, Wade?"

"What's that to you?"

"Just answer the question, make like I'm a minister."

"Yes, I love her."

"If you want her back, you'd better hurry. I understand she's seeing some guy steady."

Wade made a mark on a jotting pad, the dull tip of the pencil tearing through two sheets. "How the hell would you know that?" he demanded, and Thurston's voice came through like fluid.

"Believe me, I know."

Wade was silent. He dropped the pencil and rubbed an eye, making it sore.

Thurston said, "I'll pretend you never made this call."

———

Two weeks later Special Agent Blodgett stood stocky and blunt-shouldered in a public phone booth in Hyde Park's Cleary Square, his back to the slow grind of winter traffic. "I think it's going to happen. I'd bet my last dollar." He placed his lips closer to the mouthpiece. "Five got into a car. Blue followed them as far as the Mass Pike."

"Five?" Russell Thurston was on the other end. "That seems like overkill."

"Victor Scandura's there with two heavies—Ralph Roselli and a kid I don't know, but I'm sure I've seen him before, just haven't figured out where yet."

"That's good. That's beautiful. The kid could come in handy sometime. Who are the other two?"

"I was saving that for last." Growing excitement animated Blodgett's usually bland face. "Looks like Gardella and his sister are going along for the ride."

"Beautiful," said Thurston. "Absolutely beautiful."

"I guess you want to rethink this now."

"No," Thurston said firmly. "They get one whiff of us, it won't go down."

"Sir, this is a gift from God. We could grab a chopper and get to Greenwood before they do. We could—"

"You didn't hear me, Blodgett. Nor do you understand. I don't want only Gardella and his sister. I want the whole operation. I want the biggest bust Boston's ever seen. Cops, politicians, bankers, everybody Gardella deals with. You hear me now, don't you?"

Blodgett made a small sound.

"I want it on the national news and Ted Koppel talking about it on *Nightline*, me there, along with Webster. Get the picture?"

"Yes, sir," Blodgett said and cut the connection.

The roadhouse was an oasis of jagged neon on a country thoroughfare bordered by heaped snow. The evening sky was clear and full of stars. In the plowed lot, pickups and cars surrounded the roadhouse, a rusted Thunderbird among them, also a dark Cadillac, not the Eldorado but an old one, nondescript. In the back seat, sitting with her brother, Rita O'Dea unwrapped a cold chicken sandwich dripping with mayonnaise, and Gardella told her to be careful. He shifted away from her. "You got a napkin, I hope."

"Don't worry about it," she said.

Gardella leaned forward and murmured to Victor Scandura, "They might stay in there for hours."

"I don't think so." Scandura twisted around. He was in front between the inert shapes of Ralph and Augie. "They try to score with the girls, but they don't know how. So they get mad and leave."

Time dragged. Rita O'Dea finished her sandwich and cleaned her fingers with fierce licks, annoying her brother in a way she had as a child. It made her feel closer to him. She crumpled the wrapper and stuffed it into an ashtray, another annoyance. She whispered something to him, and he answered mechanically, his eye trained on the entrance of the roadhouse. People had gone in, but no one had come out. Finally two shuffling figures did. "Well?" he said.

Scandura squinted through his spectacles. The figures seemed to float up. One weaved. Then, near the corner of the building, they abruptly anchored themselves with stiff stances, their mackinaws thrown open. Scandura said, "That's them."

Gardella's breath caught.

Rita O'Dea watched them poison the snow and whispered, "Pigs."

"You're sure?" Gardella said to Scandura in a tightly controlled voice, and Scandura nodded.

"Definitely."

The taller of the two moved off toward the Thunderbird. The other one was slow to follow, still busy. Rita O'Dea said, "Shake it good, buster. That's the last piss you'll ever take."

The Cadillac, Augie at the wheel, cruised through the night with a soft and silent motion, well behind the Thunderbird, which traveled at breakneck speed, its taillights diminishing licks of fire. "They always drive like that," Scandura said over his shoulder. "Idiots."

Gardella was agitated. "We'll lose them. Catch up!"

"There's a fork up ahead," Scandura said equably. "If they go left, means they're heading home, except they won't go in the house right away. They'll go in the barn."

"What if they go right?"

"I've got a good idea where they'll be."

They went right and vanished.

The Cadillac followed and soon made an effortless turn onto a road that rose. The sky seemed to spread, revealing more stars than before. Rita O'Dea detected a great sadness in her brother's shadowed

features and sensed an impatience greater than hers.
His relief was enormous when they came upon the
Thunderbird. Lights out, motor idling roughly, it
was parked in a clear area right off the road where
the snow, pounded down, glimmered in the metallic
gloom of the moon and drifted off toward an abyss
of darkness. Gardella thrust himself forward. "What's
out there?"

"Nothing," said Scandura as the Cadillac crept to a
stop at a right angle to the Thunderbird. "Town
trucks dump snow off the edge. It's a hell of a drop,
lot of boulders at the bottom."

"What are they doing here?"

"Boozing."

"Stupid place to do it."

"Maybe they jack off," Rita O'Dea said in a deadly
sweet voice.

"You guys just going to sit here?" Gardella said,
and Augie opened his door and got out. As he did,
he brushed something into his mouth and swallowed
hard. Gardella saw him do it but said nothing. Outside, Augie shivered. Ralph joined him and whispered, "Don't shit your pants, kid." The Cadillac
purred in place, glued to its lights. Augie and Ralph
lifted the hood. Within seconds the doors of the
Thunderbird winged open, shedding a weak light,
and the Bass brothers showed their faces. Ralph
called out in apparent perplexity, "You guys know
anything about engines?"

The brothers shuffled forward, flaccid, carelessly
bold. Their arms hung long. The bigger of them,
Leroy, said, "We don't get our hands dirty for nothin'."

Ralph said, "We'll give you something."

The brothers angled their way between Augie and
Ralph. "Looks like a hearse," Leroy said thickly. His
brother Wally couldn't speak. His nose was full. Le-

roy plunged his head under the hood and then backed away fast. "Hell, it's runnin'. What more do you want?" Ralph smiled, his sack of a face illegible. Augie shifted close to Wally, who suddenly was nervous. Leroy, on guard, glanced sideways and said, "Who are those people?"

Scandura, Gardella, and Rita O'Dea had emerged from the Cadillac and lined themselves in a row, Rita O'Dea in the middle. Bearlike in her fur, she was smoking a cigarette; Gardella stood very straight. Scandura smiled, his teeth glittering, some more than others. He said, "I'm nobody, but these people recently buried their parents, Santo and Rosalie Gardella. Maybe you remember them."

Gardella and Rita O'Dea uttered oaths in Italian. The brothers did not know the words but were terrified by the sound. Leroy Bass rose on his toes and froze, while Wally failed to react, as if he did not know how. Ralph and Augie dredged up long objects from their coats in almost a benign way. The brothers did not respond; they felt as if they were hallucinating.

Victor Scandura said, "Good-bye, boys."

Ralph swung his tire iron and broke the flesh in Leroy Bass's face, and then he swung again and destroyed the skull. Augie's aim was off, and he merely fractured the younger brother's shoulder. Ralph completed the job for him, each wing of the iron progressively emphatic, until there was not a whimper left.

Rita O'Dea said, "Leave something to spit on."

Afterward Scandura made a quick gesture. Ralph and Augie knew what to do. He had coached them. They dragged the bodies to the Thunderbird and rammed them into the front seat. Ralph steered from the outside with an arm through the open window, the gear shift in drive and the motor snorting, while Augie pushed from the opposite side, twice falling to his knees because of city shoes. The crunch of tires over the snow was oddly musical. The two men leaped away when they neared the edge. The crash was muffled.

Gardella and his sister climbed back into the Cadillac, anxious to leave, their satisfaction scant and their disappointment great. Scandura waited outside for Ralph and Augie, who both arrived breathless. Opening a door, Scandura said, "Let's move." But nobody did. A police cruiser whirling blue and red rays veered off the road and braked behind them. In a fateful tone from the depths of the Cadillac, Gardella said, "Handle it, Victor."

The cruiser door flew open. The man who tumbled out wore a fur cap and a badge glinting off his mackinaw. Scandura murmured, "A local, alone." Ralph was ready to act, but Augie wasn't. Augie had put a hand to his throat. His lack of a chin placed his mouth too low in his face, and for the moment the face looked abject. "Get in the car," Scandura whispered to him savagely. "We don't need you."

Quickly, hands buried in his topcoat pockets, Scandura walked toward the officer, who had set himself in a defensive manner. Scandura greeted him in a clear voice and gave him a story, apparently plausible, about an accident. Officer Hunkins exclaimed, "Jesus Christ, how many in it?"

"Looked like two," Scandura said in a specious tone of cooperation. "Like I said, they were going like a bat out of hell."

The two of them began tramping over the hard snow, their breaths trailing them. Officer Hunkins said matter-of-factly, "That's Steuben's Bluff. They went over it, they're dead." Suddenly he stopped. He had a flashlight and he clicked it on and fanned the light over the ground. "Where are the skids? I don't see any."

Scandura freed his left hand from his coat pocket and surreptitiously let something fall from his fingers. "They just didn't make the turn. Kids, I think. Probably drunk."

"What kind of car?"

"Looked like an old T-bird."

"All rusted up?"

"Might've been."

Officer Hunkins shrugged. "I think I knew the suckers. Hardworking kids, but a little wild." His voice abruptly turned official and grave. "You and your friends are going to have to stick around."

Scandura stepped casually to one side, his hand slipping back into his pocket, and looked down with a mild show of surprise. "What's that?"

Hunkins bent down fast and straightened slowly. "Jesus Christ, it's somebody's roll. Enough to choke a horse." He looked at Scandura, who said nothing. "Must be a grand here."

"At least."

Hunkins started counting with trembling fingers and then quit. "More than a grand."

A moment passed.

"It's yours," Scandura said.

"What d'you mean?"

"Finders keepers." Scandura's smile was slight, off-hand, and unmistakable. He turned softly on his heel. "I'll be leaving now."

Hunkins hesitated a bare second. "Sure, why not?"

———

At three-thirty in the morning the bedside telephone in Russell Thurston's bachelor apartment rang. A bare arm snaked over him to get it. "Don't!" he said. "Don't *ever* answer my phone." The call was from a confidential source, code name Honey. The voice said, "They're back."

Several hours later, from his cubicle in the Kennedy Building, Thurston placed a call across the state. Trooper Denton came on the line. Thurston said, "I don't want you, I want your boss." At the same time he smiled at Blodgett and then wryly at Blue, who had been told little but had guessed much, which had been Thurston's intention all along, one of his ways of amusing himself. His secret was that he had more confidence in Blue than in Blodgett, which neither suspected.

When Lieutenant Wade finally came on the line, Thurston increased his smile and said, "I understand justice has been served."

Austin Coates

5

IN A BAR LOUNGE at Miami International Airport two men sat at a low table. One of them, Ty O'Dea, had a pickled Irish face and prematurely white hair that was neatly parted. His nose was drawn out at the end, as if pulled, and his smile was fake. His blue eyes blended vulnerability with caution. The other man, Miguel, half Puerto Rican and half Floridian, was small, like a jockey, with black eyes that seemed too big for their sockets. He spoke poor Spanish and fluent street English. His gaze was riveted on two figures who had hesitated outside the wide, doorless entrance to the lounge.

"Who's the guy looks like Cesar Romero?"

"That's him," O'Dea said with a start. "That's Tony Gardella."

"Who's the cunt hanging all over him?"

"Must be his wife. Look beyond him, you'll see his muscle, Ralph Roselli."

Miguel frowned. "Phone Alvaro. Find out what the fuck's going on."

"I move, he'll see me."

"You scared?" Miguel's quick smile was sardonic. "It was his sister used to beat you up, not him."

O'Dea lowered his head. "I can't call. Rita'll recognize my voice."

"She answers, you hang up. What's so hard about that?"

Anthony Gardella and his wife moved out of sight, followed by Ralph Roselli. O'Dea lifted his glass and drained it. He took his whiskey neat. Then he rose quickly and wended his way to the rear of the lounge. He had on a sky-blue suit and a matching vest and a print shirt with the collar flipped over the top of the jacket. His shoes were white. He stayed on the phone less than three minutes. When he returned to the table, he said, "He's down here on business."

"Business?" Miguel looked a shade skeptical. "And he brings his wife with him?"

"She didn't want to be left."

"I thought Victor Scandura did his dealing. Scandura sick or something?"

"Sometimes Tony likes to do things himself."

"Funny family." Miguel's manner was superior and indulgent, his face soft, and his voice a degree away from being girlish. "What's with Alvaro?"

"He says for you not to sweat. It'll be done."

———

Lieutenant Christopher Wade checked into the Howard Johnson's in downtown Boston and was in his room less than a half hour when he had a visitor. It was a black man, tall and slender and impeccably groomed. Wade shut the door behind him and said, "You don't look like an agent. You look more like affirmative action at its corporate best. What do you want me to call you?"

"Blue's good enough."

Wade sat on the edge of the bed, and Blue lowered himself into a vinyl chair. A moment of quiet passed as each sized up the other. Blue's mouth curved doubtfully under his trim mustache.

"I hope you know what you're doing."

"I don't," Wade said. "As a matter of fact I've got a sour feeling I can't get rid of. I suppose that's something you'll have to tell Thurston."

Blue shrugged. "We've leased an apartment for you, something suitable but within your income."

"That was nice of you guys. How do you know I'll like it?"

"It's better than what you're living in now."

"How do you know what I'm living in?"

"We've been through it," Blue said, and Wade flushed, partly from outrage and partly from embarrassment. "You can move in March first," Blue went on easily. "That's the effective date of your transfer. We've deposited a sum in your checking account for next year's tuition for your daughters at Boston University. You'll be pleased to know the amount includes room and board, books, and a clothing allowance."

Wade forced himself to relax somewhat. He lit a cigarette, which helped. "Should I consider you my contact?"

"Could be me, could be somebody else," Blue said effortlessly. "Thurston has a lot of moves."

"I gathered that. While we're on the subject, maybe you could give me your honest opinion of him."

"I don't tell tales out of school. But I'll listen to your opinion of him."

"You're smooth, Blue."

"Comes with the suit." Blue got to his feet. He had said all he had come to say.

"That was quick," Wade said, rising, and together they walked to the door. Before opening it for him, Wade said, "By the way, you guys got a code name for me yet?"

Blue nodded. "Sweetheart."

———

Wade drove from Boston to Wellesley, to the sedate horseshoe-shaped street off the main drag, where he had once lived. It was seven in the evening, the streetlights burning in the cold. He still had a key to the house, though no longer the right to use it. But he did, as if from habit. Gently opening the door, he stepped into the light that shone from the living room. Nothing had been changed. No new furniture had been added and none of the old rearranged, but he felt like a stranger. Though not like an intruder. He went to the bottom of the carpeted stairs and called up to his wife, startling her.

"Chris, what are you doing here?"

Her voice revealed annoyance but no anger. She was doing her hair in the lit mirrors of the bathroom, obviously preparing to go out. When he got halfway up the stairs he could see her.

"Don't come up," she said, but he did, and she faced him with a frown, wearing only a soft cream blouse and speckled pantyhose. She had a long, attractive face and a well-kept figure. Her eyes were brown and serious. "I don't appreciate this," she said.

He said, "You look wonderful."

"And you look tired. What do you want, Chris?"

He smiled. "You."

"Don't," she said and began brushing her hair. "Don't play games."

He leaned against the door frame and took in her every movement. Their years together, in his eyes, had been precious, especially the early years when they lived in a housing project and put aside every dime they could for a house of their own. Their first child arrived five months after their marriage, which put a crib in their bedroom but not a crimp in their lovemaking. It seemed he could never get enough of her. He remembered her ingenious ways of disguising meatloaf and of creating files for myriad grocery coupons. He remembered his habit of tracing a finger around her ankle when they watched television together, and he remembered her face being full of light, as if from some radiant purpose, when she tried to peer into their future. His goal was to wangle his way into the detective division, which he managed the same year they passed papers on this house. The house was her joy, his new job was his. In time she said the job was excluding her from four-fifths of his life because of his obsession with every case he handled, his irregular hours, and his prolonged absences, weeks when he was tracking down leads, months when he was undercover, times when she didn't know whether he was alive or dead. The last straw for her was his seeming indifference to his daughters, who shocked him by growing up. He couldn't fault her decision to separate, but neither could he accept it as final.

"I'm being transferred back to Boston," he said and held his breath for a favorable reaction.

"I'm glad for you," she said. "I know you don't like it out there."

"Susan, listen—"

"Don't," she interjected. "Don't say it." She put the brush down and glanced quickly at her watch. "Chris, I have to hurry."

He could tell from her tone that she did not want to hurt him but at the same time did not want to delude him. The fact was that he was already hurt and would not have minded being deluded. The question he wanted to ask would not take shape.

She said, "Go downstairs. I'll join you in a minute."

It was nearly ten minutes before she came down dressed in a pearl-gray bolero and a fitted skirt that matched it. He looked up at her slowly from his chair and said, "Who is he, Susan? Anybody I know?"

"No, Chris, nobody you know."

"Somebody at work?"

She hesitated. She was a travel agent, Benson Tours. "Yes," she said, "somebody at work."

"A nice guy?"

"Yes, a nice guy."

He said, "I suppose I could stick around and meet him. It would be the civilized thing to do."

"I don't think it's necessary, Chris."

He lifted himself from the chair, working hard to keep his emotions hidden. "I have something for you," he said and gave her a check he had written out while he was waiting. "It's for the kids' schooling next year."

Her eyes widened when she read the amount, and then she looked at him suspiciously. "Where did you get this much all at once?"

He shrugged his shoulders and gave her a story he knew she found difficult to believe. Had she the time she would have sought a further explanation. Instead she again shot a look at her watch.

"Should I deposit it, or wait?"

"Deposit it," he said.

———

He drove back to the Howard Johnson's hotel and left the car in the underground garage and then, tightening his overcoat, walked the few blocks to the Combat Zone, where he jockeyed his way through the motley crowd on narrow Washington Street and eyed the gaudy arcades, movie houses, smut shops, and girlie joints. Despite the cold, the air was carnival. Bare-legged prostitutes, some underage, all insensible to the weather, tossed out smiles like peanuts to pigeons. A small band of pimps, tall fur or felt

hats a part of their regalia, filed into a lounge as if
for a meeting; the last to enter gave Wade a curt
glance. Wade went farther up the street and entered
a joint he knew Anthony Gardella had a piece of.

It was one of the busiest, perhaps the loudest, with
a succession of three circular bars, each with a miniature stage where a young woman gyrated to music
too electronic for Wade, too ear-shattering, too crush-
ing to his nerves. Yet he stayed. He found a seat at
the second bar and wedged himself in between two
black men, who gave him furtive looks without moving their heads. The stripper noticed his arrival and
welcomed it with a sudden thrust. She had milk-
white skin and a smattering of stretch marks on an
otherwise fine belly. Wade drank bottled beer.

He was on his second bottle when the man on his
right picked up his cigarettes and left, which gave
him room to relax his shoulders. Twice, from the
corner of his eye, he spotted someone from the
Gardella organization. Their pictures were among
those in a file Thurston had given him. Mostly they
were watching the tills, occasionally the strippers. He
retracted an elbow when a young black woman
perched herself on the vacated chair and smiled at
him through gilded eyelids and dangling cornrow
braids. She said something he couldn't hear over the
music. Then suddenly her breath was in his ear.
"Hey, you a cop? People here saying you're a cop."

He leaned toward her. "Yes, I'm a cop, but don't
worry about it. I'm here to relax. Buy you a drink?"

"Sure," she said and touched his hand by way of
thanks, her nails sparkling. "But we can't hear each
other here. Why don't we go to a booth?"

His beer bottle was only half-empty, and he took it
with him. She led the way into almost total darkness.
Though it was impossible to see, the booths all seemed

occupied, but she found one free down at the end
and stepped aside for him to slip in first. Then she
crowded in on the same side as he sat at an angle, his
back to the wall. He could not see her face, only her
eyes and teeth.

"We'll wait a second, okay?"

"Wait for what?" he asked as someone leaned into
the booth. A full bottle was deposited near his half-
empty one. He knew it was there by touching it, and
he knew something was there for her. It glistened.

She said, "You sure you're not here to bust people?"

"I give you my word."

"How much you want to relax?" she asked and let
her hand fall into his lap. "I can do some awful nice
things for you right here. Depending on what you
want is what it'll cost."

"I want so much," he said in a low voice, "here
wouldn't do."

"We can go someplace, three-minute walk."

Wade shook his head. His eyes had adjusted, and
he could see more of her. "Not tonight. Another
night. Tonight I'm hurting, carrying too much inside me."

"What kind of problems you got?"

"Wife problems. Wife's two-timing me."

The young woman's teeth flashed. "There's a way
to fix that, you two-time her, that way you come out
even and both be happy again. What you think of
that, huh?"

"I think you've got it all together, I just wish that I
did." Somebody was passing by the booth. He could
not see who it was, but he sensed it was a man. "This
is worth money to you, listening to me talk."

"I get all kinds," she said.

"I'm sure."

Before he left, he slipped a ten-dollar bill onto the

table for the drinks and pressed a larger denomination into her hand. She looked at it with the eyes of a lynx and whispered, "You're an all-right guy."

On his way out, letting his shoulders droop, he glimpsed Gardella's people. Their eyes burned into his back, which had been his purpose. He knew that everything he had told the young woman would be repeated.

———

Victor Scandura leaned over a cup of capuccino inside the Caffè Pompei, his elbows on the tiny table, his glasses off. His eyes, flyspecks, seemed blind. He said to Augie, "I've got to ask you something, be nice you answer me straight. What are you on?"

Augie made a face. "What you talking about?"

"You'd better tell me," Scandura said and rubbed the pinch marks on his nose. "Anthony wants to know."

Augie wrestled with something inside himself and finally said, "So I pop a little, what's the harm? I got a lot of scores behind me. The Skelly warehouse job was mine, so was the meat truck on Route One."

"You pop. What do you pop?"

"Uppers, okay? Now and then."

"You ask the harm, I'll tell you. You didn't perform well in Greenwood. Ralph wasn't there, I don't know what would have happened. You understand what I'm saying? You dirty yourself on junk, you're dangerous to us. It wasn't for Anthony's regard for your uncle, I wouldn't be talking to you. You wouldn't be here."

Augie's chinless face, already pale, went white. He tried to lift his cup of cappuccino, but his hand shook too much. "You don't have to worry about me, I understand."

"You make a mistake in these things," Scandura said evenly, "a lot of people have to pay. No more pills."

"I promise. You tell Anthony I swear. Okay?"

"Sure." Scandura fitted his glasses back onto his face. "Now get out of here."

Rita O'Dea descended the stairs bound in a big robe, her face moist and bright from her bath. She called out for Alvaro and found him in the kitchen, where he had made himself a fruit drink in the blender and was pouring it into a tall glass. Her gaze narrowed in on him. "Who was that you were talking to on the phone?"

"It was nobody," he said. "It was somebody asking if we wanted to buy a bunch of light bulbs for handicapped people. I told them we've got plenty of light bulbs, more than we can use."

"Don't give me that crap. Who was it?"

The drink he had made for himself contained banana, pineapple, nutmeg, vanilla syrup, and skim milk. He took a long taste of it and said, "Delicious."

She said, "Was it from Miami? Was it a woman?"

"One woman at a time, Rita. That's my rule."

"That's a good rule. You break it, I'll break you."

"Hey," Alvaro said with a handsome smile, "you're forgetting something. I love you."

"Yeah, I love you too," she said with no change of expression on her face. "C'mere and give me a kiss."

Inside one of the lusher residences on Key Biscayne, Anthony Gardella sat in air-conditioned comfort and sipped coffee brewed from choice blends. The host was Sal Nardozza, his contemporary and a cousin twice or thrice removed. Perched open on a marble table was a black-and-chrome briefcase over-stacked with money, fifties and hundreds, half to be washed through a Miami bank and half to broker a cocaine transaction, the clients Cuban and Colombian. Earlier a third man had slipped quietly into the room to count the bills so that later there would be no misunderstanding. He had also shown Gardella a balance sheet, which Gardella had perused with the trained eye of an accountant and then returned without comment.

Now that their business was done, Nardozza lit a cheroot and sat back in his wicker chair. He was dressed casually, Florida-style, his shirt open to the silver floss on his chest. His voice was raspy. "I'm surprised you came down here yourself, but I'm glad you did. You're staying for dinner, I hope. I'll give you a good feed."

Gardella shook his head. "My wife's waiting for me at the hotel."

"Have her join us, why not? I had a wife like you got, I'd never leave her alone."

"We got reservations at a little place. Second honeymoon for us."

Nardozza grinned respectfully. "You're a lucky guy, Anthony.

Gardella put his coffee cup down with care, centering it in the saucer. "There's a Cuban calls himself Alvaro, used to dish out towels at the Sonesta. Check him out for me, will you?"

"No problem. Anything else?"

"How's my brother-in-law doing?"

"Ty? I guess he's doing okay. I don't hear nothing bad about him. He's tied tight with that spic Miguel, but I guess you know that."

"Yes," Gardella said, "I know that. What I don't know is what Miguel wants with him."

"You want me to check on that too?"

"No," Gardella said. "My brother-in-law's got a big mouth. He was up to something, you'd have heard."

Nardozza assumed a sober expression. "I never asked, but how did Rita ever get hooked up with him?"

"Like she meets all her guys, Sal. She's a lonely woman."

"She dropped fifty pounds, she'd be beautiful."

"Seventy-five's more like it."

"She's still beautiful. She was growing up I had a crush on her, you remember?"

"I remember."

"You give her my best, Anthony."

"I will," Gardella said, rising.

He rode back to his hotel in the car he had rented, Ralph Roselli at the wheel. Ralph Roselli carried two concealed handguns, one under his arm and the other inside his waistband. The weapons were also rented, from the same fellow who had given them the keys to the car. Ralph stayed in the lobby, and Gardella rode the elevator to the fifteenth floor. The door to his room was open, and Jane Gardella was waiting for him, vivid, chic, eye-filling, dressed to the nines. "We're late," she said.

"They'll hold the table," he told her. "Let me look at you."

She turned one way and then another and said, "Do you approve?" The question was unnecessary.

He said, "You make me feel ten times more important than I am."

They held hands in the elevator. When they stepped into the lobby, she saw Ralph and stopped short. "Tony, do we have to bring him with us?"

"Yes," Gardella said remotely. "For some funny reason I don't feel right down here."

———

From his room at the Howard Johnson's, Christopher Wade punched out the private number of Russell Thurston. It was past midnight. After Wade identified himself, Thurston said, "I don't mind you calling me at home, but not at this hour. I hope it's important."

"You've got pull inside the state police. I mean, you've shown that, right? Who's it with, the commissioner himself? Old FBI man."

"What do you want, Wade?"

"Back in Greenwood there's a trooper named Denton—big, lumbering kid—who should be promoted to corporal. Deserves it. Why don't we see he gets it?"

"Did I hear you right?"

"It's a legitimate request."

"The hell it is."

"It's important to the kid, and I owe him."

Thurston sighed with annoyance. "What you're asking is petty. It doesn't make you look good, and it doesn't make me look good, laying something like that on the commissioner."

"Are you telling me you can't do it?"

"Sure I can do it, but I'm not going to."

"Do it, Thurston. Make me happy."

Thurston was quiet for a moment. "I hope you're not going to make this a habit."

"You have my word." Wade cleared his throat. "As long as I've got you on the line, let me ask you something. Should I keep a list of my expenses or just give you a round figure each week?"

"Each month. Yes, you list them. Wade, you trying to get my ass?"

"Yes," Wade said. "I find it a challenge. See you."

"Wait a minute." There was the sound of Thurston shifting the receiver from one hand to the other.

"I might as well tell you something I was saving for later. A rumble one of my people picked up, might not be anything to it."

"Go ahead," Wade said. "I'm all ears."

"There may be a contract on Gardella."

Wade pressed a finger to his lips and then slowly let it fall away. "They'll never hit him," he said.

Thurston said, "I'm betting on it."

6

AGENT BLUE lived with his wife on the Cambridge Street side of Beacon Hill, a mere three-minute walk to the Kennedy Building. Massachusetts General Hospital, where his wife worked, was a minute closer. At the breakfast table he dawdled over his coffee, and she leafed through the *Globe*. Her eye passed over a half-column mug shot of a man and then swept back to the name under it. Pushing the paper to Blue, she said, "Isn't this the guy you were telling me about?"

The photo was of Lieutenant Christopher Wade, accompanied by a brief report of his reassignment from the detective division at the Lee barracks to the Suffolk County office of the district attorney, where "the twenty-year veteran of the state police will take up the duties of a special investigator, particularly in the area of organized crime."

Blue said, "I pity the bastard. Thurston will chew him up."

His wife took the paper back and studied the picture. "Not a bad face. I like the eyes."

Blue said, "Be better if they were in the back of his head."

"You going to help him?"

"I don't know if he's worth it."

The same report caught the notice of a mildly good-looking man at the offices of Benson Tours in Wellesley. He carried the newspaper into Susan Wade's office and, with a vaguely apologetic air, waited until she got off the phone. Then, folding the paper to the article, he slid it across her desk. "Did you know about this?"

"Yes" she admitted, dropping back in her chair. He hovered.

"What does it mean to us?"

"Absolutely nothing."

He brightened and, stepping around the desk, thrust forward a long Yankee face with comfortable creases. He prided himself on a devotion to the finer things in life, intelligent and attractive women being among them. "What's your schedule?" he asked, pronouncing "schedule" in the British way.

"If you're asking if I'm free for lunch, the answer's yes."

———

Anthony Gardella and Victor Scandura were also interested in the announcement of Christopher Wade's reassignment. They were seated in the rear room of Gardella's real estate office on Hanover Street, a block down from St. Leonard's Church. Gardella read the item twice, the second time aloud to Scandura, who said, "I'm not all that surprised. The time I saw him he hinted he was working something. He must've known this was coming."

"Yet he did me a favor."

"In a way we did him one. We got rid of two crazies for him."

Gardella was quiet for a moment. "Two ways to figure him. He's a regular guy. Or he's cute. What do you think?"

"I'm like you, Anthony. I always think the worst and work from there."

There were two leather chairs in the room, and Gardella was in the larger one. On a side table was a bag of Italian cookies bought fresh that morning from the bakery next door. Gardella ate one. "You don't like him."

"I didn't say that."

"This new job of his, Victor, it could mean heat for us."

"What can he do to us? Nothing."

"He can come on strong, or he can do it easy. I'd rather have him do it easy, wouldn't you? What do we know about him?"

"He's got wife trouble, I know that. He was in one of our joints bleeding on one of the hookers."

"Let's check on it, see if it's true," Gardella said, interested. "Wrong woman can mess up a guy."

Scandura nodded. He was once married to a woman who allowed him his pleasure only on Fridays. Now he no longer felt the need. He crossed his legs, extending a shoe foxed along the sides and perforated on the toe. He said, "You've been quiet since you got back from Miami. Anything wrong?"

"I don't know." Gardella was pensive. "I got bad feelings down there. My cousin Sal. I think he wants to make a move. I could be wrong, since I got nothing staring me in the face that says I'm right."

Scandura said ominously, "You're seldom wrong, Anthony."

"I'll tell you what it was," Gardella said, reaching for another cookie. "Remember when my sister turned sixteen, and Sal, my age, had a hard-on for her?"

"I remember you telling me about it."

"I was so mad I was going to clip him. Anyway, there we are sitting in his house in Biscayne, and he mentions how he used to like her. Can you imagine? He reminds me of it, like he's not scared anymore."

"Maybe he forgot you were going to clip him over it."

"No. A guy *never* forgets something like that."

"That's true," Scandura agreed.

"Nose around, Victor. I need to know."

———

Christopher Wade's new apartment was on the third floor of a venerable brick building on Commonwealth Avenue. It had a kitchenette, a bedroom, a good-sized bathroom, and an extra-large sitting room that opened onto a small balcony overlooking the tree-lined mall. The weather was mild, almost springlike, and Wade, perched on the balcony, imagined the trees exploding into leaf and birds winging to the balcony for the feed he'd provide, though the thought came to him that he'd only attract pigeons. When he stepped back into the sitting room he heard the person in the apartment above walk across the floor.

He checked the telephone to see whether it was working. Boston University was in the vicinity, and he considered calling his daughters on the remote possibility of reaching one of them for lunch. Both lived in the same dormitory, Warren Towers, though in different rooms. He tried the older daughter's number, no response, and then the younger daughter's, same result. In his mind's eye he tended to see them still as little girls in braids, which was the reason he was always jolted when they appeared in person as willowy young women with hard touches of sophistication, the older one majoring in child psychology, the younger in journalism. The telephone shrilled as he drifted away from it.

He wheeled around fast and snatched it up, wondering if they had divined his wishes and even his unlisted number.

Russell Thurston said, "Hello, Sweetheart. Let's meet."

They met north of Boston at a rest stop on Route 93. Thurston climbed out of a nondescript Dodge and slipped into Wade's five-year-old Chevy Camaro, his small conceit, purchased at the time he promised both daughters he'd teach them to drive but never did. Thurston gave him a lingering look.

"Why the long face?"

Wade said, "Let's get on with it."

"Sure," Thurston said easily. "First of all, I want to make certain you know what Gardella's into besides the gambling, sharking, prostitution, and pornography. He's into state contracts with that development company of his, and he's into chemical waste disposal. Every time it rains he poisons half of New Hampshire, running trucks up there to leak on the roads. He's into—"

"Thurston, I know what he's into."

"Hear me out, because you don't know half what you think you do. Lately he's been doing a lot of business in Miami. He and his cousin Sal Nardozza have been bankrolling drug deals, no personal risk, only financial, and they make sure they never get burnt. The profits, I understand, have been fantastic. He and Nardozza used to work with some middleman named Miguel, but they squeezed him out." Thurston suddenly snapped his fingers, for Wade did not seem alert. "You with me?"

"I'm with you."

"Gardella's also washing a lot of money down there, most of it his own, some of it for friends, including politicians. He's got his finger in everything."

"What was that you were saying about a contract on him?"

"It could be a hundred percent horseshit, so forget it until I hear more."

Wade gazed up through the windshield at a sky more milk than blue. "What makes you so confident Gardella will let me get close to him?"

"That's the easy part," Thurston said complacently. "Since you already did a favor for him, he'll figure you want to do more, this time with your hand half out. Let him do little things for you, nothing big. And you do little things for him. Work it into something like friendship."

"You make it sound easy."

"I've got faith in you."

"Gardella's not stupid."

"Neither are you."

"He's not going to confide in me, no matter how close I get to him."

"Don't be so sure of that. And even if he doesn't, you've got eyes and ears." Thurston reached inside his coat and produced a folded sheet of paper. "Here's a list of names, politicians and businessmen Gardella's close with and cops he gives more than just pocket money to. When this thing is over, I'm going to have all of them."

Wade scanned the list. "Some of these names surprise me."

"Nothing should surprise you. Memorize them. One cop in particular I'm interested in. Scatamacchia. Know him?"

"We've met."

A trailer truck swung in off the highway and rumbled past them, air brakes wheezing, the ground trembling. The driver pulled the truck to a stop some twenty yards away and hopped out of the cab.

Before hustling into the woods, he gave the Camaro a curious look.

"He's wondering what we're doing," Wade said with a smile. "I can imagine what he's thinking."

Thurston, not amused, said, "How do you like your apartment?"

"Fine." Wade tightened his voice. "Who's in the apartment above me?"

Thurston was impressed. "Didn't take you long to figure that out."

"It was easy. No carpet on the floor. Someone living there for real would've laid one. Who's up there, Thurston?"

"Someone to look after you."

"And, of course, after your interests."

"Why not?" Thurston said in all reasonableness. When the truck driver emerged from the woods he cast another glance at the Camaro. Thurston gave him the finger.

Wade said, "You've made my day."

———

Alvaro twitched the curtain back. From the dining room in Rita O'Dea's house he had an unimpeded view of Anthony Gardella's house and of the expansive backyard, where Gardella's wife was roaming about, inspecting winter damage to shrubs, and intermittently gazing up at the mild sky. She had on a headband, a warmup jacket, and designer jeans stuffed into leather boots, all of which made her look even younger than her twenty-three years. Her hair was loose and curly. Alvaro adored blondes.

With a soft foot he made his way to a closed door and laid his ear to it. Rita O'Dea was on the phone, business, going over figures with somebody from G&B Toxic Waste Disposal. He knew she would be on the phone for a while yet, for she loved the sound of her own voice. Quietly he let himself out of the house.

Jane Gardella looked up sharply when he approached her and set herself imposingly. She was an inch taller than he, which in no way intimidated him. Rather, he put her on the defensive, his dark eyes edging over her, a smile creeping out of his neat beard, almost as if he knew more about her than he should. "We haven't had a chance to meet," he said slowly. "I'm Rita's friend."

Jane Gardella drew her elbows in, cupping them with her hands, and checked a smile. Some little warning told her to.

"Alvaro," he said.

"What?"

"My name. That's my first name. I got too many last names for you to remember." He had sugar in his smile, more in his voice. "Rita said her brother had a young wife, but I didn't know it was somebody looks like a movie star. She should've said, prepared me."

She turned slightly away from him, her hair fluttering in a cool breeze, something nagging her, as if she'd seen him before, two years ago, three years ago, someone like him. "You'll excuse me."

"What's your hurry?" he said, and his voice held her. It was that sudden and almost that familiar, and it frightened her for a reason she couldn't fathom. His eyes danced. "How'd he meet someone gorgeous like you? Was it here, in Boston?"

She let her arms fall to her sides and watched his face, watched the way he moved his mouth, his teeth flashing inside the beard.

"Miami. Was it Miami?"

She looked through him, beyond him. Quietly she said, "I think you're in trouble."

"What?"

A shadow fell over him. He turned, but not in time to avoid Rita O'Dea's lightning grip. She said, "You've got a lot of balls, Alvaro."

He made amends many hours later, nightfall. In the master bathroom, in front of mirrors, he used oils on himself, cologne, polish. He deodorized and powdered his private places, minted his breath, and stroked his close beard until it gleamed like the pelt of the blackest animal. His eyes sparkled like the sweetest woman's. He pattered over rugs to Rita O'Dea's enormous bed, drew back the spread, and lay on the top blanket to wait for her, to surprise her. "You little whore," she whispered moments later, leaning over him, gigantic in her tent dress. Parts of him received pondering glances.

"Do we need the light on, Rita?"

"Yes," she said, "because you're a fool and I'm a bigger one." Eyes remaining on him, she reached up and loosened her luxurious hair, as black as his beard. The lamp was little and shadowed him nicely. "You don't fool with my brother's wife. You so silly you don't know that?"

"You're reading me wrong, Rita, always reading me wrong. Am I not supposed to talk to people?"

She did not trouble herself to reply. She removed her jewelry, then her dress, yanking it off over her head, and stood in a slip that looked like the better part of a parachute. "Aren't you happy here?" she asked. "Don't you like the money I put in your pocket, the credit card I let you carry around, the clothes I buy you? You really want to give all that up?"

"Come to me, Rita."

She sat on the bed's edge and propped an arm on the far side of him, her hair falling. He raised a hand and traced a finger over her full face. "Don't give me any difficult decisions, Alvaro, or we both get hurt, you more than me."

"I'll be good."

She said, starkly, "You're lucky I love you."

———

The first evening in his new apartment Christopher Wade listened carefully for sounds above him and heard none, which did not satisfy him that no one was up there. A few minutes later he quietly climbed the stairs and tapped lightly on the door. He waited more than a moment and tapped again. Then he tried the knob, but there was no give. He placed his mouth near the crack and said, "If you don't open up, I'll use my shoulder."

The door opened.

The man who let him in was thickset, blondish, dour, and his voice was barely more than a whisper: "This is goddamned dumb of you." Then, surprisingly, he extended a hand. "The name's Blodgett."

Wade shook the hand and then angled past him. The apartment was a duplicate of his but seemed larger because of the minimal furniture. He saw electronic equipment, which was what he was looking for. Two telephones were on the floor. He glanced into the bedroom, which contained only a cot, the bedding stacked on top. A card table and two metal chairs had been placed in the kitchenette. A coffee-maker, the kind Joe DiMaggio touted on TV, was set up on the counter space.

Blodgett said, "As long as you're here, you want a cup?"

"No." Wade lit a Merit Menthol. Smoke popped out of his mouth. "You could use a carpet."

"We're getting one. Take it easy, Lieutenant. You're looking at me fierce."

"I took it for granted my phone was tapped, but I didn't realize you've got my whole apartment wired for sound."

"Everywhere but the bathroom," Blodgett said. "You want to talk private, you go in there."

"I don't believe you."

"Okay. You flush the toilet. Run the shower. We're not going to hear you over that."

"What about video?"

"That's coming, if we feel we need it. You'll know about it first."

Wade moved into the kitchenette and poured himself a cup of coffee after all. The cup was Styrofoam, which he hated the feel of. He dropped in a sugar cube and peeled open a creamer, which was nondairy, not to his liking. He didn't use it. "You're going to look conspicuous moving in and out of this building. You look more like a cop than I do."

"I won't be here anymore," Blodgett said in an easy tone. "A guy and a gal will be taking over, and you don't have to worry, they won't be here every minute. They'll pass as young marrieds, a professional couple. That make you feel better?"

Wade sipped his coffee, disliking it, and drew on his cigarette, letting out a thread of smoke. He was not sure what he thought of Blodgett, whose smile was faintly porcine, otherwise relaxed and open.

"If you run into them on the stairs, nod like a neighbor, but don't get friendly. Basically they know only what they have to about the operation. Let's keep it that way. Meaning don't come up here again."

"What about the other agent I met? Blue."

"Blue's a good man. You can trust him a hundred percent. You can trust me a hundred and five."

Wade dumped what remained of his coffee into the sink, his stomach queasy. He had not bothered with lunch or dinner. "Any other vital things you want to pass on?"

"Not really," Blodgett said carelessly. "Though I hear Gardella's got an interesting wife, half his age. Watch your step with her. I hear he's jealous."

"I'll bear that in mind."

"One other thing." The voice turned grave. "Be damned careful of his sister."

7

VICTOR SCANDURA took a taxi out of Miami Airport in a rainstorm. The rain was heavy, voluble, and the windshield wipers flailed. Peering into the rearview, the driver said, "You don't look the type. For where you're going, I mean. It ain't the ritziest place in the world. Take my advice. Watch your wallet."

Scandura nodded slightly as he peered through a sodden window. The outside world churned, trees eddied in the rain, oncoming traffic ghosted by. Then the driver's head turned for a second. "If you get my drift."

"I do," Scandura said.

When they reached the storm-darkened dock area, the taxi plowed slowly through puddles that linked up into black lakes. Tandem trailer trucks, which looked abandoned, reared up between buildings fronted by curbside sacks of uncollected rubbish. Some sacks had shattered into the gutter, the trash surging away. "Down there," Scandura said, and the driver said, "I know where it is. I just don't like going down there." It was more of an alley than a street, the rain gusting through it. The taxi inched into it and stopped at a small, squat structure that looked like zinc. A half-lit sign read DINTY'S. The driver said, "Don't ask me to wait."

"That's exactly what I'm going to do," Scandura replied, peeling off a fifty and tearing it in half.

He hustled into Dinty's before the rain could pin him in place or sweep him away but not before it soaked the back of him, and he shivered as the door shut behind him with a dull thud. He recoiled from the chill, stale air of the place, which in no way had changed since his last visit, maybe two years ago. The barkeep was obese, the waiter lame. Most of the patrons were lined up at the bar, and immediately he picked out the snitches, their faces secretive, even those who probably had no secrets. Only one interested him.

Suddenly he felt uncomfortable. He was standing in a shaft of light, and he pulled away from it and made his way to a chrome-stemmed table against the wall in a corner, where he felt the draft from an air conditioner. Five minutes passed before the waiter hobbled near. Without looking at him, Scandura said, "I've got a headache. Bring me a Bromo with ice."

Nearly three minutes passed before the waiter returned, setting down the Bromo with a hard clunk, the tablet still fizzing. Scandura said, "The little guy down at the end of the bar, he called Skeeter?"

The waiter looked. "Yeah, that's Skeeter."

"I thought so. He's changed some. You go by him, tell him to come over, I'll buy him a drink."

The waiter said, "Sure, I can do that."

Skeeter appeared presently, carrying a shot of whiskey and a beer chaser, and joined Scandura with a nod. He was a nervous creature, skin and bones, bird-nosed, prick-eared, existing as if solely on his own nervous energy. From the depths of a sour-smelling suit two sizes too big for him, he said, "What's this you told him I changed some? I look the same as the last time I seen you."

"I had to tell him something, didn't I, Skeeter?"

Skeeter was Boston-born, Prince Street, a boyhood friend of Anthony Gardella's. Consumptive when he was a young man, he fled south to escape the New England weather and picked up pocket money doing odd jobs for friends of Meyer Lansky. In celebration of his regained health he began boozing and never stopped, which left him unreliable as a shooter for Lansky's people. Gradually, between burglaries and racetrack scams, he became a snitch, one of the best. How he stayed alive was a curiosity, not least of all to Scandura, who had no use for him.

"Anthony sends you his best."

"How is Anthony?"

"He's fine."

"He comes down here, he never looks me up. Only you look me up."

Scandura's elbows were damp, which sent a chill through him. His jacket stuck to his back. The last time he was here the barkeep cold-cocked a Hispanic customer for trying to pay for a drink with a peso.

Skeeter said, "You're getting bald, Victor. I remember as a kid you had light hair. We all called you Victor the Kraut. Most guys get names like that, they stick for life. Yours didn't."

"Maybe because I didn't like it."

"That's right. People didn't fuck with you."

"They still don't."

Skeeter smiled slowly, a part of his face sagging as if it were missing a bone. "I should've sucked up to Anthony more. I'd've made it big too."

"Now you've got that out of the way," Scandura said, "maybe we can talk."

"Sure, shoot."

"What's Sal Nardozza doing that's different?"

"You're asking the wrong question, you always

do." Skeeter wriggled inside his suit, as if climbing up in it. Then he downed his whiskey and shivered all over as he reached for his beer. "Ask me about Miguel Gilberto, him I know something about could surprise you. He's dealing again."

"Small stuff, we know. He's got Ty O'Dea with him, which makes it real small."

"He's dealing big, believe me."

"He's got no money to deal big. We cut him off."

"Sal didn't."

Scandura jerked his head back so that what little light fell his way wouldn't touch his face. "You telling me Sal's still banking him?"

Skeeter grinned triumphantly. "I gotta spell it out for you, you horse's ass?"

A thrill shot through Scandura's belly. Conspiracy, intrigue, betrayal always affected him a funny way, like someone brushing a finger just below his navel. Skeeter's narrow head teetered at the top of his suit.

"How much, Victor? How much you giving me?"

Scandura already had the money out, a small moist wad, which he passed under the table. He was on his feet before Skeeter knew it was in his lap, and he was through the door before Skeeter counted it. The rain pelted him. He had to pound his fist against the taxi window to gain entry. The driver flung the door open and said, "Jesus Christ, I'll never do this again!"

Scandura said, "It's the only way to live."

———

Ty O'Dea, who lived in a little metal trailer outside Miami, felt lousy and took a belt of bourbon to calm his stomach, which it didn't do. Finally he lay down in his bunk and listened to the rain. He could feel the throb on all sides of the trailer, which put him to sleep. When he woke four hours later, it was raining even harder. Flannel-mouthed, he took another swig of bourbon and waited for a cramp to pass. He was sitting on the edge of the bunk when the woman who lived with him came home from work. She shook her umbrella and closed it with a flourish as he watched with a faint smile. He was always glad to see her and worried when she was late.

"I was feeling shitty, so I slept," he told her.

"How do you feel now?"

"Better," he said, watching her rummage inside her book bag and finally come up with a comb, which she ran roughly through brown hair that was graying ungracefully. She was in her early thirties. The books that had tumbled out of her bag were dog-eared Penguins. She taught English literature and occasionally pushed marijuana at Miami-Dade Community College. "If it stops raining," he said, "I'll take you out to eat."

"I can make something here," she said. "You think about it for a while and tell me what you want."

She went into the bathroom, which was a tiny compartment, barely big enough to squeeze into, and closed the door, and he pondered supper in a leisurely way, glad that they would be sharing it. She was the first woman he had ever truly felt comfortable with and the first he had felt lonely without. He got up and spoke through the bathroom door. "Did you miss me?"

"Yes," she answered. "I always miss you."

"I feel lucky, do you know that? I feel for the first time in my life everything's going right." He wiped his white hair from his eyes and smiled cautiously. He had money in the bank, a joint account, his name and hers, both signatures required for withdrawals. "Sara," he said, leaning a shoulder against the door.

"What is it, Ty?"

"I love you."

"Good," she said, "because I think I'm pregnant."

He beamed, all of a sudden, and for a full moment closed his eyes. "I'm glad," he said. "I hope you are."

"Do you want it, Ty?"

"Yes," he said. "I've always wanted a kid. If it's a boy, I'd like him to be Tyrone O'Dea Junior, do you mind?"

"No, Ty. I don't mind."

Nor did he mind that the child would not be his. Years ago, at Rita O'Dea's suggestion and then insistence, he had gotten a vasectomy. He said with zest, "Tomorrow we look for a better place to live."

As soon as he got back from Miami, Victor Scandura reported to Anthony Gardella, who listened carefully and without interruption. When Scandura finished, Gardella evinced no sign of wounded feelings and said, "Only one way to figure it. Sal's using money doesn't belong to him."

"Stuff we give him to wash?"

"He's washing it all right, he's not that stupid, but he's playing with it first. That's the only way he could bankroll big scores on his own. Wasn't for me, he wouldn't have a penny."

"Wasn't for you, Anthony, he wouldn't even be down there. He'd still be up here stealing razor blades from Gillette. I still got some he gave me."

Gardella said, "He's got something going with this Miguel, it means what he's got going with me isn't enough for him. Maybe he wants me out altogether."

"Something to consider. He ever get back to you on what you asked him about? Rita's friend, Alvarez."

"Alvaro. Yeah, he told me this guy's a piece of slime, a two-bit hustler, and it's a wonder nobody's broken his legs and maybe I should do it, advice I don't need."

Scandura let a second pass. "About time Rita grew up, don't you think?"

"That's not for you to say," Gardella said, narrowing his eyes.

"Sorry, Anthony, I was out of line."

"Too many things hitting on me, Victor. I still haven't got over what happened to the folks. Neither has Rita. I look at her the wrong way, she's hurt to the core. Thinks nobody loves her. I love her, I almost got to put it in writing." Gardella sighed. "Then there's the thing with Ferlito's nephew Augie, which I haven't forgotten. What d'you think about that, Victor?"

"I talked to him like you asked. I say we watch him, see how it goes."

"What about the other thing? Wade. I don't want any surprises."

"He's set up in an office in the Saltonstall Building, twentieth floor, nothing on the door except *Private*. They tell me it looks real hush-hush."

"What about his wife?"

"Checks out. She's playing footsie with her boss, John Benson, Benson Tours. They've been away together on trips. Guess where? Key Biscayne."

Gardella was thoughtful, even a little pained. "A guy separated from his wife still expects her to behave. Depending on the guy, it can tear him up. What d'you think?"

"I don't know, Anthony. I can't get in the guy's skull."

"I think he and I should talk. Minute he did me a favor, he said something to me. He's smart enough to know that."

"Long as we go easy on it. You know how I am

about cops. Even Scat rubs me the wrong way. I still don't forget the time in the fifth grade he ratted on my brother about who picked the priest's pocket. Father D'Agostino, you remember him?"

"Scatamacchia is one of us," Gardella said dryly. "Wade isn't. I get the idea he's the kind of guy you don't embarrass with an offer."

"What kinda guy gets embarrassed? Mad maybe, not embarrassed."

"I just told you. His kind of guy. He doesn't want to come right out and say he'll take. Maybe he wants to fool himself."

"Somebody should tell him everybody takes."

"We can feel him out and do him little favors. He's lonely, we get him a woman." Gardella's voice rippled. "Money can come later. Gradually, naturally. But first I want to talk to him face to face. You set it up."

Scandura nodded. He had a small glass of beer in front of him. Scattered salt on the table stuck to the edge of his hand. "What are you going to do about Sal?"

"I got a choice, Victor? You tell me."

"You got to clear it first?"

"This is my business, nobody else's."

"Then the only question is whether taking Sal out is going to be enough."

"Make your point, Victor."

"If Sal has a contract on you, he must've done it through the half-breed. Miguel."

"He goes too."

"Be nice to know who his shooter is."

"I'll leave that up to you," Gardella said with a lethargic movement, some sadness in it, as if from a premonition. Scandura straightened his spectacles and lifted his beer glass.

"Then there's the matter of your brother-in-law."

"That I got to think about," Gardella said.

———

The district attorney did not know Lieutenant Christopher Wade and did not want to know him. One of his bright young assistants, magna cum laude from Suffolk Law, said, "What the hell's going on?" and the DA told him to mind his own business. The DA had been vaguely briefed by the FBI, sworn to secrecy on the little he'd been told, and promised some of the credit if the scam worked and none of the responsibility if it didn't. In his conversation with Supervisor Russell Thurston, he said, "I don't want him anywhere near me," and Thurston told him not to worry. "If he's found floating in the harbor," the DA said, "I don't want the heat."

"You have my word," Thurston said.

Lieutenant Wade was installed in a two-room office in the Saltonstall Building, where he could look out a window at the Post Office, Kennedy Building, and City Hall across the way in Government Center. The first room in Wade's office was furnished with steel desks and empty file cabinets. Wade used the top drawer of one cabinet to stash personal belongings, which included a shaving kit and a spare Beretta 9mm semiautomatic, a twin to the one he carried. Atop each desk was a telephone and a pad of paper. Mug shots of local organized crime figures adorned a bulletin board. The inner room was vacant except for a cot with bedding, in case Wade ever wanted to spend the night there, which he considered unlikely. There was a small sink but no toilet. For that, he would need to go down the hall.

His second day there, he rang up Thurston and said, "Where's my staff?"

"I'm working on it."

"I've got nothing to do."

"Pretty soon you'll have plenty to do. Right now people don't know what you're up to. It creates tension."

"So I just sit here on my ass."

"Till I say move it."

Wade clunked the phone down. He locked the office, rode an elevator to the lobby, and strode out of the building. It was the noon hour, a mild, blowy day. He stood against the percussion of traffic that surged up Cambridge Street, God help anyone in the way. He crossed the street when the lights let him. The plaza of Government Center swarmed with office workers out for the warmth, the men in shirt sleeves, the women bare-armed, tourists among them, also peddlers and vendors, the food smoking from their pushcarts. A ravaged old man, death warmed over, rattled a cup of coins, and Wade, who could never walk by a beggar without giving something, stuffed a fast dollar into the cup. A Chinese youth glided by on roller skates, skillfully, like a spirit.

With a sidelong glance Wade noticed that the beggar was trying to follow him, perhaps to thank him, or perhaps to ask for a little more. Then the beggar seemed to lose his way, to vanish, a wraith like the youth on skates.

Wade queued up to buy a hot dog at a busy pushcart. In front of him was an assemblage of City Hall types, Cro-Magnons in Arrow shirts, their conversation carnal. Suddenly they all wheeled around, their eyes darting past Wade to a sudden commotion. Wade pivoted.

He elbowed through a crowd that did not want to move, its fascination too great. "Look out!" he said and shoved people aside. The beggar was sprawled on his back, coins spilled around him, somebody stepping on the dollar. Wade crouched over him. There was dried blood on his face, not from shaving but from picking, and a yellow fringe of foam on his lips. His eyes were sightless, his fingers curled into claws. Wade listened for a beat and felt for a pulse and then, wincing, the crowd gasping, he gave the man mouth-to-mouth.

It was in vain.

He staggered to his feet as two uniformed policemen wended toward him. "The guy's gone," he said and stumbled away, again using an elbow, more emphatically this time. He bought a can of Coca-Cola, gargled a mouthful, and spat it into the gutter as his stomach turned. Somebody in passing brushed close to him.

"That's no way to make a living," Victor Scandura said from behind glaring spectacles and continued on. Then he stopped and looked back.

"You got something to say?" Wade asked.

"Another time," Scandura said. "When you're feeling better."

8

FLOWN UP from the New York office were four federal agents with newly contrived credentials that bore the seal of Suffolk County, Commonwealth of Massachusetts. Agent Blodgett met them at the airport, provided them with rented cars, introduced them into the lava flow of early Boston traffic, and escorted them to the Saltonstall Building, where they gathered into Christopher Wade's outer office and stood stiffly in look-alike suits. Each had a background in accounting. Each looked dry, distant, and difficult—perfect for the task, Wade mused. He glanced at Blodgett and said, "I assume Thurston has briefed them."

"They know their objective."

"Which is?"

"To harass, to scare."

Wade looked skeptical. "They can harass Gardella, but they won't scare him."

"They'll make him uneasy," Blodgett said in a tone low and authoritative. "That's good enough for your purposes."

"You hope."

"You worry too much."

"My nature."

"Change it."

"You sound like Thurston."

Blodgett smiled, as if he had gotten a compliment.

Within the hour Wade and two of the four agents arrived at the drab premises of G&B Toxic Waste Disposal Company in East Boston. A tank truck was parked behind a chain fence that was warped in places. A NO TRESPASSING sign clung unsteadily to an unlocked gate that swayed open when Wade touched it. The three of them strode into a cinder-block building, followed a dim corridor to its end, and made a commanding entrance into a surprisingly neat and bright office, the furniture chrome and leather. Two women stared from their desks, and a small man with lank hair and a Givenchy necktie leaped up from his.

"Who the hell let you guys in?"

Wade seemed to smile. "You're Rizzo, right? You're the manager."

"I'm the owner."

"No, you're the manager. You answer to Rita O'Dea, and she answers to her brother."

The man instantly went on guard, eyes narrowing. His tie hung past his fly. His shirt was silk. "I've seen your picture in the paper."

"Then you know why I'm here," Wade said and glanced at the women, who averted their eyes. Both were attractive in hard, uneven ways. Wade noticeably admired each.

"This is bullshit," the man said, and Wade returned his gaze to him.

"I saw only one tanker out there. Where're the rest?"

"Hauling waste."

"I heard they don't go anywhere. They just drive out of state and leak a lot."

"You hear wrong."

Wade assumed a virtuous expression. "These are

two of my assistants. This is Mr. Holly, that's Mr. Haynes. They're going to check your shipment records for the past year and audit your books. Figure them being here at least a month."

The man's eyes radiated contempt. "This is bullshit."

"Don't you believe it, Mr. Rizzo."

"You got anything to show?"

Wade flashed a court order.

A half hour later, back in Boston's business core, he left his car in a private lot and walked around the corner to an imposing office building of darkened glass, where on an upper floor Aceway Development Association had a suite, Anthony Gardella one of the principal owners, though not of record. The two other agents from New York were waiting outside the building for him. Their bogus names were Danley and Dane. The one named Danley glided forward, the dark glass reflecting his movement. "We just saw Gardella go up," he said and looked pleased. Wade wasn't. "What's the matter, Lieutenant?"

Wade glanced at the traffic, which honked and fumed. "Let's not go in yet."

"Why not?"

"I don't feel like facing him."

The agent made a face. "You afraid of him?"

"Yes," said Wade. "I'm afraid of him."

———

From a dormer window in Rita O'Dea's bedroom, Alvaro had a full view of the driveway leading to Anthony Gardella's house. When he saw the flash and sweep of headlights, he noted the time and later the fact that, as usual, Gardella entered his house through the three-stall garage, the doors of which moved electrically. He also observed that, of the two men who had arrived with Gardella, only one stayed, Ralph Roselli, who presumably would spend the night in a downstairs guest room. The other man, Victor Scandura, left in another car, his own.

Alvaro further noted that the grounds were well lit, as usual.

He moved swiftly from the window when Rita O'Dea called from the bathroom. Clad only in magenta Jockey briefs, he pattered to the door and peered through the vapors. Half out of the shower stall, she looked like a big baby picture that had burst out of its frame.

"No towels!" she cried.

He found one, terry cloth, monogrammed, one that he had used earlier, but was dry now. He spread it wide and rubbed her down, her flesh quivering. Gently he raked his fingernails down her back and gave her a shiver. She snatched off her shower cap, her hair jumping loose, and gazed at him over her shoulder.

"Sometimes you know just what to do," she said and sought his lips. The kiss was vigorous on her part, expert on his. He helped her into a massive robe and tied it for her. She reached for a brush as the telephone rang in the bedroom. "Get it," she said.

He fetched it for her. It was cordless. He stepped back to listen to her talk and immediately knew from her voice that the caller was her brother. She threw a look at him.

"This is private."

He retreated into the bedroom, but it wasn't far enough. She told him to go downstairs, which he did after squeezing into a pair of pants. He made his way into the kitchen, where polished pots and pans hung from a wall like weaponry. A knife gleamed from the butcher's block. Opening a side door, he peered out into the chill darkness. Only a couple of lights glowed inside Anthony Gardella's house. He had never been in it, but he knew it was laid out more or less like Rita's. He also knew that Gardella never lingered more than a moment near a lit window, even with the shade pulled.

He went back up to the bedroom, where Rita O'Dea was moving about with a heavy step. She was dressing and doing it hurriedly, giving only scant attention to how she looked, which was uncharacteristic. "What's the matter?" he asked and received no answer, not even a look. "Why you so quiet?"

"I'm quiet, you should be too." She shook her shoulders. Button me.

He lifted her hair and did up the back of her dress while breathing on her neck. "Where you going?"

"My brother wants to see me."

"Is there a problem?"

"Don't ask. It was for you to know, I'd tell you."

He stepped around her, forced her to look at him. His beard had a sleek look and smelled of bay rum. "What's the matter, you afraid I keep a notebook on things you tell me?"

"No, only the things I don't tell you."

"What's that mean?"

"It means my brother and I only trust each other." Then she smiled thinly. "It's how we stay in business, kiddo."

———

Jane Gardella, staring through her darkened bedroom window, saw Alvaro standing in the side door of Rita O'Dea's house and suddenly remembered where she had seen him before.

A part of her went cold.

The beard had fooled her. Slowly she dropped back from the window and only with the greatest effort restrained herself from running downstairs to her husband. It was not something she could tell him.

It had been three years ago.

She was Jane Denig then, a stewardess for Delta. She sat in the passenger seat of a red Porsche in a crowded car park at Miami Airport and watched through the windshield as her boyfriend Charlie dealt with a buyer some twenty yards away. Charlie had no choice. He was in debt, behind in his child support, the mortgage on his condo, and the payments on the Porsche. She had no choice either. She loved him, or thought she did.

She watched the deal go down while sitting safely in the car. She was unobserved, her face shrouded in shadow as the richness of the Florida evening poured in on her. Money changed hands in an almost priestly way. Cocaine was passed, though with a slight hesitation. Then in a snatch of light she glimpsed the buyer, who was obviously Hispanic, slim, clean-shaven, and very handsome. He seemed to throw Charlie a little kiss before he vanished.

Charlie scurried back to the Porsche and pushed himself behind the wheel, his face ashen. "Damn it!" he said, trembling and searching for a cigarette he couldn't find. "He only paid me half what he said he would."

"Then why'd you give him the stuff?" she asked.

"I didn't want to fool with him," Charlie said miserably. "I know what he does on the side."

She waited for the answer.

"He kills people."

———

Christopher Wade met with Russell Thurston in frail light behind a dark building where scraps of paper, fruit rinds, and flattened soft-drink cans littered the asphalt like fragments from an explosion.

Wade, catching the whiff of an alley used as a privy, said, "Couldn't you have picked a better place?"

"Call it an adventure."

"You want a report?"

"I already got one. Things went well." Thurston's smile was an ironic shadow in his steep face, and his breath smelled of what he'd eaten, which was French food at the Café Plaza. "But tell me, are you really afraid of Gardella?"

"You bet I am."

"As long as it doesn't make you too cautious. When do you think he'll make contact?"

"Soon. Victor Scandura's been nosing around."

Thurston's breathing quickened. "Gardella will want to take you to dinner, no guinea joint, but someplace nice. He likes to put on airs."

"You know his habits."

"I know guineas."

Wade experienced a quality of feeling he couldn't explain. Nor did he want to. Having it was bad enough, and watching the glint in Thurston's eye made it worse. Thurston moved closer.

"Something's breaking down in Miami that could have repercussions here. We think it involves Gardella's money operation, somebody's greedy fingers. Bodies could fall."

Wade said, "You going to let it happen?"

"How can I stop it? And even if I could, why would I want to? It gives Gardella more to think about and you more of an edge."

"That contract on him, he must know about it."

"Fits, doesn't it?" Thurston said and turned sharply. There was static from the alley, a derelict's gut-rending cough, and they moved quietly to another side of the building, the windows meshed in steel. "You know who owns this building?" Thurston asked and smiled as if from a private joke. Wade looked up and just barely made out the weathered sign that read GAR-DELLA'S COLD STORAGE.

"Damn you," Wade said. "This is my life you're playing with."

———

Anthony Gardella closed the door of his library to give him and his sister total privacy. The chairs were leather. His voice was sober. He gave an account of what had happened at G&B Toxic Waste and later at Aceway Development. "I should've been called too," she started to say, but his eyes silenced her. He gave a curt assessment of the situation, no more than she needed to know, and then informed her of happenings in Miami, which caused her to tighten. He spoke without haste, without inflection, almost—it seemed—without interest. Then there was silence. She knew enough not to break it. She also knew that her involvement in his operations—unprecedented in the eyes of his associates—was distant, token, a gesture of his to make her feel useful, valued, good about herself. He let his head drop back, closed his eyes, and said, "You got any questions?"

"I know why you told me about Miami," she said in a small voice. "Ty's there."

"What do you feel for him?"

"He's still my husband. I don't want to see him dead. I don't want to go to the wake knowing we did it."

"He's garbage."

"No, Tony. He's only weak. He's not big like you and me. And it wasn't all his fault. You remember how it was. I was never good to him. Maybe you know why."

"I don't care why."

"He made me mad. He wasn't you. I wanted you, Tony, but you're my brother."

"I don't want to hear talk like this."

"My big brother."

"You been drinking?"

"No, Tony, making love with the spic, that's all."

"I got more things to tell you. You want to listen, or you want to keep saying things that get me mad?"

"I want to be sixteen again. I want to get into a size-ten dress, and I want Papa to scold me and you to hug me."

Gardella opened his eyes and looked at her. Her dense hair gathered light; no lines in her large face, only a shadow. "Go home, Rita. I'm tired."

Much later, after receiving a succinct phone call from Victor Scandura, he climbed the stairs to his bedroom. A small bedside light was on. His wife lay well into the covers. He leaned over and kissed the top of her blonde head.

"I'm not asleep," she said.

He sat on the edge of the bed and stroked her cheek. "You were me," he asked in a weary voice, "what would you do about Rita?"

"Be good to her."

"I am," he said. "A lot of times too good."

"Tony."

"What?"

Her slim hand floated up to his face. "Thank you for asking me."

9

A CADILLAC fishtailed through traffic into the Combat Zone and eventually forced itself into a parking space, one wire-rimmed wheel up on the curb. Victor Scandura climbed out of the passenger side, leaving his topcoat unbuttoned. The March morning was mild. He walked along the sidewalk's edge at a brisk pace until all of a sudden his step faltered. There was a burning below his chest from an ulcer that hadn't kicked up in a long time. As he waited for relief, a woman police officer approached cautiously and asked whether anything was the matter. He shaped a smile of sorts. "Everything's fine. Thanks for asking."

A minute later he entered the dimness of a girlie joint. There was not much of a crowd, nothing near the numbers that would be there later. A couple of blowsy women occupied a booth, another sat at the bar. Scandura proceeded to the end of the bar, and a man with a spotted forehead and thin combed-back hair emerged from a table, where he had been checking race results in the *Herald*. His smile was effusive.

"Victor. Good to see you."

Scandura nodded, no smile. "We want a woman to do something for us. She's gotta have class, talk right, know how to throw her ass around so it don't hit you in the face. You got somebody like that?"

"No problem. I'll get on the phone, get back to you in a coupla hours. Where will you be?"

"I'll call you."

The man batted his eyes. His voice squeaked. "I hear Anthony's got trouble."

"What trouble?"

"The crime-buster thing. That guy Wade, he gonna hit on here too?"

"He does, you call me." Scandura started to turn away.

"Hey, Victor. Can I get you something before you go?"

"Yeah, get me a glass of milk."

When Scandura returned to the car, Ralph Roselli immediately switched on the ignition and looked at his watch. "Plenty of time," Scandura said, sitting back, half closing his eyes. They drove to Logan Airport, Delta terminal. The Cadillac slid to a sharp stop. Ralph Roselli, his baggy face immobile, grabbed a flight bag from the back seat and slipped out. Scandura eased himself behind the wheel and said, "Good luck."

———

Christopher Wade telephoned Russell Thurston and said, "You were wrong. He doesn't want to meet in some fancy restaurant. He wants me to take a trip."

"What are you saying to me?"

"He's got a summer house in Rye Beach, New Hampshire. That's where he wants to meet."

"I know the place," Thurston said. "Blodgett took pictures of it a few years ago. A ninety-minute drive from here. That's where he used to take his wife—the one he's got now—before he married her. He didn't let her into his house in Hyde Park till she had the ring on her finger."

"Interesting."

"When are you meeting him?"

"He wants Wednesday, the evening."

"Give it to him."

"I already told Scandura I'd be there, no promises on what I'd listen to, or even if I'd listen at all."

"Beautiful," said Thurston. "You're a Hollywood actor."

"What does that make you—Otto Preminger?"

"Make it John Ford," Thurston said. "He was my favorite."

————

Anthony Gardella took his wife to the theater, choice seats, a hit play, and later they went to a small North End restaurant that stayed open late, just for them. The owner made much of them, as did the waiters. They especially made much of her, to honor him. Later, at home, after he had locked up and checked the security alarms, he watched her remove her earrings. When she slipped out of her pumps, he placed slow arms around her. "You've been quiet lately. How come?"

"I'm happy, Tony. I don't need to shout." She smiled at him, but with care, as if to give him no wrong impressions. "How about you? Are you happy? Do you love me?"

"You know how much I love you. I loved you any more, it wouldn't be right."

Her lips grazed his cheek. "Talk to me that way always, I can live on it."

He said, "This is a funny mood you're in, but I like it."

Afterward, in bed, their hands touching under the covers, he told her they would be going to Rye Beach on Wednesday. "I have to entertain somebody," he said and told her who it would be. Her head shifted imperceptibly on the pillow.

"I read the papers, Tony. I know who he is, and what he's trying to do to you."

"The DA's behind it. He's looking to make political points, get some exposure on TV, some good ink from the *Globe* and *Herald*. Him I can't talk to. Wade I can."

"What makes Wade different?"

"He's got a heart. He let it show once."

There was a silence, no explanations sought. She was lying on one of her bobby pins, and she moved herself slightly. She let her eyes close with a flutter, as if from feelings that had uncoiled slowly, perhaps reluctantly.

Gardella said, "There's going to be a woman with us. I want you to pretend she's your friend."

She kept her voice light. "And you don't want me to ask why."

"That's right," he said and gave her hand a playful squeeze. I want you to be a real wop wife."

Ralph Roselli drove over the Southern Boulevard Bridge into Palm Beach and, turning left, drove for more than a mile on Ocean Boulevard. Then he took another left, which aimed him into a network of narrow residential streets, tiny stucco houses jammed in from corner to corner, many painted pink. Checking signs, he eventually wound his way to a street narrower than the others and parked in front of a house more rose than pink. A man in rumpled pants that once went with a decent suit was watering his meager patch of lawn. The man looked up with a start as Roselli shuffled toward him. "You're early," he said and turned off the hose.

"No," Roselli said. "If anything, I'm a few minutes late. You got my material?"

"Your material, huh. Yuh, I've got your material. It's in the garage, back of my car."

The garage was under the house, stuck in the ground, part of what passed for a basement. Roselli wrinkled his nose. "Stinks in here."

"We got problems in the ground. Stuff seeps up that shouldn't be down there in the first place. Half of Florida's poisoned. Don't drink the water."

"Hurry up," Roselli said.

The man opened the trunk of his car, gingerly lifted out a package the size of a shoe box, and passed it into Roselli's careful hands. "Want me to explain the mechanism to you?"

"I needed you to explain it, I wouldn't be taking it."

The man said, "How long you going to be in the area, Ralph?"

"Why d'you want to know?"

"If you're going to be around till Wednesday, my wife's uncle's having a big cookout. Lives in Lantana. You're welcome to come."

"Enjoy yourselves," Roselli said and returned to his car. With much care he placed the package inside his flight bag. Moments later he was back on Ocean Boulevard. He drove south to Miami, scrupulously observing the speed limit all the way.

———

On Wednesday, late morning, Miguel Gilberto was killing time with a waitress in a hotel bar in downtown Miami. The waitress, who had joined him at his table when the only other customer had drifted out, sat with her knees knocked together, her kinky red hair worn long and wild. She said, "Maybe you got it mixed up. It must've been your mother was American, not your father."

"No," he said, his enormous black eyes sinking into her, "it was my father."

"Then how come your name isn't like his?"

"Gilbert didn't go with Miguel. I put the *o* on to make it ring right."

She laughed. "I bet you're kidding me."

"I don't kid." He scooped peanuts from a dish and ate them out of his hand, then licked the salt off his palm. "How about it, you gonna go out with me later or not?"

"You're too short for me."

"I got shoes with heels," he said, "I'll wear 'em." She let out another laugh, but not as loud this time. His eyes were too sardonically into hers. He said, "Al Pacino's short. You wouldn't turn him down."

"You serious? You really want to take me out?"

He gazed beyond her, and his face abruptly changed, grew hard in a way that daunted her. "You'd better go now," he said quietly.

She got to her feet fast and went to the bar. Sal Nardozza dropped himself into the vacated chair. He was smoking a cheroot and wearing an open shirt, leafy in design, his silver chest floss showing. Leaning forward, he rasped, "Who we dealing with?"

"Couple of Cubans," Gilberto said. "I've done business with them before. Ty O'Dea knows them. You can check with him, you don't believe me."

"I'd take your word before I'd take his. How many pure pounds we talking about?"

"They didn't tell me. They just said how much money they're going to need to make it happen. Million five."

"You're kidding."

"You can't handle it all, maybe we can bring in some other people, make up the difference."

Nardozza said, "Million five is nothing to me. But I'll feel better when Alvaro does his thing."

"Alvaro does his thing, we'll all feel better." Gilberto's eyes moved restlessly. "Right now, we got this business to decide."

"I want to be eye to eye with them," Nardozza said, "let them understand they got guns to their heads every minute my money's in their pockets."

"You want to talk to them, that's easy. They're waiting to hear from me out in the parking lot, sitting in a red-and-black Trans Am, dent on top of the hood, like somebody pounded his fist on it."

"Okay, let's go."

Chairs scraped. Gilberto sprang to his full height, which was half of Nardozza's. "I'll meet you out there, I gotta say something to the waitress."

"The one you were talking to?" Nardozza gave a look. "She's got stupid hair."

Gilberto grinned. "Kind that drives me crazy."

The waitress was sitting on a high stool at the bar and doodling on a pad, her eyes blank and bored. Gilberto sidled up. He had on a short-sleeved jacket with epaulettes and redundant pockets. From one of the pockets he withdrew a thick roll of bills, big denominations. She lowered her eyes and said, "What're you showing me that for?"

"I'm going to California, live near the movie stars, I'm going to leave this bar, walk through the lobby, and catch a cab. Get me to the airport in ten minutes. You want to come, right this minute, no thinking it over, you'll live like a queen." He paused without a smile. "Up to you. Think fast."

"One chance in a zillion you're telling the truth."

"Minute's up."

She slipped off the stool. "I'm going to take the chance."

Sal Nardozza stepped out into the parking lot at the back of the hotel and immediately glimpsed the red-and-black Trans Am, two faces in it. Nardozza, chewing on his cheroot, walked closer and gestured, and the two men climbed out. One of the Cubans had a shaved head, which gave him a moronic look. The other, clad in a vested tropical suit, had a more intelligent bearing, despite mirror sunglasses. He said, "Where's Miguel?"

"Coming," Nardozza rasped. "We have to talk. Ground rules you guys got to know."

"Sure, go ahead. Talk."

"Not here. My car."

Nardozza's car was parked several rows away, a topaz-yellow Lincoln Continental with tinted windows and a bumper sticker touting Crandon Park Zoo on Key Biscayne. Beneath the Lincoln, gummed to its fuel tank, was a plastic explosive that could be detonated from across the street. Nardozza unlocked the door on the driver's side and punched a button that unlocked the others. The two Cubans appeared wary, especially the one in the suit, who said, "Let's wait for Miguel."

"Miguel's got ass on his mind. Get in."

For the Cubans and for himself, it was the worst decision Nardozza could have made.

———

At Miami Airport, near a secluded bank of telephones, none being used, Miguel Gilberto checked the tickets, then his watch, and said, "We got an hour to wait." Which did not please the waitress, who was already disquieted. He said, "Why the face?"

"You told me we were going to California."

"A mistake. I meant Mexico. You'll still live like a

queen. He grinned, exhibiting teeth he took good
care of. "You got something against Acapulco? Tell
me, so I can get it in the book of records."

"What am I going to do for clothes?"

"We get there, I'll buy you what you want." He
tucked his hand into a pocket. "You want to look at
the money again?"

She glanced down at herself, at the soiled raincoat
she was wearing over her waitress's costume and at
the bows on her frayed shoes. "I live like a queen,
right? I don't care for how long, long as it's for a
while."

"You got it."

She brightened some and said, "I've got to use the
john."

The ladies' room was across the way, down a little.
He watched her disappear into it and then picked up
a phone. He had a sister living in Boca Raton and
wanted to say good-bye to her, but there was no
answer. When he hung up the phone, he sensed a
movement behind him and spun around, then went
still. Ralph Roselli hovered.

"You took off fast," Roselli said. "You didn't even
wait for the bang."

"I did my part," Gilberto said with a sense of
dread. "What more d'you want?"

"Why you shivering?"

"Because you scare me. You scare me all to hell."

"Settle down," Roselli said and took hold of
Gilberto's arm, a grip that couldn't be broken. Roselli's
eyes seemed to sink away in their heavy pouches as
he nodded toward a nearby door marked by a NO
ADMITTANCE sign.

"Hey, I'm not going in there."

"Sure you are," Roselli said in a flat tone as Gilberto
tried to resist. Nearly lifting him off his feet, Roselli

walked him forcibly to the door and made him open it. At that moment the woman reappeared behind them.

"What's going on?" she asked with a dismal air of being cheated, the chances of something enjoyable in her life fading away. Roselli eyed her lazily.

"Who are you?"

"I'm with him."

"That's too bad," Roselli said and clenched her arm too.

———————

Several hours later, up in Boston, Supervisor Russell Thurston phoned Christopher Wade. "Just so you'll know, there was a bloodbath today in Miami. Three guys got blown to kingdom come outside a hotel. One was probably Salvador Nardozza, Gardella's cousin. It was his car. Then later at the airport a runt named Gilberto and some woman were shot in the head, their bodies found on a stairwell. Dade County cops will probably mark it up to a local drug squabble. We know better."

Wade said nothing.

"Did you hear me?"

"It's too much," Wade said. "It shouldn't have happened."

"Don't worry about it. People like that never should have been born. When you meet Gardella tonight, watch his face. See if it's satisfied."

"I'm thinking of canceling," Wade said.

"You cancel," Thurston said, "you'll wish to hell *you* were never born."

10

ANTHONY GARDELLA'S HOUSE at Rye Beach was an
old Cape that had been given a deck, a solarium, a
sauna, and, for winter use, a massive fireplace in the
extended sitting room. A fire was lit, though the
evening was mild, more like May than March. From
the start, Christopher Wade was uncomfortable there.
He was conscious of a trace of sweat on his nose and
of Gardella's watchful eyes.

Gardella gave him a drink and warned, "It's sweet.
Maybe too sweet for you."

Wade tasted it. "Like Dubonnet."

"But better. And a dollar cheaper." Gardella smiled
with handsome teeth, a noticeable separation between
the two front ones. "A toast."

"To what?"

"Reasonableness."

Wade received the word with a stare and recorded
it without thought. Somewhere a window was open,
and he could smell salt air. If he listened hard, he
could hear waves flapping.

With a sort of pulse to his voice, Gardella said, "I
want you to relax. But I don't know, is that possible?"

"For a few hours, why not?" Wade said as Jane
Gardella entered the room with hors d'oeuvres and
eyes that disturbed him. They rested on him carefully, discreetly, and, at the same time, imperiously.

Her youth more than her beauty disconcerted him, along with her poise. Her scent touched him as she offered choices on a silver tray.

"Laura recommends everything," she said.

Laura was the other woman, the fourth person in the house, a balance to the evening. At the moment she was in the kitchen, helping out. Wade lifted something flaky and hot from the tray and said, "Have you two been friends long?"

"All our lives," Jane Gardella answered and moved with the tray to her husband, who sat with his legs crossed, a black English shoe extended, the toe perforated.

He said to Wade, "Go tell her to take off her apron. Maybe she'll listen to you."

Wade rose with a strain, found his way to the kitchen, and glimpsed Laura straightening her stocking on an endless leg. She was especially slim, elegantly tall, boy-hipped, the kind of body one associated with models. Wade said, "You're wanted."

She came forward with feline grace and stunning agility, and yet she stumbled. She fell against Wade, her hands grazing his chest. He stood immobile. "I'm not wired," he whispered, "if that's what you're trying to find out."

She eyed him coolly out of shaded lids, a bold tilt to her head, though her voice was warm. "I'll tell Mr. Gardella."

"With what? A look?"

"A little one." Her eyes played subtly with his. "What's a nice cop like you doing here?"

"I'll ask myself that later on," he said in a tone consistently flat. "Are you here for my benefit?"

"No," she said. "For Mr. Gardella's."

Wade liked her, but not much.

At dinner he sat with his back to the fire, Laura

beside him, and the Gardellas facing him. He gave a
start when a log fell and then let his shoulders sink
against the heat. Gardella said, "We don't say grace
here. Does that bother you?"

"I don't say it either," he replied and ate his soup
without knowing what it was. Dover sole followed.
Gardella rose to bone and serve it. The conversation
went quietly to New Hampshire politics. Jane Gardella
mentioned the man likely to become governor,
Sununu, and said he sounded like an oil company.

"He's Arab," Gardella said. "Same thing."

Jane Gardella lifted her wineglass, and Wade found
his eyes lingering on her. He thought she looked
Dutch or Danish, or perhaps Norwegian, but toward
the end of dinner there was mention of Germany, an
aside about her father's forebears, Bavarians. Wade
wondered what there was about her that made him
uneasy.

Laura said, "I'll get dessert."

"I'll pass," Wade said.

"It's parfait," Gardella said. "Your favorite."

Wade had dessert. When it came time for coffee,
Gardella glanced at him. "We'll have ours in the
den." Then he looked at the women. "You'll excuse
us?"

Wade went to the bathroom first. The lighting was
merciless, and the mirror gave him a swollen look.
His hand moved clumsily and upset a crowd of cos-
metic bottles. As he set them right, a suspicion reared
up and settled in his mind like a cankerworm on a
leaf. The suspicion was that he was openly doing
himself in. When he unlocked the door he saw Laura
standing outside, waiting her turn. She regarded
him serenely, as if her eyes could enter him at will.

"Where's the den?"

She pointed. "You'll find it."

"No, I don't think I will."

"Then I'll show you."

It was in a distant part of the house. He peered into a hard-edged room with high windows, pointed shadows, and heavy furniture, and he entered it with a sense of weight and mass, which extended to Gardella, who looked heavier from having eaten. The coffee was poured. Wade picked up a cup and committed himself to the deepest chair in the room. Apropos of nothing, Gardella said, "Were you in the service?"

"Ages ago."

"Yeah, me too. Korean thing. I still look back at it like it was the best time of my life. I enlisted, eighteen years old, can you believe it? Guys I took basic with were older. I still remember most of the names, all from New York. Deckler from Queens, Bellia from Brooklyn, Davidson from Manhattan. Deckler, a big Kraut with hair always sticking up, got me interested in reading books, and Davidson, a Jew, got me talking about life, you know, what you want out of it. I always meant to get in touch with those guys, but I never did." Gardella sighed. "When were you in? Vietnam thing?"

"Early part," Wade said. "Actually I never left the States."

Gardella smiled. "Neither did I." Then his face turned serious, stiff, almost pallid. "Maybe you mind me saying this, but I'm going to, anyway. You showed feeling when the thing happened to my mother and father. I appreciate it. My sister, she appreciates it. She was here, she'd tell you so herself. There, I've said it. That okay with you?"

Wade looked at him directly. "The case is still open. We had two suspects, brothers, but their car went over a cliff."

"Maybe it's better that way."

"I don't know. I'm not God."

"Sometimes you have to ask yourself if there is one." Gardella's expressive eyes brimmed with light. "For me, the pain will always be there, but now I can live with it." Then he drank some coffee, the subject closed. "What d'you think of my wife?"

"She's beautiful."

"What about her friend?"

"Almost as beautiful."

"But you're not interested, I could tell."

"Sure I'm interested, but that's not why I'm here. You've got a pitch to make, and I'm curious to hear it. Maybe I'll laugh in your face, or maybe I'll just walk away, or maybe I'll have something to mull over. But it's best I warn you now. I don't do business."

"If I thought you did business," Gardella said, "I wouldn't have had you at my table. My wife wouldn't have served you canapés, I wouldn't have boned a fish for you. You're a clean cop, that's what I've been told. I respect that. I also heard about you trying to save the bum dying on the sidewalk. You putting your mouth on his. You care for people. I respect that even more."

Wade said, "I'm starting to feel like a saint."

"Few saints around, none that I've met, anyway." Gardella sipped his coffee idly. "All I know, at this particular moment, is the DA's looking to hurt me for reasons better known to him than to me, and he's using you to do it. Naturally I don't like it. I sound worried, it's because I am. I've got a lot of businesses, hard to keep my finger on all of them."

"If you keep good books, you don't have a problem."

"Come on, Wade." Gardella's smile was transient. "You and I both know you guys look long enough, you can find what isn't there. That takes up my time, gives me grief, and costs me money. It goes to court, I pay for the lawyers. In the end the judge throws out the case because you guys never had one. Who wins? No one."

"I don't look that far ahead. I just do my job."

"There's plenty of ways to do a job. Best way is to just look busy. That's how you look good, and I don't get harassed."

"I haven't heard one word you've said," Wade murmured.

"That's because I haven't said anything you don't already know twice as well as me."

"You mind if I smoke?" Wade asked and lit a Merit Menthol. He raised his coffee cup from its saucer. Someone passed by the door, and he wasn't sure whether it was Jane Gardella or the other woman. Their scent, he had realized earlier, was nearly the same.

Gardella said, "Basically, in case you haven't noticed, we're not that much different. We're family men. You got daughters, I got sons. I got a son who's a marine. I'm proud of him. I'm even prouder of my other kid, who's at Holy Cross. He's going to be better than me. Not bigger, that doesn't count, but better."

Wade listened to the voice trail off; then it came back more mellow.

"We're lonely guys, not just me, you too, I can tell. When my first wife died, I didn't know if I wanted to go on. I still wake up in the night and think it's her beside me, not Jane. I didn't have Jane, though, I'd go crazy. You know what I'm telling you?"

"That you'd go crazy."

"I'm telling you two guys shouldn't go out of their

way to hurt each other. They get hurt enough in other ways. No?"

Wade nudged his cigarette ash into a hollow of crystal he wasn't certain was an ashtray. The coffee was a special blend, a chocolate taste to it. He said quietly, "The reason I came here is I thought you might want to raise the possibility of immunity in return for your cooperation. You're big, but Angello, Zanigari, they're bigger."

Gardella did not trouble himself to reply to that or even to acknowledge with a glance that the words had been spoken. Instead he lifted his jaw in a manner that compelled attention. "Kith and kin, Wade. That's what's important to us. The people who make our lives matter, the women who make us whole. Without a woman, you're not whole. Tell me I'm wrong. If I am, I'll shut up."

Wade said, "You're not wrong, but your wife's friend—she wasn't necessary."

"Clumsy of me. Stupid, even. D'you know what I'd like to see? I'd like to see you back with your wife, where you belong. I think you'd be a happier man."

Something in Wade went cold and affected his face.

"I care," Gardella said quickly. "Should I apologize for caring?"

"Why the hell should you care?"

"You're happy, maybe I don't have to worry about you," Gardella said with a smile, as if he had come up with an ace.

Wade looked uneasily toward the door, as if he had played this hand too well.

———

It was nearly two in the morning when Wade, speeding along Interstate 95, saw the distant lights of Boston pricking the darkness. It was two-fifteen when he let himself into his Commonwealth Avenue apartment and two-twenty when the phone rang. It was his wife, one of the few people who had the unlisted number. "Are you all right?" she asked.

"Yes, of course," he said, surprised, a tense quickness in his voice. "Why do you ask?"

"Silly of me, but I had the same horrible feeling I used to get when you were working undercover and I was sure you were dead or dying. Chris . . . you're not a young guy anymore."

"Why the reminder?"

"Are you undercover again?"

"You read the papers. You know what I'm doing."

"No," she said. "I don't know what you're doing. None of my business. I shouldn't have called."

"But you did."

"Chris, please. Don't make too much of it."

"Have you seen the girls lately?" he asked, staring at their framed pictures, studio shots taken when they were ten and eleven, one a close facsimile of the other, each a fatted calf at that tender age.

"Yes, haven't you?"

"I've talked to them a few times on the phone. I wanted them to have lunch with me, but they were always busy."

"Ironic, isn't it. In the past it was you who were too busy."

He stood poised on his toes, aware that even if no one was in the apartment above him a tape recorder was operating. Ears, if not listening now, would listen later. "Susan . . . are you alone?"

"Yes," she said."

"I could come over. It wouldn't take long."

"Goodnight, Chris."

————

Wade did not sleep well, scarcely at all, and he was up early. The streets appeared raw, bruised. They needed warming up from a sun only gradually showing itself. He drove to nearby Newbury Street, left his Camaro double-parked, and went into a basement coffee shop for breakfast. He ordered Number Three without knowing what Number Three was. The tables were close. A man wearing a security guard uniform and a sidearm that looked real enough but was a toy said, "You a cop?"

Wade narrowed his gaze. "Does it show?"

"I know cops. I was one for twenty-three years. Don't ever retire. It's bullshit."

"I'm a few years from that."

"Die first," the man said.

"Suicide's a sin."

"You got insurance? Get cancer."

"You've made my morning," Wade said and changed tables.

When he returned to his car, he found Russell Thurston sitting in it. As he pushed in behind the wheel, Thurston said in a well-regulated voice, "A hell of a way to park."

"I wanted to make it easy for you."

"Drive, will you? Around the block. How'd it go last night?"

Without answering, Wade drove up Newbury Street and eased through a red light. His eyes were fixed to the windshield in the growing traffic.

"You in a bad mood?"

"A small one."

"Any mention made of Miami? It was all over the news last night."

"No mention."

"He's a cool bastard."

"He's smooth, Thurston. Smoother than you."

"Did he put a hook in you?"

"So smoothly I haven't felt it yet."

"What did he offer?"

"Happiness." Wade glanced sideways. "I can't remember, what am I getting from you?"

"Thrills," said Thurston.

———————

Unannounced, Victor Scandura entered the office of John Benson at Benson Tours and lowered himself into a chair. John Benson's head jerked up, and then he smiled. "Nice to see you, Mr. Scandura. You have no complaints, I hope."

"None," said Scandura. Benson Tours was one of the travel agencies the Gardella organization used in sponsoring gambling junkets to Las Vegas and Atlantic City.

"So, what can I do for you?"

"I understand you got a cop's wife working here."

"You talking about Mrs. Wade?"

"I want you to fire her."

John Benson colored up. "I can't do that."

Scandura went on as though the other man hadn't spoken. "I also understand you've got something going with her. I want it ended."

"You can't tell me what to do!"

Scandura lethargically lifted himself from the chair, his eyes slanting through his spectacles. "I'll tell you what, Mr. Benson. Think about it, and then do what you think is best for yourself."

Alone, John Benson pondered the problem for two minutes. Then he went into Susan Wade's office and, with a practiced British accent, said, "How about lunch, old girl?"

11

AGENTS BLODGETT AND BLUE caught up with him near a display window and cornered him in the shadow of the building's overhang. It was an extraordinarily bright day, mild, with traffic shaking the street and pedestrians thronging the sidewalk. "Hey, Augie, you know who I am?" Blodgett asked, and Augie turned fast and stood fixed in a sports jacket of fishscale pattern, a red velour shirt beneath it. His teeth protruded.

"You don't look familiar in the face," he said cautiously, "but I can guess. A fed, right?"

"You're quick, Augie. You'd be surprised the number of people told us you weren't. Right, Blue?" Agent Blue nodded as a truck boomed by. A woman with a mouth clenched as if from permanent suspicion gave them more than a passing glance. Blodgett said, "What do you think of the Miami thing, Augie?"

"What Miami thing?"

"All those people that got blown away, Gardella's cousin among 'em. When they buried him, he wasn't all together. Some parts they put in the coffin might not even have been him."

"What's it got to do with me?"

"Nothing, Augie. That was expert work in Miami. You're only good at hijacking meat wagons, though I hear you're telling people you're a shooter now."

"What the hell you talking about? Me a shooter? Come on."

"But it makes you feel good, doesn't it, us thinking you might be? Gives you bigger balls."

"Hey, I got a job. I work for my uncle. You die, I'll do you up nice, only charge half price."

"He's cute, isn't he, Blue?"

"He needs a chin, then he'd be cute."

"And he needs some sleep. Look how funny his eyes are. He must be on something. What kind of pills do you pop, Augie?"

"You got a great sense of humor. Tell the spade to quit looking at me."

"Tell him yourself."

Agent Blue pushed forward with a supple movement. "Do you have something to tell me?" he asked with lips that scarcely moved. Augie flinched under a gaze sure and deep. Then Blodgett bore in.

"You don't know who your friends are, Augie. You don't even know much about yourself. Guys like you don't make out. Blue and I, we've seen hundreds like you. You come out on the short end, you take the falls for the bigger guys, you get fished out of the river. You get tossed in the harbor, the chemicals eat you. The local cops laugh. You guys want to bump yourselves off, what do they care? But we care, Augie, not personally, you understand, but professionally. You catching any of this?"

"Yeah, I'm catching a lot of shit."

"Explain it to him, Blue."

"You're doing okay."

"No, I'm not doing good at all," Blodgett said with a pained expression. "This guy thinks he's Mafia. He doesn't know he's nothing."

"Maybe he doesn't know how it works," Blue said.

"You have to be kissed to be Mafia. Ask him if Anthony Gardella ever kissed him."

Blodgett shook his head. "I can't imagine Anthony Gardella making Augie. Most Gardella would do is use him for something—and then worry about him later. A guy who pops pills and brags he's a shooter is someone Gardella would definitely worry about, I can guarantee that."

"Especially," added Blue, "when the DA's task force is looking into Gardella's operations. Right this minute Gardella's got to be thinking about loose ends."

"A loose end, Augie, is a loose mouth. If we know it, you can be damn sure Gardella knows it."

"I'm going to leave now," Augie said, buttoning his sports jacket. "I'm going to walk away from you guys."

"You take one step," Blodgett said pleasantly, "and I'll break your head." In the distance a police car howled, or perhaps it was a fire truck. Despite its push, the sidewalk crowd seemed muted, nebulous. Blodgett said, "What it comes down to is nobody's going to protect you except us. *Us*, Augie, we're the only ones. I don't expect you to understand that, not now, not this minute, because it's obvious things come slow to you. If you'd gone to a community college or even finished high school, I wouldn't have had to explain any of this. You'd have been three jumps ahead of me."

With a rich voice, Agent Blue said, "He's not trying to insult you, Augie. He's just telling you fact."

"One last thing," said Blodgett. "You'd better tell Gardella we've talked to you. If you don't and he finds out, that'll make it worse for you."

Blue said, "Now you can go."

They watched him slice into the crowd to the street

and then pit himself against traffic. He did not look back. Blodgett said, "What do you think?"

Blue said, "It doesn't matter what I think, only what Thurston thinks. You write up the report."

———

Rita O'Dea opened the front door and peered out at the man teetering on the second step. "You look like hell," she said, and Ty O'Dea's eyes went blank for a moment. His voice faltered as he shifted his weight from foot to foot. He was unshaved, ashen, and his sky-blue suit was disheveled from the flight up from Florida, stops in Washington and New York along the way. "Don't just stand there," she said, "speak."

"I'm scared, Rita." He spoke too fast, his lips desperate. "I didn't know if I was next or not. I still don't know. You have to tell me."

"If you'd been next, you wouldn't have had time to think about it."

He shivered on the step, his chin lifting. A breeze unfixed his shock of white hair, which was in need of a wash. He said, "I came here, I didn't know what else to do."

"I've been expecting you," she said, shifting somewhat out of the doorway, the sun catching her black hair. She had on a Titian-red tent dress and furry house slippers. "I saved your ass, you know that," she said, and he nodded, blink-eyed. "Like old times, me doing it."

Her voice confused him. It was softer than he had ever heard it before, though her expression was cheerless, critical, intimidating. Her gaze swept past him to the foot of the drive, where a taxi was idling, a woman visible in the back seat.

"Who is she, Ty?"

Ty O'Dea showed grit. "It's my woman," he said. "Her name's Sara."

"You just going to let her sit there?"

He turned around and gestured with his fingers. The woman leaned forward in the taxi to pay the driver. Then she climbed out and began struggling up the drive with a suitcase in each hand. Rita O'Dea made a sour face.

"Go help her, for Christ's sake."

———

Anthony Gardella stayed longer at the house in Rye than he had intended. He and his wife stayed there through the weekend and well into the next week. Two or three hours a day, wearing bulky Norwegian sweaters, they tramped along the surf. With her Canon camera, Jane Gardella took pictures of gulls riding glittering waves and of her husband inspecting crumbs of bread sponge and lifting a length of driftwood riddled by boatworms. They walked over wet flats of sand and left behind squishy shoeprints as they vanished into the far reaches of the beach. On the final day, as they retraced their steps, a figure waited for them in the distance, near the house.

"It's Victor," Gardella said.

"You were expecting him?"

"Yes," he said, taking her arm.

"Business?"

"Business."

"I suppose I shouldn't complain," she said without hiding her disappointment. She took a wide breath of salt air. "I've had more of you than I thought I would."

Inside the house she served coffee and then left them alone. Victor Scandura sat near the lit fireplace for the extra warmth. Gardella was too warm and removed his sweater. Stark sunshine cut through the windows. "You want something stronger, say so," Gardella said, and Scandura shook his head.

"This is fine."

Gardella relaxed in his chair, one leg slung over the other. "Roselli was good in Miami. I can always count on him."

"He was very good," Scandura said. "You oughta give him something extra, show your appreciation."

"Give him what you think is right. Make him happy."

"It should come from your hand, Anthony. It would mean more."

"All right, remind me. I get back, I'll do it." Gardella compressed his lips for a second. "I've done some thinking about Miami. We're getting out of dope for a while, the wisest thing under the circumstances, but we'll continue with the washing. We don't want to screw that up."

"Who you going to put down there?"

"It's got to be you, Victor. Temporarily."

Scandura's eyes thinned into slits behind his glasses. "Give me a break, Anthony. You've got me doing everything."

"With that much money, you're the only one I can trust at the moment."

"Why don't we bring the operation up here? Wire transfers are easy. Plenty of foreign banks in Boston we can do business with."

"Up here I'm watched. Down there, everybody's doing it. You don't need me to explain that."

Scandura put his coffee aside and gazed at the fire, his head held erect. His words were quiet. "My place is with you, not down in Florida. People say you got eyes in the back of your head. That's because of me. I'm those eyes. You know that's so, don't you, Anthony?"

"Yes, I do."

"I give you a hundred percent."

"No, Victor. You give me a hundred ten."

"I give you advice. You don't always take it, but I give the best I can. Lately you've done things that worry me. I guess you know that, but you're the boss. What you say goes, like always. You want me to go to Florida, I'll go."

"Tell me again what's worrying you, Victor. Sometimes I forget."

"Hitting those punks that did in your parents, that was bad. I still haven't figured out why it was bad, but I know it was. You know it too."

Gardella spoke with dry lips. "That's something we're never going to talk about. *Capisce?* What else worries you?"

"Everything you do is quick now. Maybe too quick."

"It's the way my mind moves."

"And, you want my opinion, you should've gone to Sal Nardozza's funeral. People were surprised you didn't. Biggest bunch of flowers should have come from you."

"You're talking old fashion, old ways. I go to a funeral, I get my picture taken. I get my picture taken enough."

"But it was expected, Anthony. You near the front pew. And your sister too."

"You know what, Victor? You worry too much." The words moved smoothly over Gardella's tongue. His gaze narrowed. "But that's okay. A guy like you I couldn't do without."

Five minutes later Gardella went into the kitchen, where his wife was busy at the sink. He lifted her hair, kissed the back of her neck, and said, "I'm going to walk Victor out to his car."

"Are we leaving too?" she asked.

"It's about time, don't you think?"

"I could stay here forever," she answered with emotion.

"One of these days," he said, "we might do that."

Scandura comported himself stiffly toward his Cadillac, which was parked partly on thin grass. His face was drawn under a dove-gray felt hat. With his topcoat buttoned to the throat, he seemed embalmed in too much clothing. Gardella, in shirt sleeves, grazed a hand over evergreen shrubs struggling to recoup from winter sunscald.

"Wade's wife. How'd it go?"

"No problem," Scandura said.

"Good. . Good. I love playing angles, don't you, Victor? It's what makes life interesting."

Scandura said, "There's something I was saving for last. Your brother-in-law showed up."

"I'd have been surprised if he hadn't."

"Rita took him in."

"Predictable."

"He had a woman with him."

"Interesting," Gardella said in a manner that closed the subject. "You drive with care, you hear?" He put his arms around Scandura, embraced him hard, and then abruptly pulled back. "Jesus, Victor, all I feel is bones. You losing weight?"

"I go up and down, you know that."

"You feeling okay? Don't lie to me."

"I'm fine."

Gardella was thoughtful for a moment, a breeze moving across him. "You're right, Victor. Your place is here, not Miami."

Scandura's eyes filled. "Thank you, Anthony."

Two blocks from Government Center, Christopher Wade caught sight of his wife across the street. She was moving swiftly, painted in sunlight, and he called to her, but his voice failed to carry over the tone of traffic. When he tried to push into the street, the potency of the crowd kept him in its grip long enough for her to vanish around a corner.

Minutes later, double-timing, he glimpsed her toiling up steep steps where the city rose to another level. Again he called out, and this time she stopped, her hand clinging to an iron rail. The face she presented was white and cold, with a curious smile that seemed only half attached to her mouth. She waited until he reached the steps, and then she turned away. There was a stone bench nearby. She sat on it.

"Susan." He said the name tentatively as he joined her, and he put out a hand to touch her and thought better of it. She was a mystery to him, all of a sudden a total mystery. "Why are you here?"

"Why shouldn't I be here?" Her voice slid grudgingly to him. "Why shouldn't I go where I want?" Then she glanced away, her hands in the lap of her light wool skirt, her knees pressed together. Her stockings were dark, speckled. "I'm sorry," she said, "I'm not at my best."

"What's wrong?"

"I'm out of a job. John Benson sacked me during an otherwise nice lunch. Also, he doesn't want to see me anymore." A laugh shot out of her mouth. "His excuse is he doesn't want to tie me down. Says I should be my own person." Her throat pulsed. "I honestly thought he cared for me."

"You'll find another job," Wade said, noticing for the first time a gentle pattern of aging in her face, and he felt an extravagance of sadness, almost as much for himself as for her. She spoke rapidly, too rapidly.

"I already had an offer, the same day. Have you heard of Rodino Travel? You pass it every day. It's practically next door to the Saltonstall Building."

Wade drew his lips together. Feet shuffled by, dour Boston faces that he glimpsed peripherally. Her eyes pressed upon him.

"How did they know so fast at Rodino's that I was available? John never would have told them."

"I don't know," Wade said with the hint of a frown and a sudden wince in his stomach. He was wearing an old knit tie, and he gently tightened the knot. "Are you accepting the offer?"

"I haven't decided," she said with a stinging look. "Something's happening I don't know about. I feel somebody's pulling strings, somebody's yanking me from one place to another. Is it you, Chris?"

He shook his head.

"If it was, I'd never forgive you."

"I would never interfere in your life."

"I'd like to believe that."

"Tonight," he asked, "would you like to go to the movies?"

"No, Chris, I wouldn't," she replied, rising to her feet, regret in her voice. "There's something you've got to get through your head. I don't love you anymore."

He gazed up at her in injured silence.

"And there's something else you should admit to yourself. You don't love me."

Watching her slip away, the sun glancing over her, he murmured, "You're wrong."

———

Ten minutes later, plunged into the gloom of a cocktail lounge, Wade made himself reasonably comfortable at a miniature table, lit a cigarette, and listened to a piano player ripple out airs of the forties for a few middle-aged lovers. Flicking an ash, he stared at the bare legs of the waitress who approached with a smile too rigid to be friendly. "I suppose," he said, "you have a husband or a boyfriend."

"Both," she said. She was of indeterminate age, her hair a haze of old gold, which was almost the color of her diminutive costume, her breasts propped up by the tight top.

"Then I'll try not to bother you," he said.

"You can bother me all you want as long as you don't expect too much."

"What would I expect?"

"The world. Men do. But you I probably don't have to worry about. I don't think you're interested."

His eye turned more sensitive. "What makes you say that?"

"The way you make with the talk, it's automatic. It doesn't mean anything."

"You've been on the job a long time."

"Too long," she said succinctly. "I'm forty-one years old. Look how I'm dressed. I feel like a fucking freak. What can I get for you?"

He took a moment to concentrate. "A dark Heineken," he said, and she screwed up her face.

"That's funny. I thought you'd want something with a jolt."

"No," said Wade. "I've already had one."

A moment later he got up, squeezed by tables, found a phone, and deposited a dime too thin to work. He came up with another, which dropped true. He pressed out a number, the pips inordinately loud. The line crackled. A voice in his ear said, "Yuh."

"Gardella."

"He ain't here."

"When will he be in?"

"Don't know."

"Is he at his home?"

"Don't know."

"Is he still in Rye?"

"Look, fella, I don't know."

"Tell him I want to see him. Something personal to talk about. Tell him I'm pissed off."

"Who the hell is this?"

"He'll know," Wade said.

When he returned to his table, the waitress had delivered a bottle of Heineken and was pouring out a token amount into a frosted glass. He sat down with an air of fatigue. She tossed him a tight little look and said, "You want to know what's the most boring business in the world?"

He waited. The piano player was rendering a tune that, he remembered, Perry Como used to sing.

"It's talking to a lonely guy who doesn't know what he wants. You know what's worse?"

"I'm afraid to ask."

"Going to bed with him."

"You've set me straight," he said with a slow smile, which she more than matched. Hers was warmer.

"You should be glad. You know what I look like in the morning? Phyllis Diller." She pushed the beer glass toward him. "Drink up. It's on me."

"Why?"

"Because you're a cop."

————

Anthony Gardella and his wife left Rye Beach in the early evening, the sun still brilliant. The wide surface of Interstate 95 glistened with mirages. Gardella rested his head back and half closed his eyes while his wife drove with a solid foot on the

accelerator. At one point, during a close stretch, she
touched ninety. Gardella said, "You got a death wish
or something?"

"I'm a good driver."

"I'm not disputing that, but you're bucking the
odds. Slow down."

She slowed to seventy-five and gradually to sixty,
her hands slackening on the wheel, her mouth set
apologetically. "Did I scare you, Tony? I didn't mean
to."

"You didn't scare me," he said quietly. I simply
forgot how young you are."

"Don't do that, Tony." For an instant she held
back her breath. Her hair trembled. "Don't put me
down like that. I'm not a child."

"Then don't try to live dangerously. Trust your
instincts, never your luck."

She drove at varying speeds, down to fifty, back
up to sixty, then somewhere in between, and she
watched the sun lose its strength. Eventually the
traffic thickened and Boston loomed. It seemed
muted, unfamiliar to her, threatening in a vague
way, which made her reluctant to enter it. On Mystic
Tobin Bridge a decrepit car swerved in front of
them, youths in it, and then a pickup truck rolling
high on outsize tires eased her into another lane.
Gardella gave her money for the toll.

"Back at Rye everything seemed so simple," she
said, "so . . . right."

"And now?"

"Different, that's all." Blindly she sought his hand,
found it, and brought it up to her cheek. "Look at
me, Tony. Look at me and love me."

Soon they were on the Central Artery, a pall of
industrial smoke drifting high over it. Gardella had
liberated his hand so that she would use both of hers

on the wheel. Traffic was frantic, pounding in their ears. He said, "What's the matter with you, Jane?"

"The letdown. Being back." She spoke through an upsurge of feeling she fought to control. "And the air, Tony. None of it's fresh."

"What's really bothering you?"

"Nothing."

"Are you worried about us? You shouldn't be. There's nothing we can't handle."

In Hyde Park they drove through a neighborhood that had long ago deteriorated, past the broken metal bars of a playground fence, down a street of condemned properties, ruined sidewalks, naked lots. Then, gradually, the cityscape softened. In time they coasted into a section that preserved its charm, its orderliness, its trees, many already beginning to bud. As they neared home, Gardella turned his head around for a glance through the back window.

"How long has that car been behind us?"

"I don't know, Tony. I haven't noticed."

"You should always notice."

She shuddered, as if too much were pulling on her. Her eyes were in the rearview. "Who is it? I can't tell."

"Our friend," Gardella said, staring straight ahead, almost smiling.

"What friend?"

"Christopher Wade."

12

SARA looked done in. At Rita O'Dea's direction, Alvaro escorted her upstairs, showed her to a room, and gave her towels for a bath. Later Rita O'Dea told Alvaro to make himself scarce. She wanted to be alone with her husband. Ty O'Dea, who had avoided Alvaro's eyes, was sitting awkwardly on the sofa. Rita O'Dea approached and said, "Alvaro's my houseboy."

"Is that what you call him?" he said. He was tired, a little punchy. His head lolled.

"I was being cute, Ty." She studied him. "I think you could use a drink," she said and went to the liquor cabinet, where she dug out a bottle of Jameson's Irish Whiskey. The amount she poured was generous, and he accepted it gratefully, his hand trembling a little. She said, "You still got a liver left?"

"I don't drink like I used to," he said.

"You could've fooled me. Be careful, Ty. Everything catches up. Everything can hurt." She dropped herself into a chair near the sofa, beside a small marble-top table that held upright pictures of her mother and father. Her eyes filled. "You should've come up for the funeral."

"I didn't think you'd want me there."

"You should've come, anyway. They never liked you, Ty, but they'd have wanted you next to me. You know the way they were." Her voice broke a little. "You think they're in heaven? You think there's such a place? No, I know you don't."

Ty O'Dea peered into his whiskey, as if assessing its potential jolt. His blue eyes looked more washed out than ever. "You die, you die, Rita. That's what I think."

"I have to believe there's something more, for their sake and my own. I don't have a choice. I have to stay sane."

Ty O'Dea took a long taste. The whiskey seemed to go down slowly, warming him in odd places, his upper arms, one side of his stomach. His chest heaved as he coughed. He had a smoker's raucous cough, and he brought a fist up to temper it.

"You look like an old man," she said. The two days of stubble on his face looked like a week's worth, all of it white. His underlip quivered. "You're a case of nerves," she said.

"I'm all right now."

"All that time in Florida, you got no tan. And that cough makes me wonder if you got emphysema or something."

"I'm fine."

"You look beat. Take your shoes off and stretch out."

"I oughta go up and see Sara."

"Don't bother her. She'll want to sleep." She watched him put the whiskey glass aside and remove his shoes. He had a hole in one stocking, which he tried to hide. "No class, Ty," she quipped, and he appeared stung. His background was a poor South Boston neighborhood, where his bedroom window in a top-floor tenement had overlooked trash barrels and marauding rats. His father had spent his life in a labor pool. "That's right," she said, "lie back. Use the pillow."

Inertia set in as soon as he lowered his head. A good portion of his face collapsed.

"Look at me, Ty." She wanted him to relax, not to fall asleep. "I'm going through a lousy time," she said tentatively. "Everything I do feels . . . final."

He did not know what to say and so said nothing. He wanted to keep his eyes closed, to pretend he wasn't there.

"Things that are mine I want to hold on to harder than ever," she said ominously. Then, heavily, pound by pound, she lifted herself out of her chair. "Let's talk about the woman."

"Sara?"

"Sara who?"

"Dillon." He screwed up his courage and spoke from his heart. "I love her."

"You love her. You *think* you love her."

"No, Rita. I really do."

She stood massive, her dress clinging to her legs, which made her stance seem predatory. She took three steps, yawing on the second and hovering on the third. Her voice was deep, as if her throat were a brass pipe. "Tell me about her."

He sat up on his elbows. A bone creaked and did not sound real. "What do you want to know?"

"Everything," she said. "Your life depends on it."

Alvaro slipped into the room without knocking, leaving the door ajar so that he would hear anybody coming up the stairs. Sara Dillon stared at him. She looked drab after her bath. Blotches and blemishes stood out. Her breasts were swollen. The traces of gray in her damp head of hair made her look older than she was, which was thirty-one. "Get out," she said.

"In a minute." Though she was pregnant, which he

had surmised with a swift eye, there was a certain deadness about her. "You've been around, I can tell that," he said and stroked his beard.

She covered herself.

"You know all about me," he said accusingly.

"What makes you think so?"

"You're Ty's woman. Ty doesn't keep his mouth shut."

"You don't have to worry about me," she said listlessly and with a subtle weight shift covered herself more adequately. "You should worry about yourself."

He glided to her and stood close, giving her a whiff of piquant cologne, which he had worked into his beard. Extremely white teeth flashed from his dark mouth. "You're an unknown factor. See my position?"

"I only know my own."

"You give me trouble, I'll cut your heart out, Ty's too. Understand?"

"Perfectly."

"Good," he said with a ruttish look, "now we can be friends."

"No, we can't." She dodged his hand. "Don't touch me."

He seemed surprised.

"I don't like pretty men," she explained.

"You're right," he said. "We can't be friends."

———

Two men who worked for Anthony Gardella were inside his house; they'd been looking after it. Each stood with a hand inside his jacket, fingers on a weapon. Each gazed hard at Christopher Wade, who ignored them. "Nothing to worry about," Gardella said lightly and dismissed them with his eyes. Wade watched them leave. Gardella smiled. "You've got guts."

Jane Gardella said, "I take it you two want to be alone."

"I don't know, do we?"

Wade nodded.

"Follow me," Gardella said.

They sat in a room that was a cave of shadows, though each could clearly see the other's face. It was Wade who did not want a light on. Wade murmured, "One thing you shouldn't have done was mess with my wife."

"For your own good, and hers," Gardella said in a discreet voice. He waited to be interrupted but wasn't. Head lowered a little, he gazed at Wade speculatively under his eyebrows. "I didn't want you compromised. I figured I owed you. Right?" Again there was a pause. This time Gardella slowly retracted his gaze while maintaining his half smile. "You don't know, do you? I do business with Benson. Not much, but enough."

Wade's face faded back. "I don't know if that's true or not. I can check."

"Yes, check. This guy Benson, he's a phony in every way. He didn't even pay your wife a decent salary. Gave her fringe benefits instead. She tell you about her trip with him down to Biscayne? Hotel Sonesta."

Wade twitched.

Gardella said, "Beats me what she saw in him."

"You'd better shut up."

"Sure, I know how you feel."

Wade rested dry hands on his knees. The only light came from the open door, which gave him a sensation of being in a subterranean world that was

much too quiet, somewhat dusty, bulky in places.
The room had books.

"This is my library. I read. That surprise you?"

"Why should anything surprise me?" Wade asked
with a growing remoteness. "Why, most of all, should
you surprise me?"

"I'm glad you said that," Gardella said mysteriously.

"Is anyone hungry?" The voice came from the lit
doorway, from Jane Gardella, whose tentative entry
into the room was gentle, a few soft steps that did
not take her out of the light. She waited for a
response.

Wade said, "I'm not."

Gardella rose with a shake of his head. "I have to
get something. Entertain the lieutenant for a moment."

Left alone with her, Wade became aware of too
many details: the shades in her hair, the length of
her hands, the neat fit of her trousers over long
hips. Her eyes were disturbing, hostile even as she
smiled, and for the moment he disliked her. "At Rye
you surprised me," he said.

She stood fixed, showing careful eyes. "How did I
do that?"

"From the start I expected a Kewpie doll. You're
not that at all."

"That doesn't even come close to being a compliment," she said coldly. "Actually it's an insult to
Tony."

"I guess it is," he said, passing the flat of his hand
over his jaw, an absent gesture. "You'll have to forgive me."

"I don't have the power," she said glibly on her
way out. "Only Tony does."

Gardella returned to the room but not to his chair.
For a number of seconds he stood near shadowy
shelves of books, his back to Wade. His shoulders

slackened some as he traced a finger over titles he couldn't clearly see. "I feel a little old tonight, I wonder why." His smile was rueful as he turned around. " 'No longer mourn for me when I am dead.' A poet wrote that. I got him here somewhere. See, I told you I read."

"I never said I doubted you," Wade uttered from the gloom.

"When I was a kid, my mother and father wanted me to be a professor of something, anything, didn't matter what. They never liked what I got into, but they understood. My first wife, God bless her, never said a word, but deep down she was ashamed, I always knew that. Tell me something, Wade, what you do, is it always clean?"

"No, but it's usually right."

"Neither of us, we're not angels, would you admit that?"

Wade grimaced, the victim of a muscle cramp. Slowly he straightened a leg. "What can you do for me?" His voice was stark. "I mean, what *really* can you do for me? What have you got that I'd even consider? That wouldn't mean you'd own me forever?"

"You want to talk, talk naked."

"You think I'm wired?"

"I don't want to think about it, I want to know."

Wade brought his face forward and let it spread into view. With much effort, he rose to his full height. He removed his jacket, his knit tie, his shirt. The room was warm. He pulled his T-shirt off over his head, smoothed his hair down, and stood bare-chested, his holstered Beretta snugged against a hip. "Satisfied?"

"Peace of mind means a lot. You don't have to stay that way." Gardella's tone was mellow, his eyes hooded. "My sister was here, she'd whistle."

"You trying to fix me up with her?"

"I love my sister, but I wouldn't wish her on anybody," Gardella said without inflection and stepped away from the shelves. Wade began to redress. He had trouble with his tie; the knot went stubbornly askew. Gardella came up close and fixed it for him.

"Ever smoke a joint, Wade?"

"No."

"Back in school maybe? In the army?"

"Never."

Seemingly from nowhere, Gardella produced two roughly rolled cigarettes. The paper was dark. "These are my wife's," he said with a faint mix of amusement and sadness. "She thinks I don't know she has them. She's just a kid, you see, which I sometimes forget. Here."

Wade stared at the gift pressed upon him. He twisted it carefully around with a thumb and finger. "What do I want this for?"

"Because life's short." Gardella spoke with strange authority. "Because you're a sociable guy. Because I don't like to do things alone." A flame sprang up between them. "You smoke it like a regular one except you breathe in deeper and hold it longer."

After an almost imperceptible hesitation, Wade bent his head. "I think I can figure it out for myself," he said.

———

Rita O'Dea watched television on a small set, a Sony, which she had placed on an end table. The program was local, a segment on the effects of toxic waste that had been dumped for years in nearby Woburn. A dark-haired woman reporter, buttoned up against the breeze, cited a high incidence of leukemia. Then the camera cut to a mother with a dying son. The boy was bald. From the sofa, Ty

O'Dea mumbled, "What are you watching that stuff for?"

"Go back to sleep," she said, and he did, almost immediately. He was under a blanket, which she had placed over him earlier. Her eyes returned to the television, but not for long. For some reason her hand trembled when she lifted it to her hair, some of which she coiled in her fingers. She was restless and bothered, and when she forced herself from her chair she felt spongy and unwieldy. Before leaving, she gave her slumbering husband a haggard look.

Upstairs, in the room given Sara Dillon, she lit the small pink-shaded lamp on the bureau and, leaning over an open suitcase, sifted through Sara Dillon's things. The underwear was either black, magenta, or sheer. In a normal voice she said, "This how you turn him on?"

Her eyes open, Sara Dillon spoke from the bed. "I don't like people going through my stuff."

"You could've stopped me. You could've sat up and said something." Rita O'Dea approached the bed, and the other woman sat up. "Well, Sara, you look better than what Ty usually runs around with. You really pregnant?"

"Yes."

"You and I both know it's not Ty's. And he knows too."

"He's pretending it is."

Rita O'Dea's eyes softened, as if there had been too many mistakes in her past, too many irreversible decisions. "Yes," she said, "I can understand Ty pretending, like life's not real. The kid, it won't be black or something, will it?" She expected anger and observed indifference.

"It will be white."

Rita O'Dea's eyes hardened. "Ty's no bargain, but

I guess I don't have to tell you that. What I *do* have to say is more important. You ever hurt him, you'll both get it, you and the kid. I make myself clear?"

"I won't hurt him."

"Good. One other thing. I'm Catholic. Catholics don't get divorces."

"That doesn't bother me."

Rita O'Dea smiled thinly. "I didn't think it would."

———

The bakery was on Route 1 in Saugus, a take-out operation that stayed open until midnight, with a back section of a few tables for customers who wanted to sit down and indulge. A self-serve coffee urn was available. Victor Scandura carried three coffees on a tray to a corner table, where two men waited. "Much obliged," said one. He was wide-faced and thick-necked and had heavy pouches under his eyes. The other man, who was extremely pale, as if he feared fresh air, said, "I shouldn't drink it. Fuckin' stomach. How's yours, Victor?"

"No complaints," Scandura said, his eye going from one to the other. They were from Providence, trusted representatives of the organization, and the same age, more or less, as Scandura, who was meeting with them secretly. He glanced around. "Anthony knew about this, he'd blow his stack."

"No reason he should know, right?" the pale man said.

The one with the pouches said, "All we want is a clear picture from you, so we can tell the man in Providence everything's all right. You'd tell us if it wasn't?"

"Of course," Scandura said, stiffening a little. "What's the man worried about?"

"A lot's going on up here," the pale man said. "The Justice Department's all over the Angello family."

"That's been going on for years, got nothing to do with me and Anthony. All Anthony's got against him is the DA looking to make a name for himself."

"You didn't let me finish, Victor. You know well as I do the man don't think so much of Angello anymore and wouldn't care if the prick went down. But Gardella's different. The man's got special feeling for him, thinks of him as a son, maybe even as his successor. You appreciate that?"

"Yes," Scandura said. "Anthony appreciates it too."

"But we all know Anthony changed a little when his wife died."

"He took it hard," Scandura said defensively.

"That's what I'm saying. Then he went and married some kid, a fuckin' stewardess. There are those that say you shoulda talked sense to him."

"I advise him. I don't tell him what to do."

The man with the pouches said, "What he did to avenge his mother and father, nobody faults him, but he played it close, like he did right afterwards down in Miami. That was smooth, damn smooth, but he was lucky he didn't get burned."

"Nothing's luck with him," Scandura said dryly. "He figures everything."

The pale man drank some of his coffee, now that it had cooled. Scandura sat straight and adjusted his glasses. The man with the pouches said, with a vague look of depravity, "How's his sister doing? I remember her years ago when she couldn't keep her eyes off guys' crotches. She still that way?"

Scandura did not respond.

"She still fat?"

"She's heavy," Scandura said.

"Anthony lets her in on too much. That never went over with the man. You see, Victor, all this adds up, which is why the man worries. Something's going to fall apart up here, he wants to know about it."

"He'll be the first," Scandura said.

A few minutes later they rose from their chairs. The man with the pouches went to a display case and ordered powdered pastries and glazed cookies. Scandura and the pale man went outside and stood in shadows well away from the neon. The traffic on Route 1 was swift. The pale man said, "So you're not worried about the heat from the DA."

"A state cop's in charge of it, and already Anthony's got him half in his pocket. Tell the man that."

Presently the other one, carrying a bakery box and a bag, joined them. He cast dead eyes on Scandura and said, "By the way, you know a fed up here named Thurston? A few years ago Justice was using him against Angello and then squeezed him out, didn't like his personality. We don't either."

"I never met him personally," Scandura said, "but I know of him. He keeps his nose around."

"A fuckin' wop-hater is what he is. The man wants you to watch out."

Scandura nodded. "How is the man?"

There was a slight pause. Then the man with the pouches inched up, a careful grip on his baked goods. "Every year we think he's gonna die, and he don't."

The pale man said, "That answer your question?"

———————

From his chair, Anthony Gardella said, "You feel corrupted?"

Christopher Wade, from his chair, said, "I don't even feel lightheaded." The joint smoldered down to his fingers, and he mashed it out in a leaf-shaped dish, where it continued to diffuse its perfume. "Only dry in the throat."

"Maybe you didn't do it right. I feel good."

"You've had practice."

"Actually, no." Gardella's expression was drowsy, oblique. His voice was unhurried. Everything about him seemed relaxed, especially his smile. "The thing I tried to do for you with your wife, you still mad at me?"

"Just don't interfere again."

"You want, I'll see she gets her old job back."

"Too late for that."

"You don't want her back there, anyway." Gardella said knowingly. "She takes the job at Rodino Travel, you'll be able to drop in on her every day. Nice, huh?"

"The job is her decision. What's Rodino to you?"

"The family's Italian, that's all."

"That's enough." Wade closed his eyes for a moment. He had lied about not being lightheaded. After an unnecessary cough, he said casually, "I have an answer to the question I asked earlier."

"Ah, yes," said Gardella, his smile affable.

"I want a piece of all your action. I want a percentage. A Swiss bank account. Not the Caymans or some place close like that. I want Switzerland."

Gardella laughed. "You want the moon. Remember you're only a lieutenant."

"I don't want the account in my name," Wade went on blithely. "The money goes to the kids. My two daughters. And I want it done so they won't know about it until they're middle-aged women."

Gardella whistled, his smile steady.

Wade said, "While you're thinking about it, I should warn you the DA has ambition for higher office, which is the reason he's assigning me more men. He wants me to speed up the investigation, particularly into your laundering and pornography operations. He also wants the politicians you deal with, at least those that aren't his friends. If I come up with something juicy I can't use, he wants me to turn it over to the FBI."

Gardella's smile did not wane, but his jaw shifted to one side. "You got anything more to say?"

"The percentage is negotiable."

"Is that so?"

Wade waited, aware of a tiny break in the rhythm of his breathing. His throat was parched, to a degree that he feared speaking again. Small sounds filtered through the window behind him. It took him a while to realize it was raining and a moment more to notice the subtle change in Gardella's demeanor.

"Maybe your daughters will get together with my sons," Gardella said, rising. "Wouldn't that be something?"

––––––––––

Supervisor Russell Thurston was not alone in his apartment when the telephone rang. "Christ," he muttered, jacking himself up on an elbow, his face extremely unpleasant. A long stretch was needed to reach the receiver, which he did not accomplish without discomfort. The anxious voice on the line said, "This is Honey." Immediately he punched the Hold button. Questioning gray-blue eyes stared up at him from a pillow as he struggled into his robe.

"It's private," he explained.

He took the call in the room he used as an office, perching himself on a corner of the teak desk. The caller said, "I want to meet with you."

"That's totally unwise," he said in a penetrating tone.

"Please!"

"Where are you calling from?"

"You know where."

"You're being foolish, very foolish," he said stonily. "All right, I'll meet with you. Not tomorrow, I'm busy. And not the next day. We'll make it the day after that." He named the time and place. He heard a groan.

"I can't wait that long."

"You're going to have to," he said and disconnected.

He returned slowly to the bedroom. His bedmate was dozing, a smooth naked shoulder protruding from the covers. He leaned over and shook it. "Time for you to go."

"You're kidding."

"Not in the least."

Twenty minutes later he poured himself a glass of sherry and carried it into his office, where he sat at the desk, opened a number of file folders, and, from time to time, glanced at the phone. More than an hour later, when he was about to go to bed, it rang.

Lieutenant Christopher Wade said, "This is Sweetheart."

"You almost disappointed me."

"You knew I'd be calling?"

"I suspected. I must be psychic."

"Things look good."

"You in?"

"I'm in," Wade said.

13

RITA O'DEA, wrapped in a voluminous housecoat at the breakfast table, offered a choice of three cereals to her guests: Froot Loops, Frosted Flakes, and Raisin Bran. "I knew you would," she said when Ty O'Dea opted for Froot Loops. "You used to eat 'em out of the box, remember?" Sara Dillon, who wanted only coffee, lit a cigarette. Rita O'Dea said, "You're pregnant, you should eat. But you shouldn't, for Christ's sake, smoke."

Sara Dillon took a quick puff and dashed the cigarette out.

"You act nervous. You nervous?"

"No."

"You want eggs, I'll make 'em for you."

"This is fine," Sara Dillon said and shook a bit of Raisin Bran into a bowl. Rita O'Dea thrust a plastic pitcher of pineapple juice at her.

"Have some of this first," she ordered. "You need it."

"Leave her alone, Rita."

"You shut up. You want the kid to be born human, don't you?"

Ty O'Dea nodded submissively and dug his spoon into his cereal. His throat was torn from shaving, and a fluff of toilet paper clung to one of the cuts. As nonchalantly as possible, he asked, "Where's your friend?"

"My friend, as you call him, is getting my car washed. He earns his keep, something you never did." She smiled ironically as she poured juice, first for Sara Dillon, then for herself. "If it won't make you jealous, I'll tell you about him."

"No," Ty O'Dea said. "I'm not interested."

"And you're not jealous either," she said, more than a little bitterly.

Later, partly because he knew he wouldn't be missed, he left the women alone and slipped out the back door. The air was cool from the rain that had fallen most of the night, but the sun was strong. For a number of moments he watched a lone robin pulling at the ground, its energy endless. His own was minimal. Careful to keep out of sight of Anthony Gardella's house, he made his way to the open garage. There he waited.

When Alvaro returned with the car, he rose from the box he'd been sitting on. The car, smelling of hot wax, was a little sports job, and he wondered how Rita O'Dea fitted herself behind the wheel. He watched as Alvaro climbed out with a little smile, his hair and beard glistening. His shirt was blazing red.

"You fool."

"Watch your mouth," Alvaro said.

"Why the hell are you still here? With Nardozza dead, you've got no more contract. You'd better run."

"I run, it'll tell Gardella what he don't know."

"He'll find out sooner or later, assuming he don't know already."

"How come you're still alive?" Alvaro asked with a sidelong glance.

"I'm family. Rita feels for me. You think I'd be standing here now she didn't like me?"

"Then I'm safe." Alvaro increased his smile as if for perversity's sake. "You she likes, me she loves."

Ty O'Dea turned away. He stepped out of the garage and then looked back. "This minute," he said. "This minute she loves you."

————

Late that day Ty O'Dea was summoned to Anthony Gardella's house. His legs went weak as Rita O'Dea escorted him over. "Be a big boy," she said when he stumbled going up the front steps. She rang the bell but did not wait for a response. She had her own key. Before she opened the door, she said, "How do you feel?"

"Not a hundred percent," he admitted.

She said, "You got reason."

Inside the house he did not see Gardella at first and gave a start when he did. The measured neatness of the man's suit made him feel shabby. He smiled without meeting his eyes and gave another start when he saw Rita O'Dea edging away.

"Aren't you staying?" he asked in a panic.

"Anthony doesn't want me to."

He began moving when Gardella made an abrupt motion. He entered a long room and saw the large, baggy face of Ralph Roselli, who was reading a newspaper in a chair. Roselli did not look up. He kept walking, Gardella directing the way without a word, and soon found himself in the library, near leather chairs. Because he had not been told otherwise, he remained standing while Gardella seated himself. Finally, in a voice deceivingly soft, Gardella spoke.

"You should be dead. Wasn't for Rita, you would be."

Ty O'Dea leaned forward, as if he wanted to kiss Gardella's hand. Had he been given permission to move, he would have. "Anthony, I swear I didn't know what was going on in Miami. I was just working for Nardozza, trying to make a living. He was your cousin. I thought it was all right, cleared with you."

"What is it about you makes me sick?"

"Anthony, please."

"You trying to tell me you didn't know Sal was doing a number on me?"

"I swear."

"You trying to tell me you didn't know he had a contract out?"

"On you? Jesus Christ, no! I'd've been the first one to warn you."

"Why are you sweating?"

I'm in front of you, I always sweat. I get scared. You know that."

"You worry me, Tyrone. You always have."

"Anthony, please. I'll do whatever you say. I got relatives in Ireland. You want me to go there, I'll go."

Gardella stared enigmatically at him. "What if I asked you to go up and down the street picking up dog shit, would you do that?"

Ty O'Dea smiled weakly.

"Yes, you'd do it," Gardella answered for him. "You wouldn't have a choice. What if I told you to throw yourself in front of a car on the Southeast Expressway?"

Ty O'Dea teetered in place, his head burning.

"I'm waiting for an answer."

"Please, Anthony."

"You ever lie to me again, that's where you're going."

———

In the office of his funeral home, standing in the blue light that fed his ficus plants, his hands smelling of fluids, Sammy Ferlito glowered at his nephew Augie. "You ain't got the brains you were born with.

You wasn't my sister's kid, I'd throw you to the fuckin' wolves."

"I ask for advice, you give me garbage," Augie said miserably. "You act like it was my fault."

"No, peckerhead, not your fault, *mine!* I never shoulda asked Anthony to use you."

"What should I do?"

"You keep your fuckin' mouth shut, that's what you do. You don't say nothing to Anthony, better he forgets you're alive. And you see those two feds coming again, you run. *Capisce?*"

"That's all? That's all I should do?"

"You can pray," Ferlito said in a voice tailored to fit fear into him. "Now get to work. You got two stiffs to dress. Do the woman first."

When his nephew left, Ferlito locked himself in the office and after considerable thought picked up the telephone. He was lucky. He reached Victor Scandura on the first try, and he spoke rapidly, at length, with pain. Suddenly he interrupted himself. "Do you understand my position, Victor?"

"Sure," said Scandura. "You're covering your ass."

———

Anthony and Jane Gardella ate at an overpriced restaurant on Newbury Street and afterward went for drinks at the Parker House, where politicians sidled over to pay respect. A state senator, who owned a summer house near theirs in Rye and who prided himself on his courtly manners, kissed Jane Gardella's slim hand. He also admired her choker necklace with its subtle diamond pendant. When she realized the senator was hoping for a chance to talk to her husband privately, she excused herself and went to the powder room.

When she returned, the senator was gone. Gardella said with a small smile, "What did you think of him?"

"Such a gentleman," she said playfully. She touched her necklace and dangled the pendant. "This really impressed him."

"He probably knew what it was worth."

"What is it worth? You've never told me."

"I don't want to scare you."

"Do you think money scares me?"

His smile was light, indulgent, caring. "I don't want anything to scare you."

"Do you think I'm a baby?"

"Not at all."

She leaned forward over the dark table, her eyes teasing. "How much money do you have, Tony? Give me a vague idea. A lot? A whole hell of a lot? Or an unbelievable amount?"

He said, "Somewhere in between the last two things you mentioned." Then he stared into her face. "You tipsy?"

"A little. You mind?"

"No," he said and raised a hand for the check. "But you're shut off."

———

Her sleep was restless. Too many unpleasant dreams tunneled through it, and Jane Gardella rose well before she wanted to, careful not to disturb her husband. In the kitchen she heated old coffee and carried a cup toward the sun room. Ralph Roselli, who she had forgotten was in the house, glanced up from the chair he had fallen asleep in. She clutched at her brief wrap, and he lowered his eyes so that he saw only her calves and ankles.

In the sun room she nestled in the cushions of an enormous wicker chair, her head aching just enough to disconcert her. Her thoughts stretched back to the sixties, the bows in her hair, the Scout shoes on her feet, the hard-earned A's on her report card. With less pleasure she remembered her adolescence, the shock of her father's departure, the thrill of boys she imagined loving forever, the bitterness of her mother when she passed up a university scholarship to become a waitress in the sky. Only dimly could she recollect the first time she laid eyes on Anthony Gardella, though he remembered everything, even the flight number.

Through jalousie windows she watched a jay fly low over the lawn, and then she closed her eyes, as if assessing something in herself. Her pulse raced for no reason.

When she returned to the kitchen with her empty cup, she found that Ralph Roselli had made fresh coffee and had laid the morning papers on the table, the *Globe* on top, as if he knew her preference, which made her feel something of a princess. A note said he would be back later. She was at the table, hugging a raised knee and reading Erma Bombeck, when a voice asked, "You always sit around that way?"

The question came from her sister-in-law, an assertive presence, who had entered the house with little sound and was peering in on her. They were not close. They were, she had recognized early on, rivals. She said, "Not always," and dropped her knee.

"I don't suppose Tony's up yet."

"I can wake him," she said.

"Never do that," Rita O'Dea said with eyes that seemed to make a calculated assault on her. "Even if somebody should point a gun at him, you don't wake him. You jump in front of him."

"Is that what you would do?" she asked while trying to smile.

"It's what any wop wife would do."

"I'm trying to be one."

"You'll never make it dressed like that. Don't tell Tony I was here. It's not important."

Jane Gardella accompanied her halfway to the front door and then slowly reached out to detain her. "Sometime, Rita, when you're not busy, would you teach me to make sauce?"

Rita O'Dea tossed her hair back. "It's not your cooking he married you for."

"Then suppose you tell me what."

"Christ, I would've thought you knew that," Rita O'Dea said with eyebrows drawn in. "You're showing most of it."

————————

Lieutenant Christopher Wade, wearing a flat cap and sunglasses, occupied a box seat for the season's opener at Fenway Park. A cheer went up when the Red Sox loped onto the field. The seat next to Wade was vacant, but before the first inning was over Gardella was sitting in it. "You haven't missed much," Wade said without looking at him, and Gardella shrugged. It was not until the second inning, the Red Sox already losing, that he spoke.

"All my life," he said, shelling a peanut, "I've lived in Boston, but I never rooted for the Sox, always the Yankees. You know, DiMaggio, Rizzuto, Berra. Had to be loyal to the Italians. Though I'll admit I liked the old Red Sox. Williams, Doerr, Tabor, those were players you could care about. Now who've you got? Rice? What am I going to do, cheer for a nigger?"

"You could do worse," Wade said without sympathy.

Sure, I could root for Yastrzemski. Has-been with no class. Guy doesn't know when to quit."

"Most of us don't."

"Some of us can't." Gardella denuded another peanut and ate it, then rustled the bag at Wade, who declined. "My kind of thing you don't walk away from. Guys who take over for you think you're going to want to come back sometime, which means they don't trust you. They'd rather you be dead."

Wade kept his eyes on the field. The opposing team was Toronto, which was still scoring runs, the ball bounding between the shortstop and third baseman.

Gardella said, "Petrocelli was still playing, he'd've got that."

Wade said, "You don't sound happy."

"I'm not. Your people hit on more of my places yesterday. That I was expecting. What bothers me is the way they did it, came on like gangbusters. At Video Home Products they were throwing cassettes around worth more than the suits they were wearing. I could sue for damages."

"You'd probably have a case. I can't watch my people every minute."

"They scared the office girls. Some quit, afraid they'd get their names in the paper."

"You can always hire new help," Wade said and then, with a shade of distaste, added, "Some of those adult flicks you push go beyond raunchiness."

"Tell the Supreme Court, not me. I'm only a businessman, an investor looking for a decent return." Gardella glanced at a teenage girl stuffing half a hot dog into her mouth, wincing as if unable to chew fast enough. "Put a camera on her, and that's pornography."

"My people are more interested in learning how you managed to take over the company," Wade said and received an austere look.

"I thought we had an understanding."

"We've got nothing yet."

"What you asked for takes time. You made it complicated. The Swiss part's a pain in the ass, but we can work it through New York. What I don't do is deal in percentages."

"I'm not impossible."

"I'm not either," Gardella said. "You got a pencil?"

In silence, manipulating a scorecard, turning player numbers into monetary ones, they negotiated figures, a substantial one up front, more moderate amounts by the month. Wade gave a slight nod.

"I can live with that."

"I would think so," Gardella said tartly, which drew a slow look from Wade.

"Nothing comes cheap."

"Who the hell ever said it did? By the way, your wife took the job at Rodino's."

"I know."

"Consider it a bonus."

Wade feigned not to hear. "The Toronto pitcher's good. He's throwing smoke. What's his name?"

"I don't know," Gardella said, "but he just struck out the side."

Gardella left in the fifth inning, crumpling the scorecard and taking it with him. Wade waited until the eighth and joined many others jostling toward the exits.

———

While driving out of Boston, Supervisor Russell Thurston listened to a half inning of baseball and then tuned to a music station. His mood was good. He felt on top of things, as if no problem were too great to solve. He drove south to Scituate, to a complex of authentic Colonial buildings that had been restored and interconnected and were occupied by doctors, dentists, and various consultants. Leaving his car in the lot, he strolled to a grassy mall behind the buildings and sat on a bench. Though a few minutes early, he was surprised that Honey was not already there.

He slipped a pocket dictionary out of his coat pocket and studied a page, his lips silently shaping unfamiliar words. He was trying to learn Italian. He tucked the dictionary away when he saw a woman approaching. She was wearing a flannel blazer, a pleated skirt, and smoke-gray hosiery, and she was holding herself much too straight. Her hair was radically different, which was the reason his gaze was so intense.

"I almost didn't recognize you in that wig," he said with a touch of drollness, his smile an effective mask. He watched her eyes shift about nervously.

"This is a terrible place to meet."

"I have a dental appointment here in fifteen minutes," he said, "so let's make it fast. What's your problem?"

"I want out," said Jane Gardella.

14

PEOPLE came onto the mall. An elderly couple strolled to a distant bench, and a woman with two children let the older one run loose. A man in a colorful track suit trotted by. Russell Thurston viewed all with slight interest and returned his gaze to Jane Gardella, who sat rigidly, holding a cigarette, her knees tightly crossed. "Don't give me ultimatums," he said icily and watched her head droop. The wig she wore was reddish.

"I'm not doing you any good," she said in a dry whisper.

"Let me be the judge of that."

"It hasn't worked, and it's never going to." Her voice faltered as if from a weird mix of feelings. "Tony tells me nothing."

"You do all right," Thurston said with vindictive calm as his eyes seemed to unpick her seams. "You've got eyes and ears and a brain. Keep using them."

"Nothing is mine anymore, not even my life."

"That's your doing."

"It's yours."

"I'm not going to argue."

She smoked, spilling ash, brushing it from her lap. Listlessly she threw the cigarette away. It didn't go far. Thurston extended a foot and stamped it out.

She was silent, waiting until she could speak in a reasonable voice. Tears stood in her eyes.

"Don't pull that on me," he said. "It won't work."

She altered her angle of vision, unable to cope with her thoughts, all enervating in one way or another. The child running loose, a boy, was button-eyed. He ventured close and stared, his tentative smile vanishing when it received no encouragement. "Don't bother the people," his mother called, and he retreated.

With a shadow drawn across her face, Jane Gardella said, "Maybe I'll just end it my own way."

"That's entirely your business," Thurston said aloofly, "but it would be a waste. I know you're not stupid, but are you self-destructive?"

"You've made it so I don't know who I am."

"Would you like me to tell you?"

"No."

His voice drummed on. "You probably don't care anymore, but we can still put Charlie away. He's with another airline now, being a good boy."

"I don't care about Charlie, only myself."

"And Gardella."

"Yes, I care about Tony."

"That's what makes it all so amusing. You're such a challenge, Honey. And such a bundle of contradictions." He stood up, loomed over her. "But there's something you must keep in mind. You could never run far enough from me or Gardella. It would only be a question of who found you first."

She gazed up and could see under his chin, into his nose. He was the only person she had ever absolutely hated. For a number of seconds her eyes closed. She wanted to shut out not only his voice but his face. He reached down to touch her shoulder, but she dodged his fingers as if they were corrosive.

He said, "Are you through talking nonsense?"

Her hand moved itself without her knowing it. From her bag she removed sunglasses framed in golden metal and slipped them on. "I don't have a choice, do I?" she said and prepared to rise. "The man I told you about is still living with Tony's sister."

"I wouldn't worry about him."

"Is he a killer or not?"

"Perhaps, but he's not in your husband's league."

"Is Tony in danger?"

"Only from me," Thurston said with a note of satisfaction. There was no appreciable breeze, but the air suddenly was cooler. He checked his watch. "I'm running late for my appointment."

His voice chilled her more than the air did. She got to her feet and accepted his arm, part of the cover, which made her feel sordid. They walked toward the buildings, her step synchronized with his. Before they parted, she said, "I don't like Wade. He scares me."

"Refer to him by his code name," Thurston said lightly. "That's procedure."

"Does he know about me?"

"No, Honey. That's our secret."

———————

Agents Blodgett and Blue unthreaded their way out of a busy coffee shop in Government Center, where they'd had a late lunch. Blodgett had bolted his, an overstuffed roast beef sandwich, and was now paying the price, the discomfort inscribed on his face. He stopped short and suffered through a moment of abdominal torment as Blue watched without pity.

"It's your own fault. You eat like a pig."

"And you eat like you're in a French restaurant.

You put on airs." Blodgett breathed deeply and rallied well.

They pushed onto the sidewalk, where the pump of the crowd accelerated their pace. The Kennedy Building was across the way, but they headed in a different direction, which distressed Blue. His eye went to his watch. It was his wife's birthday, and he hoped to get home early.

"Someone for you to see," Blodgett explained.

They entered a building, mounted a flight of stairs, and traveled a length of corridor to glass doors, the entrance to the Rodino Travel Agency. Standing to one side, Blue behind him, Blodgett peered through the glass. Beyond free-standing posters of sunny scenes was a bank of desks, Susan Wade at one of them. She was tastefully dressed in a business suit. Her hair had been cut and restyled, which in effect had unmasked her. Her long face stood out, the bonework prominent.

"You see her?" Blodgett asked.

"Wade's wife, so what?" Blue craned his neck. "She looks like a nice lady."

Blodgett reassessed her. "She looks her age."

"Which is?"

"I forget."

"Then how do you know she looks it?"

"You can tell," Blodgett said with an air of worldliness and watched her answer her telephone. As she talked, she lined up pencils on her desk blotter and trued them at the points, a quiet task that touched Blue, as if it reflected a measure of her vulnerability. When she lifted her eyes, he tugged Blodgett's arm.

"Let's not get caught staring," he said, but Blodgett showed no concern.

"I was in there once. You can't see out."

"What's your interest in her?"

"Not mine—yours. Thurston wants no surprises."

"Which means?"

"You're the baby-sitter."

"Why not you?" Blue asked aggressively.

"Thurston's decision."

"Where does she live?"

"Wellesley."

"I'll stick out."

"It's night work."

They turned away, Blue with an odd twist, as if footsore. They retraced their steps, exited the building, pressed through the crowd, and crossed the divided thoroughfare between bursts of traffic. Ever-present pigeons flew up in front of them on the plaza. When they entered the foyer of the Kennedy Building, Blue said, "Do you think he'll ever get sick of it?"

"What's that?"

"Using people."

"What are you so pissed off about?"

"Thurston. He knows it's my wife's birthday."

———

On her way back to Hyde Park, Jane Gardella detoured into Dedham, where her mother lived. She parked her car hastily and badly, tucked her wig into her bag, and hurried past a privet hedge into a small brick apartment building. "It's me," she said some moments after pressing a button. Her mother buzzed open the inner door.

The apartment was airy and cool. Mrs. Denig had been napping and still had sleep in her eyes. The set of her mouth, somber and negative, hardened her jawline and took away something in general from her looks. "Sit down," she said. "I'll make tea."

"No, Mother, I can't stay."

"Then why'd you come?"

"Just a little favor," Jane Gardella said awkwardly. "There's no reason Tony should, but if he asks, I was here with you this afternoon."

Mrs. Denig's face went grim. "This is stupid of you. And dangerous."

"It's not what you think, Mother. It's nothing really. Just do me the favor."

"And not ask questions—is that what you're telling me?" Mrs. Denig moved to another part of the room and rested her hands on the back of a chair. Her beauty was gone, but she had a magnificent neck. It sprang high above her open collar. "I was foolish when I was young, but I never married an Italian gangster twice my age."

"Mother, please."

"Yes, I know, you don't want to listen. You never do."

"I'm leaving," Jane Gardella said nervously. "I don't have time to argue."

Mrs. Denig followed her to the door and placed a hand under her elbow. It was not particularly gentle. "You're my daughter. I'll do it this time, but don't ask again."

———

Agent Blue let himself quietly into his apartment. The television was playing, the end of the eleven o'clock news. His wife, still in her nurse's uniform, though without her stockings, was lying on the couch. Her dusky legs were stretched to the fullest. He leaned over her, his hand listing over the shiny synthetic fabric of her uniform. "I'm sorry," he whispered abjectly, and her face offered itself up to him.

"Have I ever bitched about your hours?"

"Never. But you deserve to, tonight of all nights."
He sighed. "I was watching a house in Wellesley."

"Putting somebody to bed?"

"It amounted to that." His tone became more
wretched. "I didn't have a chance to pick up your
gift."

"It's all right," she said. "Look what was delivered."

He straightened and turned and stepped quickly
toward a table. "Jesus. Roses." A profusion of them
rioted out of a fancy basket embellished with an
enormous bow. "They must've cost two hundred bucks
or more. Who sent them?"

"See for yourself."

He read the card, read it twice. " 'With warmest
wishes on your special day. Russell Thurston.' "

"You don't look pleased," she said, rising from the
couch, joining him. She sniffed one of the roses.

"There's a guy I can never seem to figure out."

"Why try?"

"Because I want to stay alive," Blue said.

———

Jane Gardella had nothing on except the towel she
had wrapped around her head after washing her
hair. Through the vapors the bathroom mirror returned a fluctuating image of herself. Her husband,
peering in at her, said, "I can't tell you how beautiful
you are."

"Yes, you can," she said, "tell me."

When he stayed silent, she had an acute sense that
something was wrong, though her reason told her
she was overreacting. He did not move; she did. Her
kiss was a tremble against his mouth.

"Say something," she whispered, for his silences
always disturbed her. She read too much into them.
Her damp breasts stretched into his hands.

"I love you," he said. "Is that what you want to hear?"

"Yes." Large portions of the day were vivid in her mind: Thurston's unresponsive face, her mother's dour one, one no less threatening than the other. She imagined her husband suddenly sweeping her off her feet, lifting her high, and holding her to the light, where every secret would be bared.

For a feverish second she considered confession.

Later, after they had meshed on the bed, she lay with him under the covers. The room was lit by the television, which was airing the news. He slung a lazy arm over her and said, "Something was different."

"What do you mean?" she asked warily.

"You tell me."

She adapted her breathing to his and forced herself to be calm. And to be quiet.

"It was like you were trying to prove something," he said, "or tell me something . . . or hide something. You tried too hard."

"I came."

"You always come."

She slipped away from his arm and propped herself on an elbow and looked at him with perfectly clear eyes. "Don't be mad, Tony. I've just never felt comfortable in this house. I'm getting there, but I need more time."

"Is it the house or me?" he asked in a dry voice that seemed to come out of the darkest part of him. "Or maybe you're seeing somebody," he added, and she flung him a desperate look of protest and hurt. The fear she kept hidden.

"Oh, Tony."

"Then if it's only the house, there's a remedy. Rye."

"Oh, yes," she said eagerly and dared say nothing

more. She was thankful when he blotted out the television with the remote-control device and threw the room into utter dark. She needed the anonymity. He gathered her up, and she pressed against him where the flesh had risen again.

15

On a warm day in May, deep inside the house at Rye, Anthony Gardella said to Christopher Wade, "I'd like you to meet one of my sons. This is Thomas, my youngest. Say hello to Mr. Wade, Tommy." The youth who sprang uneasily from the upholstered chair, a paperback novel in his hand, was of middling height and had profound dark eyes and neatly styled black hair. He immediately struck Wade as indrawn and shy. There was a polite handshake.

"Home from college?" Wade asked.

"Yes, sir. I finished my finals early."

"He's dean's list," Gardella interjected, slinging a proud arm around him. "I wanted him to go to Harvard, but his mother always had her heart set on Holy Cross, religious reasons. We respected her wishes. Right, Tommy?" A solemn nod was given. With a smile at Wade, Gardella said, "He's got his mother's looks, my brains."

The youth blushed.

Wade said quickly, "So you're home for the summer?"

"No, sir. I'm taking a job at the Cape."

"He's going to be a beach bum," Gardella said with an affectionate laugh.

"No, sir. I'll be waiting tables."

"He never asks me for a dime. Can you imagine

that, Wade, in this day and age? Go back to your
book, Tommy. Mr. Wade and I are going to talk on
the patio."

The patio was accessible past glass doors, which
Gardella closed behind them. The tide was out, the
beach immense. The ocean glittered hard. Some children were running along the surf at full speed, a
playful race. Some distance away, also near the surf,
was Jane Gardella, whom Wade sighted at once. She
had on a red top and matching shorts and seemed to
flame up. With no inflection, Wade said, "How does
your son get along with his stepmother?"

"We don't use that term. She's my wife, that's all.
He accepts it. It's not like he's a kid anymore."

"You going to bring him into your business?"

"Cut it out, Wade. Does he look the type?"

"What about your other boy, the marine?"

"Loves the military. Unless I'm misreading him,
he'll be a twenty-year man."

"You sound glad."

"I am. He was the one who worried me, too tough
for his own good." Gardella stepped to a table, set
up glasses, and poured from a pitcher. Then he
handed Wade one of the glasses. "It's punch, a little
vodka in it, not much. You'll like it. Sit down, you
make me nervous."

Both men made themselves comfortable in chairs
of canvas and wood. The punch tasted of white
grape and peach and of something tart.

Gardella said, "Have we got things to talk about?"

"You can breathe a little easier about G&B Waste.
We're not pursuing it anymore. The company's sins
go too far beyond the Massachusetts line for our
budget. That's the good news. The bad is the DA
wants me to send a courtesy copy of my report to the
New Hampshire attorney general's office. If you know

somebody there who'll sit on it, I'll target it to his attention."

After a half minute of silence, Gardella said, "I'll give you a name later. What else you got?"

"Aceway Development. Its county contracts, worth millions, smack of rigged bidding. And it's gotten unwarranted tax breaks for all its properties, some of which later go up in smoke. There's also a matter of tricky financing with the Union Bank of Boston, which has written off too many of Aceway's loans."

"Everything was done aboveboard," Gardella said without worry.

"I've got two good men, names of Danley and Dane, who say otherwise and think they can come up with hard evidence."

"They're hotdogs, shooting from the hip."

"They're smart boys. They've asked me to put pressure on the president at the Union Bank, a certain tax assessor, and the state senator who chairs the committee on counties."

"But you're not going to do that, are you?"

"I'm going to *try* not to do that. Remember, I can control the investigation only up to a point."

A shadow cut momentarily across Gardella's face. "By the way," he asked in a voice laced with implication, "how does it feel to be a man of means?"

"I don't know," Wade replied. "You're talking about money I'll never touch."

Gardella passed him an admiring smile. "You're really playing this cozy."

"Would you rather I be stupid?"

Gardella sipped his punch and slid a hand inside his cashmere sweater to scratch his chest. His eye lazily scanned the beach. His wife was no longer poised near the surf but drifting over the sand, the start of another one of her long walks. "I swear, she must hike ten miles a day. Yesterday I got scared and went looking for her."

"She must like the ocean."

"Loves it. Says it talks to her. What d'you say, Wade, am I a lucky guy?"

"I guess you are. You living here now?"

"She is. I commute when I can."

"Like a suburban husband."

"Almost."

Inside the house the telephone was ringing. Gardella seemed not to hear it, though a muscle quivered in his face, as if from a shift of feeling. Soon the son parted the glass doors and said, "For you, Dad."

"It always is," Gardella said, rising.

Left alone, Wade stood up and gazed out at the beach. The glare made him blink. Jane Gardella had reversed direction, as if something were dragging her back to the house. Gulls tracked her for a distance. As she drew closer, Wade noted the tense frown that clouded her face. She saw him, and he felt bitter hostility as she stepped toward him and stopped close so that he felt her breath on his cheek.

"Listen to me," she said. The cones in her pullover almost touched him as her voice thinned into something hard to hear.

"I'm listening."

She spoke; he caught only the breath of the words, which sounded like "I'm watching you."

"What?"

"You heard me."

"No." His reaction to her unyielding stare was visceral and disquieting. "I didn't hear you clearly," he said, and she spoke again, in a voice only a shade more distinguishable.

"How I hate you all."

Deftly she pulled away as Anthony Gardella returned to the patio, no longer in his sweater but dressed for travel, his son a slow step behind. She threw her husband an intense look of disappointment as he approached her. "I'm sorry," Gardella said, "but I've got to get back."

Wade also set himself to leave. With envy, he watched Gardella kiss his wife and pat her rear end, the pat meant to be secret. He heard Gardella say, "You stay, Tommy. The ocean air will do you good."

Presently Wade found himself tramping with Gardella toward their separate cars. Gardella, when chauffeuring himself, drove a baby-blue Cadillac with spoked hubcaps. He opened the driver's door, glanced back, and said grimly, "That was Scandura on the phone. There's a problem."

"What's it got to do with me?"

"Too soon to tell. I'll let you know."

Victor Scandura was tallying figures in the rear room of Anthony Gardella's real estate office on Hanover Street when he heard the front door open. He thought it was one of his people and did not look up. He was busily manipulating a twelve-digit calculator, a gift from a banker, and was particularly pleased with some of the subtotals. At the scrape of a shoe, his eyes darted up. The man peering in at him said, "Remember me?"

Scandura looked at him intently and drew a blank, though something was familiar about him. He advanced into the room, slowly, loutish in an ill-fitting suit and heavy shoes. The only thing Scandura knew for sure was that the man was wearing a weapon, for the bulge was unmistakable. "You're a cop," Scandura said impassively.

"You're getting there."

"I know more cops than I care to. Which one are you?"

"Think of me in a fur cap and a mackinaw. I got a mustache now, didn't have one then." A deep breath expanded the man's chest. "I'm your friend in Greenwood did you the favor. The name's Hunkins, you didn't get it when we met. You were too busy throwing money away."

Scandura did not bat an eye. "I don't seem to remember that. I'm surprised you do."

"I'm not the fastest guy in the world, you know what I mean?" Officer Hunkins gave out a playful smile. "But give me time and I figure things out. Then I need more time to decide what to do. That's why I'm here, finally."

Scandura sat braced, though he looked perfectly relaxed. He brushed aside two paper clips that were interlocked.

Hunkins said, "What you threw on the ground was okay, but it wasn't enough for what went down that night on Steuben's Bluff. That was no accident, pal. D'you want me to say more, or d'you figure I've said enough?"

"That's up to you."

"Maybe it's Mr. Gardella I should talk to. Maybe you don't see the seriousness."

Scandura sat back and suffered, or perhaps enjoyed, a silent moment of flatus. "What's on your mind, Hunkins?"

"I'll make it simple. I'm sick of Greenwood. I don't like the winters there. I know cops who retire early to Florida, get themselves a trailer, and live well. Nothing but sunshine. I think they call that the good life.

"And you want the money to make it happen. What are you talking—five figures?"

"Six," said Hunkins.

"Then maybe you oughta buy a Megabucks lottery ticket."

Hunkins suddenly jerked back, wrinkling his nose. "What the hell did you do—shit?"

"It's what I think of you," Scandura said evenly, watching Hunkins turn red. "You got a lot of balls but no brains."

"You think I'm a dummy coming here like this, huh?" Hunkins tore open his jacket and exposed the bulk of his holstered weapon. "This is a fucking magnum you're looking at. You guys want to fool with me, think twice."

"Relax, Hunkins."

"Then don't pull my chain. You don't want to do business, say so. I happen to know somebody who'd love my information, and I'd testify against you grease-balls in a minute."

Scandura smiled with infinite calm, his eyes cold and impenetrable behind his spectacles. "You're right. This is a decision for Mr. Gardella. How long you going to be around, Hunkins?"

"Coupla days, no more."

"Where are you staying?"

"Where I'm staying's my business, but it don't bother me none you knowing. Howard Johnson's, Kenmore Square. You guys get any funny ideas, just remember I sleep with the magnum, and if you think that's a lie, call up my wife, collect. I'll give you the number."

"I'll tell Mr. Gardella."

"Tell his sister too." Hunkins winked. "See, I know everything."

After Hunkins left, Scandura waited several minutes before picking up the phone and pressing out a

number, which included the area code for New
Hampshire. When he got an answer on the other
end, he said, "Let me speak to your father, Tommy."

———————

Rita O'Dea returned home bearing gifts from a
day of shopping. No one was there to lavish them on
except Sara Dillon, who was only half-dressed and
looked as if she had just gotten up. Ty O'Dea was
visiting old haunts in South Boston, and Alvaro was
playing softball for a Hispanic team in Brighton, or
at least that was what he had told Rita O'Dea. She
had only partly believed him and did not much care
if he was doing something else. "What do you think
of this?" she asked, ripping the lid off a Jordan
Marsh box and pulling out a man's powder-blue
sports jacket with silver piping. "It's for Ty."

"Yes," Sara Dillon said tactfully. "That's Ty's taste."

Rita O'Dea had an ear. "But not yours."

"Yes, I like it too."

"Wait till you see this." She plucked up an elegant
little case, clicked it open, and offered up for show a
gold Seiko watch. "That's for Ty too. I got one just
like it for Alvaro so that nobody gets jealous."

"Why are you doing this?"

"My mood. Don't question it." She reached for
something behind her. "This is for you," she announced and produced earrings from Shreve, Crump
& Low. "I got myself a pair too. Cute, don't you
think?"

"I don't know what to say. Rita, I—"

"Now comes the important stuff," she interposed
and upended a voluminous shopping bag. Within
the moment she was displaying booties, belly bands,
and all the other tender little garments for swad-
dling an infant. "I picked pink. I play the odds."

Sara Dillon's eyes filled. "It's a girl I want."

"There are ways of telling now."

"Ty wants to be surprised."

The two women were kneeling on opposite sides of a cocktail table, wrappings thrown around them. Sara Dillon's breasts, which had swollen in the past week, were visible. Her abdomen had begun to thicken. Rita O'Dea could almost feel the heat of the pregnancy. She said, "Ty never had to have himself fixed. I couldn't have had a kid anyway. I should've known."

"I'm sorry."

"Nobody's fault but mine. I screwed myself up when I was a teenager. Bad abortion. A late cousin of mine arranged it. That's something my brother doesn't know, thank God."

"I'm surprised you've told me."

"We're women, aren't we?"

A silence fell as Sara Dillon began smoothing wrappers, tidying up, her unbrushed hair dropping over her face. Rita O'Dea struggled to her feet, fought a charley horse in her left leg, and swabbed her moist face with a large sleeve. Her stomach lurched, and she experienced a mild dizziness. Her smile was rueful.

"It's like I'm pregnant, not you."

———

Inside Russell Thurston's office in the Kennedy Building, Agent Blue said, "It's a waste of time, believe me. She doesn't go anywhere. She works late, goes to bed early. No boyfriends. Besides, we've got her phone tapped. What more do we need?"

Thurston, making a show of patience, tilted back in his executive chair. "You're being belligerent. Why?"

"I'm working a lot of extra hours."

"Take the mornings off. I'm not unreasonable."

"We're using Wade. Why do we have to use his wife too?"

"Get your facts straight, Blue. The wops involved her, I didn't."

"Why do you call them wops? Shouldn't we be above that?"

"Let me make it simple for you. Not all Italians are wops, but all wops are Italians."

"I see. With that logic, you could also say—"

"Yes, I could, Blue, but why press it?" Thurston's smile, like his voice, was smooth. "By the way, you never mentioned if your wife liked the roses I sent her for her birthday. I waited for you to say something, but you never did."

Blue evinced surprise. "She sent you a note. Didn't you get it?"

"Oh, yes," Thurston said in a way that was at once playful and serious. "Nice, neat penmanship. If I didn't know better, I'd have thought she went to a Catholic school."

"So what's the problem?"

"You should know the rules by now, Blue. It's you I should've heard from."

———

Twenty minutes later Thurston left the Kennedy Building. Waiting for the lights to change at the pedestrian crossing, he turned his nose away from the fumes of fretful cars, daredevil taxis, and burdensome tourist buses. The man next to him, a derelict, spat green. When the lights turned, he crossed the thoroughfare at a brisk pace and let the pump of the crowd carry him up Tremont Street to Park. Halfway up Park Street he returned with disdain the glance of a goateed black man who seemed to be wearing lipstick. He crossed Beacon Street, passed through that part of the General Court used as a public way, and approached the front of the State House. Christopher Wade stood nearby, a conspicuous figure, with an elbow on the rail overlooking the parking area for the privileged.

"You're late," he said.

"A little," Thurston conceded cavalierly. Workers were leaving the State House for the day, the men in nubby sports jackets, the women in pastel pantsuits and flat shoes. A uniformed policeman from the Metropolitan District Commission strode by. Wade tossed away his cigarette.

"I don't like standing here with my face out."

"There's a reason for everything," Thurston said, lifting his eyes. The lieutenant governor emerged from a private exit with a claque of aides groomed and tailored in his image and in passing gave a cursory glance at Thurston, then a longer and scrutinizing one that took in Wade.

Wade said, "You don't give a damn who sees us."

"Before it wasn't good. Now it is."

"That's why we're meeting here."

"Exactly."

"The lieutenant governor's not on your list."

"True, but we'll let him think he is. Great way to keep him off balance. Right now he's wondering and worrying."

"Not if he's clean."

Thurston snorted. "There's not a politician alive who doesn't have some shit on his soul. J. Edgar Hoover himself said that."

Another group emerged from the same private exit: pinstriped doyens from the financial field, quintessential Bostonians. They had been meeting with the governor and now were moving smartly toward waiting limos whose drivers were throwing open doors. With an unnecessarily sharp nudge, Thurston said, "The tall one, that's Quimby, president of Union Bank. His people came over on the *Mayflower*."

"Does he know you?"

"Sure he knows me, but he's pretending he doesn't see me." Thurston swayed slightly, as if from a sensation of well-being. "When you talk with him, I want you wired."

"He doesn't look like the type who'll incriminate himself."

"No, but he might whine. I want to hear it."

"You want his blood."

"Every blue drop. A man of his background dealing with scum like Gardella deserves nothing."

More people were leaving the State House. Wade recognized Senate President Billy Bulger, Sheriff Dennis Kearney, and a representative he had thought dead. He also saw a couple of lawyers he knew. Thurston tapped his arm.

"Look to your left, down on Myrtle Street, the stocky gentleman talking to the two ladies. That's Senator Matchett, known for his courtly manners and dictatorial control of the committee on counties. Sexually, he's in his second childhood. So's his wife. They got a summer place in Rye, near Gardella's."

"You want me wired for them too?"

"Sure, why not? They think Gardella's some kind of god. They don't know that if you squeeze him you get olive oil."

Wade, with a dark look, reached for a cigarette and came up with an empty pack. "Do you mind if I ask you something?" he said.

"Sure, go ahead."

"It's personal, isn't it, what you've got going against Gardella?"

"Personal? Sure it's personal. I don't like wops who think they're white."

Over plates of pasta at Francesca's on Richmond Street, Anthony Gardella and Victor Scandura discussed the problem of Officer Hunkins. Scandura said, "The guy comes in, I don't believe it. Who would be so stupid? He opens his mouth, I think I'm hearing things. He's carrying a cannon, he shows it to me. Like a cowboy."

Gardella poured wine from a wickered bottle. "No brains."

"None at all."

"An asshole."

"That's what we're dealing with."

Gardella drank and ate reflectively. They were in a booth, their privacy ensured by a solicitous waiter. "If it was another time, I'd say hit him. But right now it's not the thing to do."

Scandura nodded his agreement. "That's my feeling too. Maybe your friend Wade could—"

"No, I don't like that."

"I didn't think you would, but it was something to consider." Scandura tore his bread in two and sopped up the clam sauce left on his plate. A friend of theirs gave a wave from a table across the room. Scandura scarcely acknowledged it, Gardella not at all.

Gardella said, "What I think we should do is compromise him. That way we get him off our backs, and maybe a year from now we'll feel better about hitting him."

"We need people," said Scandura. "How about that woman Laura?"

"She might be too classy for him."

"She's an actress, Anthony. She can do anything, the money's right."

"The money's always right. Use her."

"And Scatamacchia?"

"Him too." Gardella lifted his wineglass. "Now I

feel better. We finished with business? I want to enjoy."

"One more thing," Scandura said. "Sammy Ferlito did what you wanted. He sent Augie to Montreal to relatives and told him to keep his nose clean. He stays there till you say different."

"The way I feel that might be never."

"That's what I told Ferlito."

"He's responsible, did you tell him that?"

"If you'd seen his face, you'd know I didn't have to."

———

In a cafeteria in downtown Wellesley, Agent Blue carried his cup of coffee to a corner table where two Wellesley police officers were seated, the remains of a ham and bean supper on their plates. They pulled in their feet as Blue joined them, and each gave him a lazy smile. One of the officers, who had a red bush of a mustache, said, "They still making you watch that place?"

Blue nodded.

"That's a bitch."

He had met them his third or fourth night of keeping an eye on Susan Wade's house. Their cruiser had rolled up silently behind his colorless unmarked car, and they had come at him with drawn revolvers, forcing him out of the car and making him assume the position. His identification had not impressed them. A phone call to Thurston had been necessary.

"Pass the sugar," he said, and the other officer, older, tougher-looking, accommodated him.

"We're divorced, but a guy like you, married, it must be tough working nights," the officer with the mustache said. "If you want, for a few bucks each week, we'll drive by the place on the hour. It's right on our route."

Blue stirred his coffee slowly, with great care.

"Anything comes up, we'll call you right away, right, Harold?"

"Sure," said the older officer. "No problem."

"How much money you actually talking about?" Blue asked.

"Hell, we're not looking to get rich. Give me twenty bucks. Harold and I will split it."

Blue stared intently at one officer, then the other, and pushed his coffee cup to one side, spilling some. "Tell Thurston it was a nice try," he said, rising, "but it didn't work."

"Hey, you don't want the favor, forget it!"

"I already have."

They watched him leave the cafeteria, his shoulders stiff. The older officer said, "Fucking coon, he's smart."

The officer with the mustache said, "There goes our two hundred bucks."

———

In bed that night, lying flat on her back, Sara Dillon felt swollen from the pressure of her pregnancy and chilled from a growing apprehension. "I don't like it," she whispered to Ty O'Dea. "I don't like her buying us things. I don't know where she's coming from."

"It's just her way," Ty O'Dea said in a voice thick from drinking. He had spent most of the day in taprooms in South Boston. He freed an arm from the covers, the Seiko watch glowing from his wrist. "You have to understand her. Sometimes she's all heart."

"Ty, I think we should leave."

"We will," he said, "soon as the kid's born, I promise."

"I think we should leave now."

"It's ... it's not that easy. Besides, think of the money we're saving."

Sara Dillon brought a slow hand to her face. Her forehead was hot and her skin felt rough, as if blemishes were standing out. "Ty, it's like she's taking over my body."

"What kind of talk is that?"

"And she's making too much about the kid."

There was no answer from him. Seconds later he was asleep, his breathing cluttered, raucous at times. Eventually she drifted off, perhaps for a whole hour, and then she woke with her head hotter and her gown sticking to her. The window, which had been raised, was lowered, and the door, which had been shut, was ajar. She knew she had been looked upon, perhaps for several minutes. She knew this with utter certainty, as if Rita O'Dea had left the imprint of her face in the humid dark of the room.

16

THE UNION BANK OF BOSTON was an imposing structure of Victorian-Gothic architecture. Formidable in age and history, it was a monument in the city's financial district. Despite much interior modernizing, it remained staunch and venerable with its mahogany and marble and its brass plaques honoring past presidents and chairmen, a notable number of them Quimbys. Christopher Wade had an eleven o'clock appointment. He expected to be ushered to an elevator and propelled to a posh suite of offices with original art on the walls. Instead, he was kept waiting in the main concourse, where he gazed through glass at automated teller machines. The people were using them with obsessional intensity, as if the money they drew were free. He turned with a lurch when someone touched his arm.

"This way." The voice was smooth and solid, the privileged face untouched by ordinary worry and care. John Quimby guided Wade beyond a polished rail to a desk that nobody happened to be using at the time. Wade sat beside it, Quimby behind it. "I hope this won't take long."

"I can't see any reason it should," Wade said. "As you know, I've been looking into some of Anthony Gardella's business enterprises, Aceway in particular, and some questions have come up that you might be able to answer."

"Yes," Quimby said brusquely. "Mr. Gardella warned me a week ago you'd be bothering me. He assured me the inconvenience would be minimal."

"Mr. Gardella takes a lot for granted."

"I doubt that," Quimby said with a slight inflection.

Wade took out a pocket notebook, seemed to refer to it, and then put it away. "The bank made a number of bad loans to Aceway. Some were written off, some settled, and a couple of others renegotiated. The bank took a bath."

"That's ancient history."

"I'd still like to know about it."

"Nobody's infallible, not even bankers. Errors in judgment were made. The loan officer involved resigned, which satisfied both the federal and state examiners. But apparently it doesn't satisfy you."

"Where is this loan officer now?"

"He died of a heart attack. Do you want his widow's name? You might want to bother her."

"A number of years ago," Wade went on, "the bank handled a number of large money transfers for Gardella, if not directly, indirectly. Millions were involved."

"Possibly. There was nothing wrong with the practice back then. Now there are stiffer regulations, and the bank doesn't do it anymore."

"Now he shuffles his money through Florida. Would you know anything about that?"

Quimby sighed. "No, Captain."

"I'm a lieutenant."

"Your rank doesn't interest me. You're lucky I'm listening to you."

"How well do you know Gardella?"

"Socially, not at all. I know his credit rating, what I

read about him in the *Globe,* and little else. I have no firsthand knowledge about his alleged criminal connections."

"The FBI has an old photo of you two eating on the deck of a restaurant at Rye Beach, New Hampshire. You had scrod, he had scallops."

"I'm impressed," Quimby said with an austere face, like that of a Trappist monk. "I didn't think the FBI opened its files to you lesser fellows."

"When it suits their purposes."

"But it doesn't suit mine to listen to you any longer," Quimby said and gave an open glance at his watch. On cue, two bank officers, senior to Quimby in age but junior in everything else, appeared outside the rail with documents in their hands, as if their business were pressing. Quimby signaled that he would be only a moment more and switched his eyes back to Wade. "What was your father? A milkman? A plumber?"

"Close," said Wade. "He was an electrician."

"A worthy craft," Quimby noted with icy insincerity. "You should have followed in his footsteps."

"In a way I have. For your information, I'm wired."

"What?"

"It's routine."

Both men rose. "If you have any more questions, Lieutenant, direct them to my lawyer."

Five minutes later Wade was in his Camaro, a victim of the kinetic orneriness of Boston traffic, whose haphazard lines clogged with false stops. It took him an ungodly long time to reach Interstate 95, where he tuned the radio to old music and cut into a passing lane. Though he had no reason for haste, he raced toward Rye.

No one seemed to be home. After ringing the bell several times at the front door, he ambled to the side of the house, where the shrubs were juniper, bayberry, and beach plum. The beach plum was in flower, delicately white, and he glanced over it into windows that hurled back his reflection. The patio was deserted. Down on the dazzling emptiness of the beach, misty near the surf, he guessed at a direction and chose north, which proved right. Some distance around the bend, shielded by boulders, was a pebbly beach that existed only at low tide. That was where he found Jane Gardella.

He startled her.

Seated on a low, flat rock, she was plunged so deeply in private thought that she did not see him until he was upon her, and then she leaped up, confused and unprepared, like someone rousted from a heavy sleep.

"Tony's not here."

"I know," he said, his eyes full of her. She stood with her weight on one leg and threads dangling from her denim shorts. The sun had darkened her face and bleached her eyebrows, making her look even younger than usual and reminding him of certain vivid blond girls he had exalted in high school. Nancy Gleed. Margie Waitt. Terry Swedler. It amazed him that he conjured up the names so readily.

"What do you want?" Jane Gardella asked.

"I'm not sure," he said, which was true or partially true. The air was pungent with the smells of brine, washed-up weed, and dead shellfish, some of the odor emanating from her. Earlier she had been poking about among the rocks.

"You must have come here for something."

"I understand Senator Matchett and his wife have a place near here. I thought I might run into them."

"It's too early in the season for them," she said quickly. "But I think you knew that." He hovered, studying her in a way she did not like. "If you're thinking of making a pass, *don't*. One word to Tony . . . I'd destroy you."

"Why are you so suspicious?"

Her silence was formidable as she cast her eyes to one side.

"Why are you so antagonistic?"

She rubbed one wrist and then the other, as if for circulation. "You get on my nerves," she said. "I see too much of you."

"How much has your husband told you about me?"

"Enough."

"Then you know I'm a reasonable guy."

"Don't try to sell yourself to me," she said, scathing him with a look. "It won't work."

"I'd like us to be friends," he persisted.

"Fine. We're friends." Her smile cut. "Do I bother you, Lieutenant? Is there something about me that you can't figure out?"

He regarded her intently. "Yes."

"Good," she said. "Let it gnaw at you."

She turned away with a quick stride, and he, after a pause, followed. "Look here," he called after her, but she did not listen. She leaped effortlessly over a tidal pool and clambered over heaped pebbles that were wet and shiny. Wavelets were beginning to wash in. Swiftly she glanced back and told him to watch his step, but it was she who should have been careful. She gouged the sole of her foot on the point of a shell, stiffened sideways in pain, and lost her balance. Pebbles clattering, she fell on her shoulder and rolled. Within seconds Wade was crouched over her, her foot in his hands and her blood on his fingers.

"Don't be scared."

She shivered. "Is it bad?"

"I've seen worse," he said as she squeezed her eyes shut. He leaned over her. Her grimacing did not distort her youthful beauty; it gave it another dimension. The smell of summer was baked into her skin. At once he felt foolishly boyish and terribly awkward, as he had at his first school dance with a girl whose name he could almost remember. It was a tingle away.

"Is it still bleeding?" she asked.

"A little," he said and tenderly traced a finger around her ankle.

"Don't!" she said, but he could not stop himself. Leaning closer, he kissed her.

———

High in the Union Bank building, inside a spacious office where a Klee and a Kandinsky vied for attention from opposite walls, John Quimby tested his tea and nodded approval. His aging secretary, who had been with the bank since her graduation from Katharine Gibbs, waited until he sampled a scone and again gave a satisfied nod. Her tiredness showed, also her feelings for him, which he had never noticed and did not now. "I don't want to be disturbed," he said as she departed. After he consumed the scone, he picked up the phone and placed a call on his private line. When, after a considerable delay, he reached his party, he did not bother to identify himself. His commanding voice and cultivated Yankee accent, honed by a Harvard education, was identification enough. He said, "I don't ever want that cocksucker of a cop in my bank again."

There was utter silence on the other end. From Quimby came the rattle of cup and saucer.

"Did you hear me?"

"Never talk to me that way," Anthony Gardella said. "Never."

Quimby heard the line go dead.

Officer Hunkins was enjoying himself. He was in one of the larger girlie joints in the Combat Zone, with a choice seat at the bar and a strategic view of the stripper, who had shed the last spangly remnant of her costume and was gyrating to amplified music. Her smile seemed especially for him. Also, the bartender was good to him, would not let him pay for his shots of Canadian Club and beer chasers. The bartender, a towering man weighing well over two hundred pounds, wore granny glasses as if to present himself as a gentle giant. He said to Hunkins, "A cop comes in here, he gets everything for nothing. That's the way we operate."

Hunkins said, "How d'you know I'm a cop?"

"You guys, you got a bearing about you. It's kinda like military."

Hunkins glowed. Sitting next to him in a brilliant red dress that shrilled her presence was a young woman of intimidating attractiveness. She looked like a model. Screwing up his courage, he said, "How about the lady here? Can she get one free too?"

"That depends," the bartender said. "She with you?"

Hunkins leered at her. " Are you?"

"Like the man said"—her voice was deep and raspy—"it depends."

"I think it's settled," the bartender said, and served her what resembled a mixed drink chunky with ice. She rested her elbows on the bar and gently brought her slender hands together. Hunkins spoke close to her ear.

"What's your name?"

"Laura."

"What did you mean, it depends?"

Her eyes sank into his. "What do you think I meant?"

"How much?" he asked, and she quoted a price. "Jesus Christ," he said. She shrugged. Ten minutes later they left together. The bartender cleared away their glasses and then lumbered to the telephone and made a call.

———

Victor Scandura took it. "That's good," he said and afterward made a call of his own. He was in the Gardella real estate office, which he left presently while tightening his tie and donning his suitjacket. He crossed Hanover Street and walked up a way to the Caffè Pompei, enjoying the soft evening air. Anthony Gardella was seated deep inside the café with a fresh cup of cappuccino and a newspaper he was about to read. Scandura said, "It's all set."

"Good."

"You want me to oversee it?"

"I'd feel better."

Scandura left as unobtrusively as he had arrived. His car was parked nearby. Mere moments after he drove away, Supervisor Russell Thurston clumsily maneuvered his nondescript Dodge into the vacated space. A tire shrieked against the curb. He got out and locked the car under the derisive eye of a youth strenuously chewing gum, salivating, and spitting. Thurston threw him a foul look.

He entered the Caffè Pompei and proceeded nimbly, almost like a dancer, past the elaborate jukebox that pompously resembled furniture with its woodlike veneer and pastoral picture painted on its raised lid. He picked his way deftly between tiny tables and sat down at Gardella's without being asked. "We've never met," he said, "but I think we know each other."

Gardella cast aside his newspaper, examined the narrow, intolerant face, and nodded. Thurston made himself comfortable in an obviously insolent way.

"Do you know how many times I used to hear your voice on wiretaps?"

"Plenty, I'm sure," Gardella said easily. "What good did it do you?"

"I know. You're cute. You're careful, but you ought to tell that young wife of yours to be careful too. We got pictures of her sunning herself down in the Caribbean, not a damn thing on."

Gardella refused to react.

"If you want the pictures, I'll get them for you. Black guy who works for me keeps them in his desk."

Except for the sudden rigidity of his jaw, nothing in Gardella's expression changed. His darkish hands, resting on the table, were perfectly still, vaguely ominous.

"Don't take offense," Thurston said with a bogus contriteness. I know how you guys get. Remember the story about Hedy Lamarr's husband? The poor cluck tried to buy up all the reels of that movie of her prancing naked through the woods. But I can understand that. Nobody wants the whole world looking at his wife's ass."

All of Gardella's reactions were inner, unseen, tethered, though every nerve was strained. His eyes were hooded. Thurston reached forward and felt the baby-soft fabric of Gardella's sleeve.

"The coon I mentioned wears suits like yours. You'd think the both of you clerked at Brooks Brothers. Me, I buy my stuff off the rack. I pay top price, but I don't put on airs."

Gardella spoke in a muted tone. "You got anything more to say to me?"

"I don't know. Maybe you don't want to listen. After all, you've got a lot on your mind, like the DA's organized crime unit. The cop running it, Wade, probably isn't the brightest guy in the world, but he's a plugger. If he comes up with something on you, maybe you ought to come see me. Who knows, I might be able to offer you a deal. Something for both of us."

"You want a cappuccino? They put whipped cream on it if you ask."

"See, you're not listening." Thurston rose slowly and stood gracefully immobile. "Which is too bad. You might be uneducated, but you've got a brain. We could've had an intelligent talk."

Gardella, sotto voce, spoke in Italian.

"I know what you said," Thurston declared, flashing a proud smile. Gardella reopened his newspaper.

"Then you know what I think of you."

Thurston pointed a triumphant finger at him. "I got to you, didn't I?"

"Yes," Gardella conceded. "You got to me."

———

As soon as they got into his room in the Howard Johnson's Motor Lodge, Officer Hunkins pulled Laura close to him and pressed an urgent hand into the front of her red dress, below the waist. She squirmed free. "We don't touch until you pay." He paid with crumpled bills, which she smoothed out and counted carefully and then pressed into her large leather shoulder bag. The bag looked Mexican. Her hand lingered in it. "Do you mind if I have a joint? It helps me get in the mood."

"You kidding?" His face expanded. "I'm a cop. You know that, you heard."

"Right now, you're a john," she said and lit up. Closing her eyes, she took a deep drag and exhaled with a slow sigh. He circled her and came up behind her, his hands trembling for her. His palms were clammy, which made her flinch. She turned around, and he kissed her, ate her lipstick. His stubble scratched her.

"Don't tear my dress."

"Then take it off," he said. She wore black under the red. He quickened when he saw the garter belt. "Lemme help." With awkward fingers, he worked her bra loose while she avoided his breath. The white of her breasts was a purer white than the rest of her. He began stripping, his black police shoes first, then his wrinkled sports jacket. He placed his magnum on the dresser. "Don't touch it," he said. "It's loaded."

She looked at her watch.

"What are you doing, timing me?" He yanked off his trousers, skinned away his skivvies and, placing his hands on his hips, grinned. "What d'you think, huh?"

"Let me finish the joint," she said and reached toward the ashtray.

"No. Put it out."

On the bed, his senses taken by her, he used his tongue low on her body. "You don't want to do that," she advised in a flat voice, which did not stop him. It seemed to urge him on. "I was with somebody earlier," she explained with the same flatness, and he jolted up on stout arms.

"Jesus Christ, did you have to tell me?"

She heard what he failed to and glanced at the door, which he thought was locked. A second later the door crashed open, and two uniformed Boston police officers burst into the room with drawn revolvers. One was a patrolman in leather boots, and the other was Deputy Superintendent Scatamacchia, whose uniform, with its abundant braid, looped lanyard, and gold insignia, made him look like a rear admiral. He thrust the barrel of his revolver inches from Hunkins's stricken features and said, "Move and you die!"

Hunkins, a blob of naked flesh, did not breathe. Laura covered herself with the sheet and looked at Scatamacchia as if to say What the hell took you so long? The officer in the boots strode to the dresser and said, "The guy's got a cannon."

"I'm a cop," Hunkins said weakly.

"Shut up!" Scatamacchia said.

The officer inspected the ashtray. "Also we got ourselves the remains of a controlled substance," he said, holding up the butt.

"Pot party, huh?"

"No," said Hunkins, and Scatamacchia glared.

"I told you to shut up."

The officer opened the leather bag that looked Mexican and poked inside. Laura stared at the wall. "What have we got here?" the officer said, plucking out a plastic packet held together by a rubber band. He undid it, sniffed inside, and then, wetting a finger, took a taste. "Coke," he said. "Somebody's pushing."

"It's not mine," Hunkins said, and Scatamacchia instantly struck the side of his face with the revolver, just hard enough to break the skin and bruise the bone.

"Twenty years," Scatamacchia said coldly. "That's what you're going to get. Check his pants. See if he's really a cop."

The officer lifted Hunkins's trousers and extracted a bulky wallet. A moment later he said, "Yeah, I guess he is. He's a hick. Greenwood PD. Where's that, near Pittsfield?"

Hunkins, collapsed on his side and clutching his face, said nothing. His belly made glugging sounds. Scatamacchia prodded the callused sole of his foot and said, "Nothing I hate worse than a crooked cop. Did you hear me, hick?" Hunkins raised himself up on an elbow and hung his battered face out as if for a spoonful of kindness. Scatamacchia snorted. "Get dressed. I'm sick of looking at you."

Hunkins moved warily off the bed and stumbled for his clothes. He put his pants on and stuffed his underwear into a pocket. He thrust naked feet into his shoes. The woman did not move. Scatamacchia beckoned to his officer and spoke in a whisper. "Cuff him and take him outside. Talk to him like I would."

"You mean—"

"I do." Scatamacchia winked. "That magnum. It's mine now."

"Yeah, you always wanted one."

"I now what you're thinking," Scatamacchia said with a grin, "and you're right. I'm too cheap to buy one."

After the officer led Hunkins away, Laura got off the bed, dragging the sheet with her. Scatamacchia reached around her and drew her close by cupping her bare bottom. She frowned instantly and stood with her back rigid. "This wasn't part of the deal."

"Sure it was," he said with a leer. "You just didn't pay attention." When she tried to step away, he gripped her at the waist and walked her backward to the bed with his thumbs pressed into her pale skin. She cursed him, and he smiled with half of his mouth. He dropped the smile when she fought him.

Outside the motor lodge the officer guided Hunkins smartly away from the lights and halted abruptly where the shadows were the deepest. "Where's your car?" he asked, and Hunkins gestured with his man-

acled hands, his wrists hurting. The right side of his
face, which had swelled and yellowed, looked gro-
tesque. His nose was leaking. The officer said, "You
know how to get to it fast?" Hunkins stared uncom-
prehendingly. "If you don't know, I'll tell you. You
run."

Hunkins stood rooted. "What are you telling me?"

"Gimme your hands." The officer produced a key
and removed the cuffs. "What I'm telling you is the
deputy's giving you a break, you being a cop and all.
We're letting you escape. But we're not forgetting
you. We ever see you back here again or hear anything about you, you're dead."

Hunkins trembled. "I run, you'll shoot me."

"You got it wrong. You don't run, I'll shoot you."

Hunkins ran.

Twenty minutes later Deputy Superintendent
Scatamacchia emerged from the motor lodge. He
signaled to the officer sitting in an unmarked car to
wait and walked a short distance down the street to a
darkened Cadillac parked at the curb. He looked in
at the lone occupant and said, "Tell Anthony he
owes me."

Victor Scandura said, "You really want me to put
it to him that way?"

Scatamacchia grinned. "It's just a figure of speech."

Scandura gave a quick glance over his shoulder.
"Where's the woman?"

"She could use a little help," the deputy superintendent muttered and walked away.

Scandura climbed out of his car, looked furtively
around, and then moved at a fast pace toward the
motor lodge. He tapped on the door to Hunkins's
room and opened it. The room was in darkness. He
found the wall switch and swiftly shut the door be-

hind him. The woman lay on the bed as she had been left. Scandura bent over her. "Can you hear me?" he asked, and her head moved a little. Her eyes were blackened and swollen. She could not see, nor could she speak. Her jaw was broken. "I'll get you a doctor," Scandura whispered.

———————

Christopher Wade had a sub for supper, which he ate on the balcony of his apartment while absently watching traffic on Commonwealth Avenue, the cars shadowy with people he couldn't see. Later, in bed, he watched a Jack Nicholson movie, *The Last Detail*, which he had seen twice before. He watched the eleven o'clock news and dozed off during *Nightline*. He dreamed of his wife, his daughters, and Jane Gardella. In the dream he was himself, a grown man, but curiously like a child who needed his hand held. He rose early and breakfasted at the usual place on Newbury Street, where he lingered over a second and then a third cup of coffee. One of the waitresses, whose mother had died the previous week, said, "Thanks for the flowers."

Wade gave her a warm smile. "How are you doing?"

"No one should lose a mother. After that, really, you got no one." She snatched up his check and folded it. "It's on me."

"I can't let you do that," he said.

"Sure you can. You're a cop."

When he arrived at his office he found Agent Blodgett sitting at his desk. "Make yourself at home," he said with instant annoyance. Blodgett pushed a photograph across the desk, a five-by-seven glossy, the product of a zoom lens.

"Who is this guy?"

Wade picked up the photo and studied it longer than he had to. "Who wants to know?"

"Who the hell do you think? Thurston. We took the picture of him a couple of days ago coming out of your friend's real estate office. He looks familiar, but we can't place him."

Wade returned the photo. "His name's Hunkins."

———

At the real estate office Victor Scandura said, "I got somebody to wire her jaw. It's broken in two places."

Anthony Gardella, preoccupied, murmured, "So what do you think we should do about Scat?"

"I think we should break his in three places."

"Scat's an animal. He figured she was there, she was his. What we'll do is send her off to someplace nice to recuperate, with a nurse and all. Scat can pick up the tab."

"That's letting him off easy."

"What would you have me do?" Gardella asked impatiently. "Cut off his balls?"

Scandura pulled back, and Gardella went to a window to look out at the street, his shoulders drawn tight, his arms behind his back. Two passersby from the neighborhood saw him and waved, but he peered through them. Finally Scandura said, "What's the matter, Anthony? I know something's bothering you."

"That fed Thurston." Gardella gnashed out the words as he wheeled around. "First he shows up at my parents' funeral and sends a nigger into the church. Then last night he comes into the Pompei and insults me worse."

"Take it easy, Anthony."

The tendons in Gardella's neck seemed to have a life of their own; his chest heaved. "I want something on him. I want it bad. You hear me, Victor?"

Scandura looked doubtful. "Guys like Thurston are usually clean, nothing there."

"Nobody's clean," said Gardella. "That's a universal truth."

17

RITA O'DEA AND ALVARO made arrangements through Benson Tours and went away for five days. They could have gone to Atlantic City, which would have reduced their hours in the air, but Alvaro argued for Las Vegas. He had never been there before. They checked into Caesar's and made the rounds. Rita O'Dea, her mouth ablaze with a new color she was trying, wore large frilly dresses with tulle fronts and ate filet mignon at the best restaurants. They went to shows where glittery Wayne Newton sang silly songs and dough-faced Buddy Hackett told toilet jokes. Alvaro lost ten thousand dollars of Rita O'Dea's money shooting craps. Rita O'Dea, impatient in all things except cards, won a thousand at the blackjack table. She cashed in the chips and waved her winnings at Alvaro. "This is for the kid," she said.

"What kid?"

"Ty's."

"The thing ain't even born yet, and who says it's his? You going to take *her* word for it?"

She regarded him with good-natured condescension and said, "There are some things you can't understand, pet, so don't try."

On their next to last day there, she spent much time at the pool. Using a rubber doughnut, she floated on her stomach. Alvaro, tiring of the sun and of ogling young women, went up to their room. A half hour later she followed him up and found him slouched in a chair with the latest *Penthouse*. Conscious of her derisive glance, he said, "I don't buy it just for the snatch."

"Tell me another," she said, shedding her sodden bathing suit. There were ridges in her skin where the suit had been too tight. Her breasts looked waterlogged, hurt. She massaged them with her palms. He threw aside the magazine and got up.

"Let me do that." The butts of his fingers brushed her. His lightweight trousers were so tight at the crotch that his penis did more than suggest itself. "I'm horny," he whispered. "How about you?"

She shook her head. "I'm tired. I need a nap."

He took the refusal in good grace. He picked up the magazine and stuffed it into a drawer. His smile was careless, his teeth brilliant. "Then I might go out for a while. Can you spare a coupla hundred?"

"Is that what a piece of ass costs here?" she asked with an air of detached interest, and he colored. She pointed to her pocketbook. "Give it to me."

"Look, you want me to stay, I'll stay."

"The pocketbook!" He handed it to her, and she gave him two crisp hundred-dollar bills.

"I'm going to play the slots."

"Have a good time," she said. "That's what counts."

At the door he looked back at her as she wrapped herself in one towel and began rubbing her hair in another. "Rita, I got a serious question for you. You getting tired of me?"

Her eyes narrowed. "You want me to be?"

"I'm just asking."

"If I wake up at three in the morning, I want to know you're there."

He winked. "What if I'm not?"

"God help you."

———

At the house in Rye, Anthony Gardella sat in a distant room with two visitors from Providence, men wearing silver-gray suits with metallic tints that made them look like tin soldiers. Jane Gardella hovered in another room, where she could catch murmurings and from time to time glimpse faces. She heard mention of Miami, bits about money and island banks, and something vague about cocaine. She heard names mentioned, but only first names, nicknames. Solly. Skeeter. Chickie. Buster. She heard her husband, in a slightly irate voice, say, "Maybe I ought to talk to Raymond myself," and then the reply, "He's not feeling so good."

Later, business apparently over, voices grew louder and lighter. There was laughter. She glimpsed the profiled face and thick neck of one of the visitors. "You remember Mikie's brother," she heard him say. He was an exuberant speaker. Spit flew. "He was squeamy about getting his finger pricked, and he closes his eyes when they do it. Then they tell him he's a *soldato* now, *long live!* but he don't hear none of this, he's looking at his fuckin' finger and getting ready to faint. Someone holds him up. They don't want him making a donkey of himself. True story, no shit!"

Her husband's laugh was genuine, full-throated. She could tell when he was letting himself relax.

The other visitor, a pale man, said, "The third brother, spur of the moment, wants a new car to drive to California. He goes to a Pontiac place and buys a Firebird, but it's a lemon and breaks down someplace in Oklahoma. So he flies back, goes straight to the showroom, and shoots the salesman right between the fuckin' eyes. Maniac!"

"I can understand the frustration," Anthony Gardella said. "Getting back to Raymond, does he still wear white socks all the time?"

"Has to, he's got funny feet. Can't put nothing dark on 'em," the pale man said. "Remember when Raymond had to go to Washington and testify before that Senate committee? It was right after they made Puzo's thing into a movie, and the chairman says to Raymond, 'Tell me, Mr. Patriarca, how much of *The Godfather* is actually true?' and Raymond clears his throat and says, 'Senator, it's pure *friction*.'"

During the guffaws, Jane Gardella slipped quietly out of the room and out of the house. An ocean breeze blew her hair about and cooled the bare backs of her legs. She hiked up the road to Philbrick's store and, with coins ready, placed a call to Boston from an outside phone. When a voice asked whom she wanted, she said, "Thurston. Tell him it's Honey."

Thurston, who had been expecting her call, came on the line without delay and listened without interruption. When she finished, he said, "Describe them," and she did so in a low, quick voice, mentioning the pallor of one and the thick neck of the other. "You sound nervous," he said.

"I'm always nervous." She covered an ear against traffic.

"Can you give me any idea what they talked about?"

"No."

"You must have picked up something. A word. A name."

"Nothing."

"I wouldn't like to be lied to," Thurston said. Then his tone mellowed. "How's he been?"

"Who?"

"Who else? Your husband."

"Fine." She hesitated. "But quiet. Like he's annoyed with me about something, but I don't know what."

"Maybe it's your imagination," Thurston said with a measure of satisfaction that he did not quite conceal. "You got anything more to tell me?"

"Yes. Tell Sweetheart to keep his hands off me."

She hung up the receiver slowly, her gaze drifting well beyond the road. High above the beach a multicolored kite throbbed in an air current, its tail twitching. At the same time, absently, she was aware of a car creeping by, an endless Cadillac. Her knees went weak as she drew back. The driver was Victor Scandura.

––––––––

The Greenwood police chief, who had a stubborn and pious face, cornered Officer Hunkins inside the little police station, displayed a dry, rigid smile that wasn't really a smile at all, and said, "I want a straight story from you. What the hell's going on?"

"I don't know what you mean," Hunkins said, all innocence, while tugging at his gun belt and trying to keep the damaged side of his face from the chief's view.

The chief said, "You've done something wrong, I don't know what, but you'd better tell me."

Hunkins issued an abused look. "I still don't know what you're talking about," he protested.

"Let me put it another way," the chief said. "Are you a good cop?"

"Yes."

"A clean one?"

"Yes."

"Then why for the love of Christ is the FBI asking questions about you?"

Hunkins went ashen.

———————

Victor Scandura gave a short wave to the two Providence men, who were leaving in their Hertz rental as he arrived in his spotless Cadillac. He parked in their space, climbed out, and ran a hand over his scant hair. "How'd it go?" he asked Gardella, who stood just outside the house, near a rose bush, cool air swimming against his face.

"They want more control and more of a cut of the Florida thing."

Scandura stepped nearer. "There's enough for everybody down there."

"That's not the point. They're pushing."

"Maybe they just want to know you're reasonable."

"I'm always reasonable."

"Then I guess they want to be reassured." Scandura averted his face and let out a ragged cough.

"What's the matter?"

"Allergy."

"You're a bundle of complaints."

"Nothing I can't get over."

"You doing anything yet on Thurston?"

"It's going to cost you something," Scandura said with a small bronchial wheeze. "A detective agency in New York, run by guys who used to be feds themselves. They're good, probably the best. They want fifty grand up front, and they give no guarantees. If they come up with anything, they negotiate the rest of the fee."

"They sound like barracudas."

"They are. Top guy's an ex-narc."

"Do it," said Gardella.

They walked around to the ocean side of the house

and sat on patio chairs. It was breezy, too cool for
swimming, but a woman was in the water anyway.
She had on a frilly bathing cap and leaped up each
time a wave rushed at her. Finally she threw herself
into one.

Scandura said, "I have to tell you something you're
not going to like. Augie got busted for breaking and
entering up in Montreal. Sammy Ferlito almost didn't
want to tell me."

Gardella's eyes rolled. "Stupid shit!"

"That's not the worst. He jumped bail. Ferlito
doesn't know where he is."

Gardella's jaw seemed to shift. "Put the word out.
I want him."

Scandura nodded. "The kid's a loser, Anthony. I
think it's about time we admit that."

"I just did." People trickled by on the beach.
Gardella glared at his watch. "Where the hell did my
wife go?"

Scandura, surprised, pointed. "Isn't that her in the
ocean?"

"Jesus Christ, Victor, get yourself new glasses. That
broad's fifty years old. It's Senator Matchett's wife."

————————

Jane Gardella took a long, unmeasured walk that
kept her out until dusk. When she returned to the
house, there were no cars in the drive except hers
and her husband's. He was on the patio waiting for
her, casually dressed in a thin cashmere sweater and
charcoal slacks. When she saw the hard look in his
eye, her heart turned over. "Where were you?" he
asked, and she remained perfectly still, dry in the
mouth and damp under the arms. She was not confident she could speak normally.

"I didn't want to be in the way," she said pain-
stakingly.

"Everybody's long gone. From now on, tell me before you just take off like that." His arms went out to her. "I was worried."

Her sense of relief was electric, and she pitched toward him. The kiss she gave him was as passionate as if they had been in bed. Knowing that he had to return to Boston, she edged a trembling hand under the sweater and slid it up into his chest hair. "Do you have time?" she whispered up into his face, and he stared at her so starkly that her fears raced back.

"Do you know why I have time?" he asked and, in a soft voice, answered himself. "Life is short."

———

Three hours later, in Boston, Gardella said, "Excuse me," squeezed between two waiting couples, and penetrated the dimness of the upstairs lounge of the Union Oyster House. The bar was lined and every table was taken. The patrons were mostly young, in their twenties and early thirties. A waitress with drinks tried to maneuver by him, and for an instant, inadvertently, the wide front of her thigh lay warm and hard against him. "It's okay," he said dryly. "I'm a married man." Seconds later a voice stretched out to him and he pivoted toward it. A chair was edged out for him.

"You're late," Christopher Wade said dourly. "I almost left a half hour ago."

"I'm glad you didn't." Gardella dropped into the chair. "What are you drinking?"

"I'm nursing my second Heineken. Here, you want it?"

"The only person I drink after is my wife."

"Then buy your own."

Gardella rested his elbows on the table. With forced good humor, he said, "Quimby from the bank called me. That visit of yours pissed him off. I take it you went out of your way to make yourself look clean."

"I have to protect myself."

"I hope you'll be more diplomatic with Senator Matchett. He's made of softer stuff."

"I'll see what I can do. Incidentally, that's a nice sweater you've got on. What is this, your casual look?"

"I've got three more like it, different colors. You want, I'll tell you where I buy 'em. Second thought, what's your size? I'll send you some."

"You're in a rare mood."

"Not really. I've got a serious question to ask you. This guy Thurston, the fed. What do you know about him?"

"He's a zealot. That kinda says it."

"He calling any of your shots?"

"Sure he is, indirectly," Wade said in a muted voice. "He's got the DA's ear."

"You never spelled that out for me before," Gardella said accusingly.

"Maybe you didn't listen."

"Don't play it close with me." Gardella spoke in a low, guttural tone. The waitress who'd had contact with him approached with her order pad. He looked up fast and said, "Not now, later!" Wade lit a cigarette. Gardella said, "Thurston doesn't go for the throat, he goes for the balls. I don't like a guy who does that."

Wade glanced at other tables, pretty women. "What exactly did he do?"

"Came at me with shit about my wife. The man's mind worries me. Tell me, Wade, why would he do that?"

"That's easy," said Wade. "He hates you."

"That's something else you never told me."

"I'm rented, not bought."

Gardella also looked at other tables, pretty women, their handsome escorts. The chatter was vigorous. "One of these days," he said quietly and reflectively, "you've got to make a choice."

"Meaning?"

"I think you know," Gardella said and motioned for the waitress.

18

TY O'DEA sipped a glass of vodka and grapefruit juice for breakfast and smiled uneasily at Rita O'Dea as she entered the kitchen in one of her voluminous robes, her black hair hanging long and loose, the bulk of one breast exposed like a target. She snatched up a cup, poured coffee from a Silex, and joined him at the table, the cane chair groaning as she settled in it. He eyed her cautiously. Years ago she had not allowed him to speak until she had finished her coffee. After a tentative clearing of the throat, he said, "How was Vegas?"

"Lousy."

"You must have lost," he said with sympathy.

"I won. I always win."

"Alvaro?"

"He lost. You know he's a loser. Look what he's stuck with—me."

Ty O'Dea did not know quite where to cast his eyes, for never before had he heard her deprecate herself in such a fashion. She put a fixing hand to her hair and tightened her robe, making herself more presentable. Her face was puffy.

"Our last night there I had bad dreams, and I woke up with the sweats. I don't sleep good anymore, Ty. Sometimes I lie awake and hear voices, like from the other side. I hear Ma's voice a little and Pa's the loudest. Honest to God, I do."

He did not know what to say and said nothing, which for a fleeting second made him feel strengthless, useless, parasitical.

She said, "It's the way they went that I can't deal with."

"At least they went together," he offered haltingly. "They weren't alone.

"What's your idea of heaven, Ty?"

"I'm not sure I have one," he answered nakedly. "What's yours?"

"Pink and blue—baby colors." Her eyes went sightless for a moment and grew moist. "Do you know what I mean?" He didn't, but he nodded anyway while wishing mightily he had stayed in bed. He lifted his glass and drained it. She said, "That stuff's killing you."

He grinned sheepishly.

"You die, it'll be bad for the kid. What would Sara do with it alone?"

"I'm not going to die."

"Are you going to love it?"

"Yes," he said solemnly, as if under oath to a judge and jury. He wanted to fill his glass again but didn't dare.

"Do you still love me, Ty?"

Fear was the only emotion he truly associated with her. She had never been a wife to him, more like a shameless and incestuous sister explosively generous one moment and humiliatingly tyrannical the next. "There'll always be something between us," he fudged.

"It could be like it was." Her hand shot across the table, grasped his, and squeezed it. "No. I don't mean that. It could be better."

"You're hurting me," he whined like a woman,

and instantly she eased the ferocious grip of her fingers. Her eyes were soft, and her robe was loose again, this time with both breasts visible and rolling against each other.

"I'm big, Ty. I'm like an elephant, but I'm not whole. Do you know what I'm telling you?" He did not want to know, but he could not tell her that. He felt a small measure of relief when she withdrew her hand. "What time is it?" she asked. "Look at the watch I gave you and tell me."

He obliged.

She nodded, gripping the edge of the table. "Where's Sara, still in bed? I think it's time I speak to her."

"About what?" he asked in alarm.

"The future," Rita O'Dea said.

———

Anthony Gardella took a call from Miami in his real estate office. Victor Scandura handed him the phone and said, "It's Skeeter." Skeeter's voice came through in a quick rasp.

"Guess who I saw down here?"

Gardella said, "I'd rather you tell me."

"How much is it worth?"

"Cut the shit," Gardella said without patience.

"It's the kid," Skeeter said. "The one you're looking for. He's holed up in Ho Jo's, the one near me."

"That's sweet news."

"I thought it would be." There was a cough, a rough one.

"How are you doing, Skeeter?"

"I got rotten lungs. Otherwise I'm doing good."

"I'm sure you know who my new guy is down there. Tell him to give you the usual and something extra."

"He's new, Anthony, he might not know what the usual is."

"Nobody's that new," Gardella said and disconnected. Scandura stood stolid. "Augie," Gardella said in a muted voice, and Scandura evinced surprise.

"That was fast."

Ralph Roselli, who was sitting near a window, put aside his newspaper and shuffled to his feet. "No," said Gardella, "not you, Ralph." Roselli dropped back down into his chair, leaned toward the window, and killed a silverfish on the sill. Scandura threw Gardella a puzzled look and received a thin smile. "Don't you know who, Victor?"

"Yes," said Scandura all of a sudden. "It's only right."

"Then what are you waiting for?"

Scandura left the real estate office, crossed the street, and walked up past St. Leonard's Church to the funeral home. Sammy Ferlito was arranging flowers at a casket in one of the viewing rooms. In the casket was the corpse of a middle-aged nun in full habit; everything there, crucifix, beads, missal; the fixed face so shiny it looked like pure wax. "Rosie Riciputti," Ferlito said with an uneasy gesture of sadness. "Cancer. Nine, ten years old, she used to show her twat for Clark bars, then she grows up and becomes a nun. How do you figure that?"

"Some things you don't," Scandura said.

Ferlito stepped away from the flowers, the cloying scent clinging to him, which gave him an intoxicated air. "Something's the matter," he said. "I can see it in your face. Is it Augie?"

Scandura nodded. "He's in Miami."

"I'll take care of it. I'll go down there and put him on a fuckin' plane to Alaska."

"Can't be that way," Scandura said. "He's wanted, and sooner or later the feds will grab him. The kid can't do hard time, which means he'll deal."

"Okay, I understand," Ferlito said, holding himself rigid. "You guys do what you have to do."

"Anthony wants you to do it."

Ferlito shuddered. "Victor, please. Not my own blood."

"Don't beg, makes me sick." Scandura stepped to the casket, dropped to his knees, stared at the nun, and said a prayer. Then he made the sign of the cross and rose. "You and Scat used to give her candy. I never did."

"Victor, it's twenty years since I clipped anybody."

"It'll come back."

There were tears in Ferlito's eyes. "I don't even own a piece."

"You don't need one."

'What the fuck am I going to use—my hands?"

"No," Scandura said. "Bad dope."

"I don't understand why you're looking so sour," Russell Thurston said. "I pulled you off it, didn't I? You should be happy."

"I'm happy," Agent Blue said.

"If anyone was to ask me, I'd swear you had a hair across your ass, though I'm wrong occasionally. I honestly thought you'd enjoy looking after Wade's wife. A fine-looking woman. You must've peeked in her windows a couple of times. No?"

"You really don't know a damned thing about me, do you?"

"I know the basics. I know you like being a federal officer. You like the status and the salary, and you like the way your neighbors look at you. There's respect in their eyes, despite what might be in their hearts, right, Blue?"

"I don't appreciate what you did."

Thurston pointed a finger. "Don't accuse me of what you can't prove. But remember this, my friend, in this business you've got to be tough, and you're always going to be tested."

"You tried to set me up."

"It was clumsy, I'll admit."

"No, it was smooth, and you know it."

Thurston smiled. "Thank you, Blue. Now I'll let you in on a little secret. I might be the only pal you have here. How does that go down with you?"

"No problem," said Blue. "I know exactly where we stand."

"No, you don't," Thurston said, slightly altering his tone of voice. "In fact, neither do I. Now get out of here. You and Blodgett have things to do."

Christopher Wade breakfasted with his daughters in a greasy spoon kind of place near Boston University. The older, Cindy, who wore her kinked hair long and wild, told him over scrambled eggs that she was going to Israel for a month with her boyfriend. "I see," said Wade, trying to sound sophisticated and then immediately abandoning the attempt. "Why Israel?"

"Philip is Jewish."

"You could get killed there."

"So could you, Dad, in what you do. We used to think when you didn't come home that you were dead. Remember the clothes Mom burned, all the blood on them?"

Yes, he remembered, but he was astounded that she did, for she and her sister were little more than infants then, and he was working undercover in the Worcester area, mingling with the worst, buying drugs, worming his way in, except that he rubbed somebody the wrong way, an offhand remark that some junkie in the group took offense at. The next thing he knew was that he was sitting between two trash cans and watching a section of his shirt brighten and bleed. The pain hit him everywhere, even in the fillings of his teeth, especially there. A Worcester cop came upon him and deduced that the knife wound was bad, life-threatening. But the cop thought he was a druggie and took his time calling for an ambulance. It was a delay that nearly killed him.

Wade said, "I've never met your Philip."

"You'd like him," she said. "At least I think you would. He's going to be a lawyer. And he's not *my* Philip. Nobody belongs to anybody else. We belong only to ourselves."

Wade munched toast. "All the same, I'd like to plead my case to him about not going to Israel at this particular time."

"Dad, he's six-foot-five. I don't think you have to worry."

"Size is no defense against weapons," he countered without effect and looked for support from his other daughter, Barbara, who was aloof and taciturn, probably shy. She was, in a way, his favorite, perhaps because at birth she had looked so ugly. Now, like her sister, she was astonishingly good-looking.

She said, "I hate to tell you, but Tel Aviv is probably safer than Kenmore Square at night."

"And who don't you belong to?" he asked with a smile.

"His name's Larry," she said and no more. It pained him to think they wanted to share as little as possible with him and had little wish for him to meet their boyfriends. It pained him more when each finished eating before him and peeked at the time.

"I wonder if we might do this again sometime," he asked but learned that Cindy was leaving for Israel within the week and that Barbara was starting a summer job at a resort in the White Mountains.

"Maybe in September," he said. "The four of us. Your mother."

Cindy said quietly, "You'd better check with Mom first."

Barbara, coming to his aid, said, "Mom won't mind." Then, after a tense pause, she added, "I'm glad she doesn't see that Mr. Benson anymore. I hated his phony accent."

He gave her a warm look. They had shared something. He picked up the check and stood in line to pay it while they waited outside. He could see them through the glass: Cindy taller than her mother and beautifully proportioned, and Barbara shorter but no less trim, each with a touch of worldliness that he found jarring. When he emerged from the restaurant, Cindy drew him to one side.

"Dad, I wonder if . . ."

"Of course," he said, angry at himself for not being quicker. "How much do you need?"

———

Sara Dillon was asleep. Rita O'Dea woke her. "Sit up," she said. "I've brought you some orange juice. Real stuff, not the junk made from concentrates." Sara Dillon rose up gradually, fixing a pillow behind her, and accepted the juice glass reluctantly. Her face was blotchy, her hand shaky. She wanted a cigarette but was afraid to ask. All of a sudden, greedily, she drank the juice, spilling only a little on her pajama top, which Rita O'Dea impulsively put a hand to. "You're getting bigger here. Pretty soon you'll be my size."

"Why did you wake me?" Sara Dillon squinted at her watch. "Is it that late?"

"You can stay in bed as long as you want. You're pregnant, kid, which makes you the queen here. I proclaim it."

There was a slight, uneasy movement from the bed, a drawing up of the covers, and then a tightness of voice. "Almost any woman can get pregnant."

"But we're talking about you." Rita O'Dea pushed a padded chair close to the bed and sat on it ungracefully. "How many abortions have you had? One? Two? At least two, right?"

"Only one. I was very young."

"How young?"

"Thirteen."

"But you didn't get messed up like I did."

"In a different way," Sara Dillon said.

"I'm not interested in the mental crap. What I'm trying to do is tell you something, so listen close. You relax while you're here. Take good care of yourself. But after you have the kid, Ty stays. You go."

"Have you talked to Ty about this?"

"I don't have to. I'm prepared to give you a substantial amount of money."

Sara Dillon, her voice trailing, said, "Are you telling me you want to buy your husband?"

"No," said Rita O'Dea. "I'm buying your baby."

19

SENATOR MATCHETT poised himself near the flagpole in front of his Rye Beach house and gave a quick little salute as the Stars and Stripes convulsed in a random breeze too hot to have come off the ocean. "I'm patriotic," the senator announced in a rapid and nervous tone of voice. "Voted for Reagan and will again. Love the man. I'm a Democrat, naturally, but the country comes first." He smiled tentatively through the heat, the June sun lying hot on his neatly barbered and sharply parted white hair. His face was large and puffy, with dark eyes embedded in the soft flesh. Suddenly he squinted. "Listen, Lieutenant, I've nothing to hide."

"I'm sure you don't," Christopher Wade said.

"I've nothing to fear."

"You certainly have nothing to fear from me, Senator."

"Call me Joe." His smile was cautiously bright. "You can understand my uneasiness. Some people think all politicians are fair game.

"I thought it best to see you here in New Hampshire," Wade said. "Less awkward for us."

"I appreciate it. God knows what the *Globe* would make of it. Honest men have a hard time surviving these days. Look, may I call you Chris?"

"Of course."

"Come," said the senator, guiding Wade by the elbow. "I'd like you to meet my wife."

Mrs. Matchett, down on her knees in her garden, lifted herself up from among her freshly planted annuals already in full color. She had pinks, whites, and blues, and the blues were the best, the tones royal. "Lovely," the senator said, proud to show off both the garden and his wife, who was wearing a cotton top held up by elastic. Her plump shoulders were lightly freckled, and her hair was frosted. He introduced Wade.

"Goodness," she said, "I hope you're not here to arrest us."

The senator laughed. "He wants a private pow-wow to pick my brain."

"If this has anything to do with Massachusetts politics, Lieutenant, you've picked the perfect person."

"Call him Chris, dear."

"I love the name Chris." Mrs. Matchett removed her garden gloves, which were scarcely soiled from her work, and offered a soft hand. "It's a beautiful beach day. I do hope you'll go swimming with us later."

"That's a great idea," the senator interjected. "And he should stay for supper."

"Any friend of Tony's," Mrs. Matchett said knowingly, pushing her sunglasses into her hair, "is a friend of ours. Isn't that true, Joe?"

The senator and Wade entered the house through the breezeway and moved toward chairs in a long room dominated by glass panels that muted the sunlight while providing a panoramic view of the beach. While the senator poured brandy from a gift bottle, the ribbon and tag still around the neck, Wade made himself comfortable near a writing table that held a tray filled with notices, some with DEMAND printed across them. Wade knew, from a file, that the senator was bad about bills. The smaller they were, the less likely he was to pay them.

There was a clinking of glasses, a toast. "To the United States of America, the Commonwealth of Massachusetts, and the State of New Hampshire," Senator Matchett said grandly. Then he sat down. "Ask me anything you want."

In a theatrical voice, a nice cadence to it, he denied any irregularities in awarding county contracts to companies in which Anthony Gardella had an interest, and he frowned with indignation that anyone might suppose he had engineered the sale of certain public properties to the advantage of Aceway Development Association. "Good God, is that what people think?"

"It's been rumored."

"Rumors are like rats, you can't get rid of them. Even the USS *Constitution* still has them. I know because I toured her last month."

"There are rumors you and some colleagues use Gardella to conceal money you don't want to pay taxes on. The money's supposedly channeled through you."

"Absolute nonsense."

"That's what I thought," Wade said and continued with his questions. With a flourish, the senator denied a hidden interest in Gardella's porn operations, and Wade said, "I'm sorry I had to ask you that."

"Don't be. It's your job."

"I'm glad you understand."

"But let me make one point clear, Chris. Though I'd never associate myself in a business way with pornography, I pride myself in not being a prude about it. It has its uses. My wife and I both believe there's nothing on this earth that isn't here for a reason."

"That's hard to argue with, Senator."

"I guess you don't want to call me Joe."

"It just doesn't come natural," Wade said. "I guess I have too much respect for you."

The senator's eyes filled. "Thank you for saying that."

There was a noise behind them. Mrs. Matchett came a few steps into the room and smiled. She had on a black bathing suit and a frilly rubber cap that made her head look long and gave her face an exotic dimension. The freckles on her shoulders repeated themselves on her breastplate. Her knees were dimpled. "Well?" she said.

The senator said to Wade, "I'll get you some swim trunks.

Wade, who was wired, declined. "But I'll stay for supper." he said.

———

As soon as Sammy Ferlito stepped out of the Delta terminal in Miami, the heat hit him hard, threatened to suffocate him. Three minutes later in an air-conditioned cab, his body sopping inside his suit, he said, "How the fuck d'you stand it down here?" The driver, who was Hispanic, did not respond. Ferlito rasped, "Dinty's, on the dock. You know where it is?"

Strangely, despite tenseness and discomfort, he drifted off during the drive, a jerky little sleep just deep enough for the raw start of a dream in which someone, maybe the parish priest or the nun he had buried, touched the back of his neck, made him turn around, and blessed him with blackened fingers. "Jesus!" he said, waking with a jolt and digging into a pocket to pay the driver with one of several crisp bills he had drawn from an automatic teller that morning in Boston. Stumbling out of the cab, he fell over a rubbish sack. He didn't hurt himself, but he let out a sob, as a child would.

Inside Dinty's he peered through the chill, stale air at the obese barkeep and the lame waiter. Then, slowly, he took in the odd collection of faces at the bar and found Skeeter's, though he did not recognize it at first. It was skin and bones. He went to a table, and the lame waiter brought him beer.

"It's on Skeeter," the waiter said.

"I want a shot too," Ferlito said.

The waiter returned with one, and he tossed it off immediately. Skeeter, after using the men's room, joined him and said, "I ain't paying for the shot."

"Nobody asked you to."

Skeeter smiled. "You still in the undertaking business? A year, two at the most, you can bury me."

Ferlito let out another small sob, not for Skeeter and not for himself, but for his nephew. He said, "You know why I'm here."

"Never thought they'd send you, but it makes sense."

"It ain't right."

"Don't involve me." He reached for the beer glass and drank from it. "That makes it mine now. You'd never drink after me." He wiped his mouth. "The kid's not at Ho Jo's anymore. He's shacking up with a broad."

His face drawn with futility, Ferlito noted the address. "Skeeter, you do it for me. I'll pay you good."

"There ain't enough money, whole of Miami."

"And I'll bury you free, pay all expenses bringing you back."

"There's water here, Sammy. All I gotta do is fall off the wharf."

Ferlito's head sagged. He had a headache and a

chill, and something moved fiercely through his stomach. Skeeter prodded him.

"By the way, you can walk it."

"What?"

"Where you're going."

Ferlito, in the heat, hiked a block and a half to a small rundown stucco house that looked little bigger than a shed. He rang a bell that barely worked, rattled a screen door that fell open, and entered a filthy kitchenette, empty beer cans everywhere, the remains of meals festering on paper plates. The biggest cockroach he had ever seen was in the sink. The bedroom, void of furniture except for a whirring fan and a mattress thrown on the floor, was where he found them. His nephew, nearly naked, in need of a shave, was sleeping soundly and noisily. The girl lying beside him, also wearing little, opened her eyes.

"Who are you?"

Ferlito did not look at her. His eyes were full of his nephew, the muscular arms, the slack belly, the stout, hairy legs. "I'm his uncle," he said finally. "Don't wake him."

The girl—for that was all she was, sixteen at the most—sat up, resting her bare back against the wall and making herself modest with what might have once been a sheet. Her eyes, a kind of amethyst, were not truly focused, and her lower lip was swollen with a fever blister.

Ferlito, feeling lightheaded, said, "He was five, I took him to the Stoneham Zoo, that's north of Boston."

"I'm from Wisconsin, originally," the girl offered almost cheerily.

"He was nine, I took him to see the Sox play the Tigers, but he probably don't even remember. I mean, what's gratitude? You know what gratitude is?"

The girl said, "I had my picture taken with my father's prize cow at the state fair."

"Shut up," Ferlito said. "Just shut up." His head sagged. He was tired. "All of us," he said, "we're in a bad way, ain't we?"

The girl smiled vacantly. "You got any money?"

"No money, but I got this," he said, pawing into his suitcoat pocket and producing a plastic bottle that once held aspirin. He tossed it. "Dexies. He's going to need 'em."

The girl squeezed the bottle. "Thank you."

"Don't thank me." His hand moved again. "Here," he said with another toss. "A little coke too. Tell him it's the last thing I'm going to do for him."

"Enough for both of us," she said with a little laugh.

"Yeah," he said, backing away mindlessly, "enough for both."

Russell Thurston, strolling in the Public Garden, stopped twice to glance casually over his shoulder. Later he spent a minute or so admiring flowers bloated and bright, their stalks heightened, their leaves extended. He listened carefully when somebody walked by whistling an up-tempo tune. The tune was from the early fifties, which gave him an idea of the age of the person. A quick look verified it.

On Arlington Street he found his way to a public phone, got in touch with the agents who were going by the names of Danley and Dane, and told them to meet him in the bar at the Ritz. At the Ritz he stirred his drink an inordinately long time and never did taste it. The waiter stopped by twice and was unctious, which pleased him. Danley and Dane arrived just as he was becoming irritated by the wait. Coughing on a peanut, he said, "I'm going to leave, walk toward

Beacon, and return to my office. I want you to see if anybody follows me."

He took his time. He sauntered. He had strong legs and felt good about himself. On Beacon Street he vainly enjoyed his reflection in a long panel of glass that also pictured the slow float of traffic in the heat. Eventually he picked up his pace, all uphill, but he had no problem with his wind. Handball kept him in shape. At the top of Beacon, he paused with legs apart and stared up at the golden dome of the State House as if he were capable of taking on the governor, the attorney general, and the full membership of the legislature. In his office on the twenty-fourth floor of the Kennedy Building, he waited for Danley and Dane.

"Nobody," said Danley, the first to enter the cubicle. Dane soon backed him up.

"You're sure, absolutely sure?" Thurston asked, and they both nodded. He shrugged. "Well, I could've been wrong."

————

Officer Hunkins left his cruiser at the roadside and walked into the woods to take a leak. The woods were hot, sticky, rank, and teeming with mosquitoes. One bit into him. He killed it and wiped the blood from his cheek. Then he opened his trousers and drenched a blueberry bush. When he came out of the woods he saw a car parked behind his cruiser and two men waiting for him.

"You had us worried," one of them said. He was white, the other was black. The speaker, Agent Blodgett, showed identification. "We thought you were going to eat your gun."

"Why the hell would I do that?" Hunkins said, trembling.

"Cops have been known to take that route," Agent Blue said. "Cops with a lot on their minds."

Blodgett said, "The report we got on you says you wear a magnum, but that's a thirty-eight I see."

"Maybe he lost the magnum," Blue said.

"Maybe somebody took it away from him. What happened to your face, Hunkins? You trip and fall?"

"What the hell do you guys want?"

"We want to know what you were doing in Anthony Gardella's real estate office," Blodgett said. "That's out of your league, not to mention your turf."

"I don't know what you're talking about."

"You want the proof? We got a picture."

"I don't care what you got," Hunkins said, his anxiety telling on him. His mouth twitched as he tried to show a nervy little smile.

Blue said, "You can't play with wise guys in Boston. They'll eat you up. They already took a bite out of your face."

"Maybe you'd better tell us all about it," Blodgett said, stepping closer. "Otherwise we might have to fish you out of Boston Harbor."

"Nobody kills cops."

"No?" Blodgett reached into his jacket, came out with a snub-nosed revolver, and shoved the barrel into Hunkins's belly. "I could close you out right this second. Who'd know? Who'd care? And get this. You're not a cop to those guys, you're a yokel. And yokels got no rights. Even black guys got more rights than you. Isn't that so, Blue?"

Blue nodded, and Hunkins winced as if too much noise were running into his ears. "Fuck you all," he said.

"What did you say?"

Hunkins staggered back, his lightweight cap falling off. He did not pick it up. "I'm not scared!"

They watched him leap into his cruiser and speed off, the vehicle skewing to one side of the road and then to the other before it got on course. Blodgett said, "First he loses his piece, now his cap."

"I think we did it wrong," Blue said.

"What'd we do wrong?"

Blue picked up the cap. "I think he's cracking up."

———

Christopher Wade helped Mrs. Matchett clear the supper table, his insistence. "I never helped my wife do it," he explained. "Sometimes I wasn't even there for supper. So I guess I'm feeling guilt."

"You mustn't feel guilt," Mrs. Matchett said, her violet eyes jetting up at him. "All of us are too vitally human to be dragged down by it, though some of us let it happen. Don't you, Chris."

He smiled.

She smiled wider. "The Lord loves those who love themselves."

"You're sweet," he said, nearly meaning it.

"I always have been. You can ask Joe."

In the kitchen he helped her load the dishwasher. She seemed to have in stock every appliance and device imaginable, from the latest microwave oven to a glittering array of Japanese knives advertised on television and available only through toll-free telephone orders. She ran a hand across one of the knives. "They're not as nice as they lead you to believe."

"Things seldom are."

"How long have you been separated from your wife, Chris?"

"I think from the day we married."

"But you have children, you said. You got together for that."

"That's always easy."

"Do you miss her, Chris?"

"Now more than ever, though I'm growing philosophical about it."

"Starting right this minute," Mrs. Matchett said, her voice charmingly low, "you'll always have Joe and me. I want you to know that."

He soon joined the senator in the room where they had talked privately. The senator, back on the brandy, was sitting with his feet up on an ottoman and staring out at the beach, where shadows were lengthening. "It was nice of you to give her a hand," he said, his voice and mood mellow. "And, please, help yourself to the brandy."

Wade poured only a little, diluted it with ice, and sat down with a glance at his watch. "I'd better be leaving soon," he said, and the senator threw him a distressed look.

"We were hoping you'd stay the night. In fact, we've planned on it. A bed's already been made up for you."

"It wouldn't look right."

"Who'd know?"

"You can never tell."

The senator sank a little deeper into his chair and shifted his sandaled feet on the ottoman, crossing them at the ankles. "I'm at a time of my life when things are especially good. I hope they're good for you too, Chris."

"I can't complain."

"We owe it to ourselves to be comfortable. To be healthy of body and happy of heart. That's what's important, not power, though God knows I have it. But I'm not interested in it. I'm interested in a glass of brandy, and the way my feet feel when I stretch my toes, and the way I react when my wife whispers in my ear. What interests you, Chris?"

"I guess those same things, more or less."

"I'm glad to hear that, because life's short, no matter what your age is. You've been to high school reunions. You know what the talk is? *Who's gone.*"

"I hope you're not getting morbid, dear," Mrs. Matchett chided as she slipped into the room, her frosted hair arranged a little differently, in a manner that made her seem a shade more matronly. She peered at the brandy bottle. "He's not going to fall asleep on us, is he, Chris?"

The senator stretched an arm out for his wife's hand and gave it a small squeeze. "I thought we might entertain Chris with one of Tony's tapes, though I wouldn't want him to take it the wrong way. Some people get a little uptight."

"I don't think Chris will," Mrs. Matchett said confidently, with a brief look at Wade, as if an understanding had passed between them in the kitchen.

The room went dark as Mrs. Matchett lowered the blinds over the glass panels, shutting out the ocean and the world. From another part of the room she unraveled a wall screen and activated a videocassette. Then she floated toward a chair closer to Wade than to her husband and dropped into it, drawing up her legs and curving them under her. On the screen appeared the images of deep-waisted women and muscular men.

"Say the word," said the senator, "and I'll turn it off."

"No," said Wade. "I'm interested."

"Gardella won't watch his own stuff," the senator said with a snort. "Thinks it's disgusting."

From the depths of her chair, Mrs. Matchett said, "I think it's cute."

The senator had seen it before and, with reedy laughs, anticipated scenes. "This is good . . . watch this . . . she's terrific." On the screen a young woman, naked and vivid, parted herself, first in private, then with others. "She's the best," the senator whispered with evident excitement, as if caught up in a moving experience, deep-felt, indelible.

"What they won't think of next," Mrs. Matchett murmured after a prolonged silence.

"Shhh," the senator said, and his eyes stayed glued to the screen until the tape ran out. Then his head dropped back as if from exertion. Mrs. Matchett rose quietly in the gloom and took the empty brandy glass from his hand and stroked his hair, which did not in the least disturb him.

"He's such a dear."

Wade also rose and was amazed at how quickly sleep had absorbed the senator.

"He's a kind and thoughtful man, Chris. He's hard-fisted with money, but I've never wanted for anything. Neither have the children. We have one at Harvard, you know."

Wade leaned against his chair, waiting for the proper moment to leave. She approached him with short steps and stood close, as if she wanted to touch his face.

"Aren't you staying?" she asked, and he shook his head. "Maybe that's for the best," she said. "We trust you, Chris. Maybe we shouldn't, but we do. Don't ever deceive us. Promise?"

Wade, with a twinge, promised.

———

A light showed from the house, but somehow he knew she was not inside. Leaving the Camaro on the side of the road, he walked around to the patio, and her voice wafted out of the dark. "Why are you bothering me again, Lieutenant?"

He made out only an edge of her face and the tip of her fine nose. A cool draft from the ocean bathed him as he inched toward where she was sitting. "I didn't plan to," he said.

"But here you are."

"I was visiting the Matchetts."

"That must've been fun."

He let that slide. He could see more of her now, the shine of her fair hair, the length of one arm, like a smooth flow of water. Her hand cupped a cigarette, which he knew was not an ordinary one. "May I sit down?" he asked.

"For a while. But don't come near me."

He felt for a chair and dropped into one. "How's your foot?"

"Fine."

"Obviously you didn't mention everything to your husband."

"What should I have told him? That you gave me a little peck on the mouth?"

"It was more than that to me."

She did not finish the joint. She flipped it into the dark, and they sat in silence. The silence grew, mixing with the restlessness of the ocean and threatening to drown them. She said, "Why are you trying to make me? It's really stupid of you."

"Why is it stupid?"

"Answer that yourself."

He felt inside his sports jacket for his Beretta, simply to reassure himself that it was there. "I'll admit your husband scares me," he said, "but he should scare you more. No matter how you cut him, there's a dirty streak."

"You see him one way, I see him another." Through the dark she made a present of her smile, a vacant one. "What I see is an old-world *magnifico*. Do you know what the word means?"

"I can guess, but does it apply?"

"Oh, yes," she said and went quiet as if from a proliferation of feelings too difficult to deal with.

He said, "Are you expecting him?"

"What if I say yes?"

"I'll leave."

"I'm expecting him."

"You're lying."

"But you don't know that for sure—and do you know why you don't know for sure? Because you don't know me."

She walked him to his car, headlights from the boulevard sweeping over them, paralyzing their features. They avoided each other's eyes. She looked at the Camaro. "It doesn't seem like your kind of car."

"Sometimes I don't feel like my kind of man—whatever the Christ that is."

He walked around to the other side of the car and climbed in quickly because of the traffic. Then he rooted for keys as she peered in at him from the passenger side, her face a pool in the square opening of the window. "Do me a favor," she said quietly.

"Name it."

"Tell Thurston he's giving me too much to deal with. Tell him he's an obscene son of a bitch."

Wade stared at her as if his ears didn't belong to him.

She said, "Goodnight, Sweetheart."

20

THE MAN Victor Scandura approached in the plaza in Copley Square was slick-haired and moon-faced and wore a tropical suit wrinkled from the heat and the concrete ledge he had been sitting on until he stood up to scratch his behind. His name was Deckler, and his car, which bore New York plates, was parked nearby. Scandura said to him, "Got anything yet?"

"I got four guys on him," Deckler said. "You know why four? I respect him. He's smart."

"Maybe you should have eight guys. We're paying enough." Scandura glanced around. People were sunning themselves near the spray of the fountain: youths with their shirts off, businessmen with their ties loosened, women with their skirts hiked up. Scandura said, "When can we expect results?"

"Maybe never. Like you were told, no guarantees."

"But what's your feeling?"

"Thurston's a funny guy, very private. I knew him when I was a narc. Did him a favor."

"Small world," said Scandura.

"Smaller than you think." Deckler grinned. "I was in the army with your boss. Haven't seen him since. I always thought our paths would cross, but they never did."

"Now they have."

"Yeah, now they have. You tell him, okay?"

Scandura told him a half hour later in the real estate office. Anthony Gardella had the television on and was watching the noon news. He listened to Scandura without removing his eyes from the pretty anchorwoman, though his expression altered subtly, disappointment replacing nostalgia.

"You never know how people are going to turn out, do you Victor?"

"Maybe I did the wrong thing."

"No," said Gardella. "I think the guy will come through for me."

———

Russell Thurston, lunching with agents Blodgett and Blue in the cafeteria in the Kennedy Building, laid a clipping on the table, *Miami Herald,* the day before's date. "We lost him," he said in a reproving tone. Blodgett read the clipping first, slowly, and then Blue did, quickly. "We had him, you know that," Thurston said. "All we had to do was find him."

"We didn't figure him for Florida," Blodgett said defensively, "not this time of year."

"We could've squeezed him dry," Thurston said angrily. "Gardella knew that. He found him first."

Blodgett, rereading the clip, said, "Overdose. That's what they think it was."

Blue said, "The girl was only fourteen."

Thurston had a dish of garden salad before him, nothing else. He explored it with his fork and said, "We've still got Hunkins. Or have we? You two tell me."

Blodgett said confidently, "I think he'll jump into our lap, just a matter of time."

"And what do you think?" Thurston asked Blue.

"He's going to do something. I don't know what."

"Okay. Put more pressure on him."

"Blue thinks he'll snap," Blodgett said.

Blue said, "I think he's already snapped."

———

Deputy Superintendent Scatamacchia left his office in the Area D station in the South End and, with an occasional eye in the rearview, drove several blocks to a dry cleaning shop, where he placed a bet on a horse named Laura's Boy. "I got a good feeling about this animal," he told the bookie and left with a smile. On his way into Dorchester he glanced in the mirror and saw a car leap ahead of another. That was when he suspected he was being followed.

He left his car in an alley, skirted the rear of a derelict tenement house, and entered a small cinderblock building by the back door. The place was a private social club. The only people at the bar were two off-duty firemen talking baseball. He sat at a wall table, and the waitress took her time coming over to him. She was red-haired and green-eyed and the mother of seven. "How you doing?" he asked and glided a hand beneath her bottom.

"You get away with murder, d'you know that?" she said sullenly.

"What's the matter, you mad?"

"You haven't shown your face here in a month."

"I've been busy."

"I can imagine. You want a beer?"

"I want a beer," he said, "and I want a frank, lots of mustard. Any sauerkraut? Put some of that in too."

When she returned with his order, she sat down with him. The frank was sloppy with mustard. The bun was loaded with sauerkraut. With a minimum of bites he finished it off while she smoked a cigarette.

"How's your hubby?" he asked, in need of a napkin, which she pushed at him.

"Find him a job," she said. "That would do a whole hell of a lot for me."

"I could find him twenty jobs, he wouldn't keep one of 'em. He's a lush."

"Don't remind me."

"I'll send him a note. Where does he take his mail? Detox center?"

"Don't be nasty."

He downed his beer and used another napkin. "You busy?"

"Doesn't look that way," she said with a shrug, and he grinned.

"You want to?"

"It's up to you."

They got up from the table, moved to the rear, and climbed the stairs to a narrow room that contained a neatly made-up army cot. A Currier and Ives adorned one wall, Norman Rockwell another. He looked at his watch and said, "I haven't got that much time."

She kicked off her shoes, skinned away her white pantyhose, and lay on the cot. Her toenails were painted pink, and he traced a finger over them, his only frivolity. He didn't make love to her; he jackhammered her. Afterward, she was slow to get up and even slower to make herself decent.

"How was it?" he asked, getting himself together.

"I wish the hell you wouldn't ask me that each and every time. One of these days I'm going to tell you and end a perfectly good friendship."

"Friendship, hell," he said. "C'mere."

She stepped forward, and he tucked a twenty-dollar bill into her frayed bra.

With an added sense of himself, he left the club by

the same door he had come in. In the harsh, bright
sunlight his step turned cautious, and he scanned
every window of the abandoned tenement house before passing it. He entered the alley from a different
direction, falling into a semicrouch, knowing the obvious spot where anyone might be waiting for him.
The man had his back to him, but he recognized him
at once.

"You fucker," he said.

Officer Hunkins twisted around with a .38 revolver in his hand but never got a chance to fire it.
Scatamacchia shot him with his own weapon, the
magnum.

———

Rita O'Dea was a surprise visitor to the real estate
office. She nodded to Victor Scandura, who was
sitting with his glasses off, and gave her brother a
heavy, wet kiss half on his mouth, which embarrassed him. She had on a flouncy yellow sundress
and a lacquered straw hat. She took the hat off and
dropped it on her brother's desk. "Would you mind,
Victor? I'd like to talk to Tony in private."

Scandura did not move until he got the signal,
almost imperceptible, from Anthony Gardella, who
then viewed his sister with infinite patience. She drew
up a chair and sat in it with her large legs crossed.

"Do I look happy, Tony? I know I do. I'll tell you
why in a minute. First I want to talk business," she
announced, and he regarded her warily. "I was talking to Rizzo," she said. "He tells me you're not going
to sell G&B."

"I was thinking of it," Gardella said in a casual
manner, "but the heat's off it now. And Rizzo's negotiated some pretty big contracts. Better we keep it."

"Tony, G&B's my company, isn't it? I mean, mostly
mine. You said it was."

"It is," he said. "I just make sure things go right."

Her face came forward. "Tony, I'd like to run it straight from now on."

"We run it straight, we don't stay in business. You know that, or at least I thought you did. What's the matter, Rita?"

"I want to know where we're dumping the waste now."

His eyes rested carefully upon her. "A place way up in New Hampshire, so far up the people only speak French, but they understand dollars. They lead our trucks into woods with dirt roads that come out to gravel pits. That's where we unload the poison, hurts nobody."

"People up there drink out of wells, Tony."

"Not where we dump. Nobody lives anywhere near it."

She shook her head. "The stuff doesn't just stay in the ground. It travels."

"Nobody's dying up there."

"Not yet." Her eyes clouded. "Kids are dying of cancer in Woburn. You must've seen it on TV."

"Woburn's got nothing to do with me. You come in here saying you're happy and then hit me with this. You want to explain?"

"It's simple," she said in a voice charged with a sense of occasion, celebration. "I'm concerned about children, little babies. I'm going to have one." His stare was disbelieving, his silence somber. "Actually Sara Dillon's having it," she explained, "but it's going to be mine."

He was no longer looking at her. He spun a pencil around on his desk, as if from a need to gain time. He straightened slips of paper filled with figures.

"Tony, I deserve it."

"There could be trouble."

"There won't be. I swear."

"Can I talk you out of it?"

"Tony, please!"

Something in her voice made him lift his eyes. He got up from his chair and held his arms out to her.

When Russell Thurston returned to his office from the cafeteria, he found Christopher Wade waiting for him. Wade was leaning against a spare desk, a large envelope under his arm, and staring straight at a wall. "I'll take that," Thurston said, freeing the envelope, which contained a report of Wade's activities and a tape of his meeting with Senator Matchett. "I should've had this at nine o'clock."

"I slept late. Very late."

"And you should've sent Danley or Dane over with it. You're bending the rules."

"I didn't know we went by any," Wade said, and followed Thurston into the cubicle, closing the door behind him. Thurston gave him a backward look.

"Do we have something to discuss?"

"Jane Gardella," Wade said, poising himself behind a chair and gripping the top of it, as if for support. His breathing was barely detectable. "Tell me about her."

Thurston carefully read Wade's face and leisurely seated himself. "I can see you know. She told you. I figured she would in time."

"Why didn't you tell me?"

"Maybe it amused me not to." Thurston reached behind for an accordion-pleated file folder. "Would you like to read about her? Her code name's Honey."

"I want *you* to tell me."

"You do, do you? Your arms are shaking. Why?"

"You really don't want to know," Wade said grimly.

"Okay," Thurston said. "You relax. You sit down."

Wade stayed as he was, his eyes squarely on Thurston. He seemed to be seeing the man for the first time, as if before he'd been only a voice.

"We recruited her when she was Jane Denig and a flight attendant working the Florida run and Gardella was a regular passenger. That was the year he was setting up his Florida operation with his cousin Sal Nardozza. It was also the year he lost his wife. I heard he cried like a baby. That surprised me. I didn't know those people felt things like us. Anyway, he was a lonely man, and Honey was—is, of course—a good-looking woman. I suppose you could call her beautiful. Would you call her beautiful, Wade?"

"Yes," said Wade, "I'd call her beautiful."

"Gardella was interested in her, we saw that right away. He always went out of his way to talk to her. She had something going with her pilot boyfriend, a guy named Charlie, up to his ears in debt. They used to hide dope on the plane, run it up to Boston. We knew all this, you see, but Gardella didn't. I talked the narcs into busting them and then letting me have them. It worked perfectly. I mean, what could go wrong? You want me to continue?"

"Yes," Wade said. "Continue."

"My proposition to her was her boyfriend would walk and she'd work for me, nurture Gardella's interest, get something going. Do you know what my code name was during all this? Cupid!" The word popped out of Thurston's mouth like a cork from a bottle. He seemed delighted with himself. "When she first told me he wanted to marry her, I didn't believe it. I thought she had flipped out. But they were in love with each other, can you imagine that?"

"Yes," Wade said. "I can imagine it."

"There was a while I didn't know which way she'd go. A couple of times she went hysterical on me, threatened to blow it all. The possibility of a crisis," Thurston recalled with excitement, "was constant."

"I get the impression you liked it."

"Loved it. No sense lying to a smart fellow like you."

"It's blood sport. If Gardella ever finds out, he'll kill her. He won't have a choice."

"Nobody's safe in this world. If a car doesn't get you, cancer will."

Wade's stare was stony. "I don't want her to die."

"Of course you don't. It'd be a shame if she did, so we'll all do what we can to prevent it."

"I'm going to protect her."

"You protect her all you want, so long as you don't tip your hand. I've worked too hard on this to watch Gardella walk away."

"Then I'd better warn you, I've got feelings for her."

"You think I don't know that?" There was a flatness in Thurston's smile, a deadness in the way he sat at his desk. "You've got a muscle in your pants, why shouldn't she arouse you?"

"It's more than that."

Thurston flexed his jaw before he spoke. "I don't doubt it for a minute. And I appreciate the irony of it, but I'm busy." He made a movement toward papers on his desk. "See you later, Wade.

"I've a feeling," said Wade, "we might see each other in hell."

Two police officers arrived in a beat-up van. The one driving quietly backed it into the alley, stopping a few feet away from Deputy Superintendent Scatamacchia's unmarked car. They hopped out quickly and yanked open the rear doors of the van. Scatamacchia flung open the trunk of his car, in which lay the body of Officer Hunkins.

"Get rid of it. I don't care where or how, but get rid of it."

The two officers, struggling, lifted the body out and deposited it in the back of the van. Swiftly they shut the doors.

Scatamacchia said, "His car's around the corner. Get rid of that too—take it to a chop shop."

Twenty minutes later he swerved off the central artery and left his car on Commercial Street. Passing tourists and children with balloons, he hiked to the end of one of the wharves and, when no one was looking, reluctantly dropped the magnum into Boston Harbor.

When he returned to his office in the Area D station, he picked up the phone and called the bookie at the dry cleaning shop. "How'd Laura's Boy do?" he asked.

"You're a lucky son of a bitch, Scat. It paid twelve to one."

"It ain't luck," Scatamacchia said. "It's instinct."

21

INSIDE A CAMBRIDGE HEALTH CLUB, Russell Thurston came off the handball court breathing hard, sweating profusely, and scowling. He grabbed a bottle of spring water out of his locker and took a long swig. His opponent, a rangy young man who had beaten him decisively, said, "You don't like to lose, do you?"

"That's exactly right," Thurston said, putting the bottle back and pulling off his sodden T-shirt. "It's not my style."

"It's just a game."

"That's what makes it so important," Thurston said cryptically. "Give me another couple of days, I'll beat you."

The young man grinned. "Want to put money on it?"

"You could lose, kid."

"I'm faster."

"I've got better reflexes," Thurston said and looked at the young man squarely. "You're a Harvard boy, aren't you? You've got the world by the balls. I hope you realize it."

"You make me want to apologize."

"You'd be a jerk if you did. Just learn when and how to squeeze, you'll never go wrong."

They pattered into the shower room. A woman in

a white smock looked in on them and smiled. Thurston asked her whether she had towels, and she brought in two. "Either of you going to want me later?" she asked, and the young man shook his head.

Thurston said, "Probably."

Moments later he bent his head under a hot needle spray, as hot as he could bear, to the point where he felt afire. Then, gradually, while lifting his face, he cooled it. By the time he dropped his hand from the dial, the water was ice-cold, and he was benumbed.

"How the hell can you do that?" the young man asked.

"You have to be special."

The woman in the smock was waiting in an adjoining room. Without a word, he stretched out on a padded table for a body rub. She oiled her palms and went to work. "You've got nice muscles," she said professionally, "almost as nice as the kid's."

"When I was his age," Thurston murmured, "you couldn't have compared us."

"Jesus," she quipped. "You must've been Superman."

He disdained to reply.

When she finished she slipped a pillow under his head and he closed his eyes. "Wake me in twenty minutes," he said.

————

Ty O'Dea took a taxi home. The driver had to wake him. He responded at once, blue eyes popping out of a scarlet face, and paid the fare with a balled-up bill. He walked precisely up the brick path and swung his arms just so. As he was searching for his key, the front door flew open and Sara Dillon pulled him inside. Her mouth quivered. "Damn it, Ty. Don't do this to me!"

"I'm all right," he said. "I'm perfectly all right."

"No, you're not," she said, gripping his arm. "You're loaded. How can we talk?"

"What are we supposed to talk about?"

"Her. Us." She shut the door and pushed him deeper into the house. "The baby. She's not getting it."

"Shhh," he said, his eyes rolling.

"It's all right, we're alone," she said, but he was not totally convinced. Apprehensively, he looked one way and then another, as if expecting Rita O'Dea to pounce upon them. Sara Dillon said, "You have a decision to make."

"I've already decided." He gathered up one of her hands in his and kissed it. "I love you. The baby's ours."

"What's talking Ty? The booze or you?"

"Me."

"Then we'll pack up and leave now. Just leave."

"It's not that easy," he said sadly, "believe me."

"Then what do we do?"

"I have a plan," he said, and seemed to shudder. "Let me work it out."

———

The day turned hot, temperatures creeping well into the nineties, the humidity oppressive. Christopher Wade stayed in his air-conditioned office in the Saltonstall Building. He read newspapers, *Sports Illustrated*, and two-thirds of a spy novel about a professional assassin who didn't know whether he was working for the CIA or for a confederation of American corporations. The telephone rang periodically, once at length, but he never answered it. Mid-afternoon, he went into his inner office and napped for an hour on his sleeping bag. He woke when he heard agents Danley and Dane banging out reports that were not for him but for Thurston. When one of them looked in on him, he said, "Put in your report that you found your boss sleeping."

After they left he washed his face in the sink and slicked his hair back with wet hands. He did not quite know what to do with himself. He considered leaving for the day but did not want to face the heat. He returned to the novel and identified with the protagonist. As he was ending a chapter, the outer door opened and a woman walked in. It was his wife.

"I tried phoning, but there was no answer," she said as he rose to greet her. She was wearing a simple shirtdress, a part of it damp. "Don't you even have a secretary?" she asked, and he shook his head. Her eyes roamed. "This doesn't seem like your place. It doesn't seem . . . worked in."

He drew a chair for her, but she did not want to sit. She had come to tell him something and wanted to do it fast. He was not sure he wanted to hear it.

"I'd like to sell the house, Chris. Do you mind?"

He minded very much, but his expression did not change. "Where will you live?" he asked, his eyes dwelling on her. She was distant, enigmatic, no longer someone he knew.

"I'd like to get away for a while," she said. "Probably California. It'll be a whole new world for me," she added, and he felt a growing chill.

"How will you support yourself?"

"No matter where I go, I'll find a job, Chris. I know that much about myself now."

"You're a whole new woman."

"Not quite."

"Why do you want to leave?"

"You're still too much of a shadow over me, Chris. What you do—and I don't even know what it is anymore—comes at me."

"I don't know what you mean by that."

"It's not important," she said, standing inflexible. They gazed at each other without expression.

"Is it really necessary to sell the house?" he asked, and she nodded. "I suppose," he said, lowering his voice, "you want a divorce."

"When you feel up to it."

He looked away, his forehead wrinkling. "Please, do me a favor."

"What is it, Chris?"

"Get out," he said softly.

————

She walked out into the swelter, the heat of the city rushing at her. With a light head and a stunning sense of freedom, she floated into the crowd, found it congenial, allowed it to dictate her direction, which was to the plaza of the Kennedy Building. At first she did not recognize the black man coming toward her. He was wearing dark glasses and had his suitcoat slung over his shoulder. They jostled each other. The impact was slight.

"I know you," she said. "You were baby-sitting me."

"You knew," he said without surprise, his face shining from a patina of sweat. People slid looks at them in passing. She nodded.

"I called the Wellesley police when I was sure you were watching my house. They told me not to worry about it. They said you were keeping an eye on the neighborhood, to prevent break-ins. That made me feel safe, even though I knew it was a lie."

"Why did you think I was there?" he asked.

"Something to do with my husband. Maybe somebody was trying to get at him through me. I've been a cop's wife for a long time, you see. Or maybe I'm reading this all wrong. Who are you?"

"I'm a special agent, FBI."

Her face darkened. "Is my husband in trouble?" she asked, and Agent Blue immediately shook his head. "We're separated," she said, "but I still worry about him."

"I understand," Blue said. The crowd pushed them closer. Two teenage girls shuffling by in sandals stopped abruptly to peer at him for a second, as if they thought he might be a celebrity of sorts, a singer or a comic.

Susan Wade said, "Will you let me take you to dinner? I don't feel like going home and eating alone."

He looked down at his shoes.

"I'm sorry," she said quickly, "I should've asked if you're married."

"Yes," he said, meeting her gaze. "I am."

"Your wife could come too. That would be nice." She paused, aware of her own growing embarrassment. "No . . . I guess she wouldn't understand."

"I think she would," Blue said and offered his arm.

————

The sun vanished, but the air was still stifling. In the North End people sat on kitchen chairs placed in front of buildings and fanned themselves. Anthony Gardella, leaving his real estate office, spoke to people he knew, which was nearly everybody. A woman smiled at him proudly. She was sitting with a fat, bald-headed baby who looked like a miniature masseur. The baby, wearing only a diaper, had an unsightly rash, which did not prevent Gardella from petting the child's head. The woman said, "That was terrible about Augie."

"Yes, it was terrible," he said and turned a censorious eye on a passing dark-haired girl whose underpants, patterned with daisies, blossomed through her tight, thin shorts. It was the woman's niece. "Tell her," he said, "if she leaves the neighborhood that way she won't be safe."

He crossed the street, spoke to others, and entered the Caffè Pompei. A table in the rear was cleaned off for him, and a glass of lime juice topped with crushed ice was soon served. Cigarette smoke spiraled at him, and he asked the man at the next table to reposition his ashtray. Instead, the man ground the cigarette. Halfway through his drink he sensed a movement beside him and glanced up sharply. "What are you doing here?"

"I've got a right."

"Sure you do," he said as Christopher Wade sat down. "I'm just surprised." He gestured to a waiter. "Usually I'd recommend a cappuccino, but on a night like—"

"What you have looks good," Wade said, and the waiter brought him one. He wrapped his hands around the glass as if to cool them.

"That's a nice ring you've got," Gardella said. "I meant to mention it before."

Wade looked at it, seemed to study it. "Emerald, my birthstone. My wife gave it to me years ago."

"Okay, Wade, what's the story? We got a problem?"

"No."

"Something you want to tell me or ask me?"

"I don't think so."

"I see," Gardella said dryly. "You dropped in for nothing."

"I didn't feel like going to my apartment. No air conditioning."

"I'll tell you your problem," Gardella said. "It's what I told you a long time ago. No guy should live alone. You live alone, you don't eat right, you don't make your bed, you don't pick up after yourself. Pretty soon you start looking seedy. You want to know something? Right now you look seedy."

"It's the heat."

"It's going to be hotter tomorrow and stay that way through the week. I'm beating it. I'm leaving for Rye tomorrow afternoon. You're smart, you'll come with me. You could use a few days' rest."

Wade was silent for some time. He was wearing a body microphone and a tape recorder beneath his clothes. For a giddy second he considered opening his shirt and exposing them. "You're sure I wouldn't be in the way?"

Gardella laughed. "That happens, I'll tell you."

———

Russell Thurston left his car in the dark off Dewey Square and walked to South Station, whose grandeur was now confined to its Ionic columns and its weathered eagle perched atop the building. Inside, vagrants momentarily got in his way, shuffling toward him like gray ghosts and then drifting off, as if they could tell from his face that he was not the sort to give. The floor of the concourse was cracked and grimy. Merchants' booths were boarded up, some for the night, some forever. People waiting for Amtrak trains were few. Thurston looked for a woman wearing a headscarf and saw her right away. Dropping down beside her on the bench, he said, "Do I know you?"

"You will," she said in the same slow and forced voice that she had used much earlier on the telephone. Her voice had intrigued him, along with what she had to say.

He said, "What's the matter with your face?"

"My jaw was broken. I still have some wire in it."

"I still don't know your name."

"Laura will do."

He scrutinized her carefully, openly, from the polish on her mouth to the pumps on her feet. He estimated the cost of her clothes, the rings on her fingers, and the bracelet on her incredibly thin wrist. Her scent was subtle, which also told him something. "You look too intelligent for the business you're in," he said.

"You don't know what business I'm in."

"Do you want me to tell you?"

She retreated from his stare by gazing off toward a section of the station where marble had been sledge-hammered away, as if in a burst of energy from a workman without purpose. An Amtrak patrolman, finishing off a candy bar, tossed the wrapper into the rubble. She said, "Are you ready to listen?"

"That's why I'm here."

She talked without looking at him, in her labored voice, which had soft breaks in it, sudden catches, at odd times a wheeze. Her mouth began to look sore, then her whole face. "Rest if you want," he said, but she continued talking. When she finished, he again scrutinized her, this time as if she were someone much more valuable. He said, "This is bigger than just Scatamacchia, you understand that. If you give me him, you've got to give Scandura too, maybe even Gardella."

"No," she said, "you take what I give you or nothing."

"We'll work something out," he said. "We'll do it slow and easy, okay?"

"There's a condition," she stated flatly. "When you arrest him, I want to be there. I want him to see me."

Thurston's smile was instantaneous. "You know something, Laura? I could learn to like you."

Christopher Wade left the Caffè Pompei and returned to the deserted Saltonstall Building, where a security guard let him in and walked him to the elevator. When he learned that Wade was staying the night, he joked with him. "What have you got up there, a bed?"

"No," said Wade. "A bag."

In his office, after giving a quick look at his watch, he plucked up the phone, pressed numbers, and held the receiver hard against his ear. He counted the rings. When Jane Gardella picked up on the fifth, he said, "This is Sweetheart." There was silence. He said, "Your husband's joining you tomorrow."

"Why are you telling me something I already know? Why are you even calling?"

"I'll be there too."

"No," she said. "I don't want you up here."

"You can't stop me."

"I'll leave."

"No, you can't do that either."

"Why can't I?"

"You need me," he said.

———

The body, meant to rest forever in the bed of the river, wriggled free of its weights, floated serenely to the surface, and drifted with the current. Two boys fishing for hornpout and dragging up nothing but eels spotted it in the moonlight. The river was the Shawsheen in Andover.

Local police were presently at the scene and, using poles, coaxed the body out of the sedge where it had settled and guided it to shore, where they stretched it out on the bank. A state trooper, who just arrived from the Andover barracks, bent over it with a flashlight and illuminated the face. "He couldn't have been in the water long," he opined. The mosquitoes were brutal. Swatting at them with his free hand, he flashed the light on the sodden shirt and said, "That looks like a bullet wound, what d'you think?"

An Andover policeman, who had never seen a bullet wound before, said, "Could be."

The trooper, a corporal named Denton, returned the light to the face. "I used to be stationed in Lee," he said. "I swear, there's a cop in Greenwood looks just like this guy."

22

CHRISTOPHER WADE AND ANTHONY GARDELLA walked over wet flats of sand, leaving behind squishy footprints. Gardella had the wider foot. Wade had the longer one, the lighter one. He was unencumbered, unwired, at ease for the present. He had packed brilliant swim trunks and was wearing them, along with a loose and open short-sleeved shirt to protect his shoulders from the sun. Gardella, bare-chested, darker-skinned, didn't worry about the rays. He said, "How are you doing?"

"Enjoying," Wade replied, his eye glancing over people they came upon, a mother doling out sandwiches from a basket, a girl improving her tan.

"Good," said Gardella. "I want you to relax."

"Any special reason?"

"Does there have to be one?"

"Sometimes it helps."

Gardella veered away and waded into the surf, dipping a hand into the water to bless himself and then hurling himself headfirst into the onslaught of a wave. Stripping off his shirt, Wade followed but was slow to plunge in. The current around his legs was frigid. It was only when he saw Gardella watching him that he doused his face and challenged a wave. When they came out of the water, Gardella said, "I could live here."

"You've mentioned it."

"Year round. Forever." Gardella gave Wade a sideways look of irony. "But I could be kidding myself."

"People do that." Wade, still wet, put his shirt back on. Gardella flexed his arms, letting the sun dry him.

"Since my first wife died, maybe I've been kidding myself a lot."

"Meaning?"

"I'm thinking out loud, Wade. Pay no attention."

They walked on, past children using shovels and pails. Gulls, which had arrayed themselves on the beach as if for a charge, scattered reluctantly but soon regrouped, like tactical geniuses.

Gardella said, "My boys were little, they couldn't wait for summer to come here. They knew every inch of the beach. Then they got older, you couldn't drag them here. How do you figure that?"

"Typical, I guess."

"My oldest son, the marine, he's too cocky for his own good. He got promoted and demoted in the same week. Two black guys in the mess hall gave him a hard time, and he went at them both. Could've got himself killed. But I don't worry about him. He's tough. It's Tommy I think about—you met him, the tender one. His mother always thought I'd be hard on him because of the way he is, but the truth is I favor him."

"What's the matter with him?'

"Nothing," said Gardella darkly. "Nothing you'd notice."

When they returned to the house, Jane Gardella began preparing a small meal for the three of them. She set a table on the patio, laying out cornflower-blue napkins to complement the color of the crockery. She looked especially leggy in an overlarge sweatshirt that covered her shorts. Slipping an arm around her, Gardella drew her close and smiled at Wade. "Don't you think I'm lucky?" he said with something ambiguous in his voice that caused Wade to look away.

"I hope you like crabmeat," Jane Gardella said quickly to Wade.

The table was slightly unsteady and trembled throughout the meal, the conversation guided by Gardella, who kept it casual, interesting, at times witty. Bantering about Ronald Reagan, he said, "I finally figured out what he's really got against the Russians. They're there." He told a joke. "What's endless love?" he asked, and answered, "Ray Charles and Stevie Wonder playing tennis." He nodded to his wife. "I'll have some more bread." She passed the plate, eyes lowered.

When the meal was over, Wade excused himself. He was out of cigarettes, he said, and was going to Philbrick's to buy some. Gardella said, "Pick me up a paper."

Outside Philbrick's, he counted his change and telephoned Thurston, reaching him after a short delay. "In case you're wondering," he said, "I'm in Rye. I'll be here for a few days."

"Good for you," Thurston said. "While you're there ask Gardella why he wasted Hunkins."

Wade went cold in the heat. "What are you talking about?"

"Get yourself a newspaper. You can read about it." Thurston seemed in a strangely good mood, which chilled Wade even more. Listen, I'm glad I've got you on the line. I want you to think back to the first time you went to Gardella's place in Rye. You had dinner. He had a woman there for you. Called herself Laura."

"I gave you a full report."

"Now I've got questions."

Agents Danley and Dane drove Laura thirty miles out of the city to a Holiday Inn, where they checked her in under a fictitious name and checked themselves into the unit next to hers. Dane took his shoes off and stretched out on one of the beds to watch television. Danley went next door to see how she was doing. She was undressing. "Next time knock, for Christ's sake!" she said and snatched up her robe.

"I'm sorry," said Danley. "I thought you might be hungry. If you don't like the food here, I can go out for something."

"I can't chew. All I can have is soup or something soft."

"You tell me what you want, I'll get it."

"What I want to know is how long I'll be here."

"You have to ask the boss that. Could be a while. But anything you want, all you have to do is ask. Those are his orders."

She said, "I want Deputy Superintendent Scatamacchia's balls on a platter."

Danley, blushing a little, said, "Yes, ma'am."

"But nobody else's. I don't think your boss understands that yet."

"Yes, ma'am," he said, reaching for the door. "I'll pass that on to him."

"One other thing," she said. "Don't patronize me."

Sara Dillon, standing on the landing, could hear Rita O'Dea's voice in the room being converted to a nursery. "I want pretty things on the wall, lots of bright colors. Babies, soon as they can see, notice those things." Rita O'Dea's voice was fluting, breathy, aggressive. She was instructing an interior decorator, who had arrived with a flourish but had wilted fast. "Mobiles we want, right? And the furniture's going to be white. I like white."

Sara Dillon heard a sound on the stairs behind her and turned to see Alvaro, who was also listening. He said, "I bet you wonder about us. Me and Rita."

"No, I don't wonder at all."

"In bed, I mean. It's an experience, I'll tell you."

"I'm not interested."

His eyes traveled over her. "You're getting big in the belly," he said and passed a hand over it.

"Don't do that."

"My mother was pregnant, she always let us kids touch her. Feel. Listen. Put our ear right there. She said it was a miracle."

"It is," Sara Dillon said, "but I'm not your mother."

"My mother used to show her tits. Used to shake 'em at us. At the time it made me sick. Now all I do is think about it."

"I'm sorry," she said. "I can't help you."

"I'd pay you."

"Go away, Alvaro," she said with a throb of discomfort. Her legs were swollen and her back was bothering her. For a moment her eyes failed to focus.

"Go ahead, fall," he said. "I'll catch you." She reached for the rail. He said, "You were my lady, you'd still be getting your lovin', believe me."

"If I were your lady, I wouldn't have a future."

From the room came Rita O'Dea's voice, sharply pitched. "Who's out there? That you, Sara? Come in here, I want your advice on something."

"She's crazy, you know," he said.

"No," said Sara Dillon, looking at him a little sadly. "She's as sane as you are.

———

In his office at the Area D station, Deputy Superintendent Scatamacchia had stripped off his uniform shirt and was sitting at his desk in a coarse gray T-shirt, the sort athletes wear. At his elbow was a half-consumed can of Pepsi. He was about to turn the page of the police newsletter he was reading when he sensed eyes upon him. A man was peering in from the open doorway.

"Remember me?" Russell Thurston asked. Behind him was Agent Blodgett. "We were in the neighborhood, thought we'd drop in."

"Yeah, I remember. Fed with a smart mouth. You came here to see me, too bad. I got no time for you."

Thurston raised a hand and exhibited a space between forefinger and thumb. "This thick, we've got a file on you."

"You guys got files on everybody, like the fuckin' Gestapo. All you got against me are the vowels in my name."

Thurston smiled with unlimited confidence. "I've got plenty on you. In a week, maybe two, I give it to the U.S. Attorney, and he passes it to a grand jury. In the meantime, my friend, you sweat."

"You're fuckin' crazy," Scatamacchia said with a degree of discomposure.

"You know why I'm taking my time? I want to make sure everything I got on you is perfect, airtight. When that happens, there'll be somebody wanting you to look at her, but it's me you'll be seeing. *Me*, Scatamacchia. You'll come on your knees and ask to deal."

Upsetting the Pepsi can, Scatamacchia rose from his desk and stood with a deadly stillness. "I'd stick my face in a bucket of shit first."

"You'll do that too," Thurston said. "Then you'll give me Gardella."

Leaving the station, passing ranking police officials, who regarded them warily, Blodgett said, "Maybe you shouldn't have warned him."

"It's the best thing I could have done," Thurston said.

———

Anthony Gardella and his wife were in the sauna, wrapped in vapors, their bodies moist-to-wet, when Christopher Wade rapped tentatively on the door. "Come on in," Gardella said cavalierly through a cupped hand. "Jane's not bashful." She shot him a look of surprise and distress.

"Stop it, Tony." She grabbed a towel and twisted it around herself. He stayed naked. "Why are you doing this to me?"

"Doing what?" he asked in a tone of innocence as her eyes lunged at him through the steam.

"The way you've been acting toward me. It's different."

"I wasn't aware of it. Sorry." He called out, "Hold up, I think she is bashful. You'll have to wait."

"I don't want to come in," Wade said. "I just want to know how long you'll be in there."

"Why?"

"Something's come up."

"You want to talk to me?"

"Yes."

Five minutes later they walked down to the surf, where a young couple were frisking in the waves, the boy splashing, the girl squealing. Wade had a suburban newspaper under his arm. He unfolded the paper and passed it to Gardella, pointing to a headline. Gardella, squinting as dark clouds shortened the day, read only two paragraphs and said, "I swear to God, I know nothing about it."

"I don't believe you."

"I lie when I have to, I never think twice about it. This time there's no need. That's the truth, Wade."

"But you know something."

"No, nothing, but I can make guesses."

"What are they?"

"They're not for your ears." Gardella slapped the paper back into Wade's hands. Wade looked at the young couple in the water. They had quieted down, as if the clouds had tempered their mood. The girl was floating on her back, hair awash. Gardella, also looking, said tightly, "Why do they do that?"

"What?"

"Show their stuff." Gardella reached out. "Give me the paper back. I'm going to take it with me."

"Where are you going?"

"Boston. I won't be back until late tonight, maybe not until early tomorrow. Depends."

"I'll leave too."

"You don't have to."

"Then I'll stay," Wade said.

———

Gardella sped from Rye through thunder and lightning but no rain and arrived in the North End within the hour, slipping out of the air-conditioned Cadillac into the savage heat of the street. He phoned Victor Scandura from the Caffè Pompei, waited for him at a table, and shoved the newspaper at him when he arrived. "Why didn't I hear from you right away on this?" he asked in anger, watching Scandura quietly place the paper to one side.

"I'm sorry. I was tied up most of the day at Mass. General."

"What were you doing there?"

"My stomach, Anthony. You know."

"You okay?"

"Yeah." The waiter came, and Scandura asked for milk and got it.

Gardella said, "Was it Scat?"

"Yeah."

"That fucking fool," Gardella said in a whisper. Scandura drank the milk, which gave him a creamy mustache.

"He said he didn't have a choice. You know I don't particularly like Scatamacchia, but I believe him on this. Too bad the body came up."

"He did it right, it wouldn't have. Otherwise, was it clean?"

"He says so."

Gardella propped an elbow on the table and rubbed his brow against the heel of his hand as if he had a headache. "What are we going to do?"

"I don't know what we can do, Anthony. I guess just let it lie."

Gardella lifted his face and stared at a table of tourists, the children spooning up spumoni, the mother wiping mouths. "Would you like to be young again, Victor? Have everything to do over?"

"I don't know," Scandura said. "I don't think about it."

"Give me some good news, Victor. Make me happy."

"The thing in Florida is better than ever. The new guy knows his stuff."

"How about the people in Providence? They happy with their cut?"

"It's fair, Anthony, they gave us the guy. We shouldn't begrudge them."

"I don't begrudge anybody anything. Everybody should be happy. Rich. Have nice children."

"You okay, Anthony?"

"Sure I'm okay. I was not okay, I'd be home in bed, thermometer in my mouth. You're the one doesn't look so hot. Go home, Victor. Sorry I dragged you out.

Scandura stood up, his face gray, his eyes small behind the spectacles. He wanted to leave. "How about you? You going back to the beach?"

"I got more business to do," Gardella said.

———

At the health club in Cambridge, members gravitated to the handball court to watch the match, which almost looked as if it were being waged for blood. The play was furious, the ball a blur ricocheting off walls and ceiling. Bets were made. The woman who gave rubdowns said, "The older guy's going to win, you watch."

Russell Thurston made an impossible return and said, "You can't beat me, kid. I'm on a roll." He had lost the first game after playing out a tie but was winning the second with demon energy and uncanny moves. It was no contest. In the middle of the final game he turned an ankle and lamed himself, but he continued to play and continued to win, exhausting his opponent.

"I don't believe this," the young man gasped.

"Believe it," Thurston said and executed an unreturnable serve.

As they left the court, Thurston limping, they were applauded. In the locker room the young man said, "Will you take a check?"

"No checks," Thurston said, inspecting his ankle. "Make it dinner."

The young man hovered. "I just want to know. How'd you do it?"

"Willpower," said Thurston.

———

"Something's different between us," Jane Gardella said from a high-back deck chair on the patio. The clouds had long passed, and the beach lay refulgent in the moonlight, seeming limitless in its stretch. The air was sea-drenched. "I don't know what it is," she said in a hollow tone, as though something had died deep down inside her. Christopher Wade, from his chair, peered at her.

"Maybe you're imagining it."

"Maybe," she said, "he knows."

"No," Wade said immediately. "We wouldn't be sitting here."

Her eyes were hard upon him, an eerie smile passing across her lips. "He likes you, you know. Doesn't that bother you?"

"Yes," said Wade, "it bothers me."

"But not enough," she said, and he did not reply. She tightened her hands on the arms of the chair. "He loves me, but I don't kid myself. It's a narrow love, no room for the unexpected. All of this is bizarre, isn't it, Wade? If only it could be unreal too." Her unnatural smile returned. "I wonder if he feels it sometimes, the knife in his back."

"Why don't we talk about something else?"

"There's nothing else to talk about." She drew herself forward and sat erect, her blond hair quivering in the light breeze. "Would you like to go for a swim, Lieutenant. Would that please you?"

He shook his head.

She said, "Do you mind if I do? I have a small thought of swimming beyond the buoys."

He looked up with alarm. "Are you joking?"

"Fantasizing."

He reached over the side of his chair for her hand. She gave it impassively and sat quietly with her private uninfringeable thoughts. He found the silence haunting, as if a physical part of her had drifted off. He said, "Maybe I can help you."

"Why should I trust you? And what could you do? Nothing. Thurston is everything." She pulled her hand away and forced herself from the chair. When she raised her arms over her head to tie her hair, he felt entrusted with an intimate moment.

"You need me."

"That's for me to decide," she said and kicked off her sandals. "I'm going for that swim."

"Don't do anything foolish," he said.

———

Agent Blue was returning to his apartment building from the drugstore when a voice called to him from the dark of a car. A man climbed out the driver's side and came onto the sidewalk where Blue could see his face in the lamplight.

"Do you know who I am?" Anthony Gardella asked.

"Sure I know who you are," Blue said.

"Do you know my wife?"

"Personally? No, I don't know your wife."

"But you've got pictures of her."

Blue smiled. "We've got lots of pictures of her, all on your arm, mostly coming out of restaurants. You live well."

"I'm talking about the pictures in your desk."

"I've got none in my desk. What are you talking about?"

After a long hesitation Gardella whispered, "I should've known better."

Blue threw him a curious look. His mind moved fast, but he spoke slowly. "I think I get it. Something my boss said?"

"Yeah, something Thurston said."

"You're right," Blue said. "You should've known better."

———

There was a TV in the room, and Wade was watching it. He lay atop the bed in his undershorts, one arm crooked under his head. He could hear the occasional sound of traffic but nothing of the ocean. The room was on the boulevard side of the house. There was a knock on the door, and Jane Gardella looked in on him. When he reached to cover himself, she said, "I'm not embarrassed."

She advanced into the room, letting the door close behind her. "Is that wise?" he asked.

She said, "Tony wears the same kind. They don't keep him in either."

She stood with her head tilted and rose up on her toes as if to keep her feet from sticking to the hardwood floor. The wrap she wore was damp and clung to her.

"You want me, don't you?" she said.

"Of course I want you," he replied, "but the question is whether you want me."

"No," she said, "that's not the question." She looked at the television. "What are you watching?"

"Nothing."

She switched it off, which put the room in darkness. He tried to keep sight of her, but she paled away. Then he felt her settling beside him, relapsing on her side. "Who am I?" she murmured. "I'm not sure I know."

"Honey," he said as she lengthened herself. "You're Honey."

The traffic on the boulevard grew more intense for a time, or perhaps they merely became more aware of it, the danger. At one point a number of motorcyclists thundered by, some shrieking, as if a few crazies were among them. Then a quiet settled, as if the hour dictated it.

"What if he walks in on us?" Wade asked, lying

skin to skin with her, a part of him drying on her. His hand curved and slid over her.

"Then we die," she whispered. "It will solve everything."

The fear he felt was vital but did not make him move. "You'd rather have him think you betrayed him this way than the other?"

She did not move either, her drawn knees still pressed under him, her silence her answer.

———

Anthony Gardella did not return to Rye until the morning. On his way into the house he saw Wade on the beach and waved. In the master bedroom, treading on quiet feet, he approached his wife, drew the sheet from her shoulders, and gently raked his fingernails down her long, bare back, giving her a chill.

"Wake up," he whispered.

"I am awake," she said, not moving, her eyes open.

"I'm sorry," he said softly into her ear. "Sorry about a lot of things." His hand slipped into the small of her back. "Sometimes I'm such an idiot."

She spoke into the pillow. "Why are you saying that, Tony?"

"Sometime when we're lying together on the beach I'll tell you," he said and straightened up. She lifted her eyes. He was undressing, smiling. He winked at her. "You have to go to the bathroom, go now."

"Why?"

"I'm going to make love to you," he said, and she began to cry.

Two hours later, eating breakfast on the patio, he said to Wade, "I'll tell you something, I'm fifty years old, and I still don't understand women."

23

DECKLER, the private detective from New York, waited in the car while the two men working for him went into the attractive brick apartment building where Russell Thurston lived. The man who lived alone in the apartment next to Thurston's was an electrical engineer twice divorced and deep in debt from court orders requiring him to support two families. It was his bell that the two detectives rang from the foyer and his door they went to. He let them in after they flashed identification, Internal Revenue Service. He suspected the identification was false but didn't care. They were offering him five thousand dollars for the use of his apartment for a week, with the provision that he would keep the entire amount if they vacated the place sooner, which they said might well happen. Having presumed he would agree, they had booked a room for him at the Colonnade, the tab prepaid.

"Jesus," the man said. "As long as what you're up to is legal."

It was, they assured him and helped him pack.

"I don't want to get into any trouble."

"You won't."

Deckler climbed out of the car and unlocked the trunk when he saw the man drive away. In the trunk were suitcases of special equipment, which he and his two assistants carried up to the apartment. When they began sorting things, he wandered into the kitchenette, poked about, and, though he would have preferred something better than bologna, made himself a sandwich. Eating it, he went into the bedroom, where his assistants were waiting. A dresser had been pushed away from the wall. He picked up the bedside telephone, tapped out Thurston's home number, and after many rings hung up.

"Okay," he said, "start drilling."

———————

Outside the State House a hand dropped down on Senator Matchett's shoulder and a voice said, "That's a nice tan you've got, Senator." The senator spun around with an automatic smile that slipped when he saw who it was.

"Ah," he said, as if he needed to jar his memory to put a name to the face.

Russell Thurston said, "This heat wave won't quit. You should've stayed at the beach."

"Can't abandon my duties," the senator said jauntily and felt his arm being taken, the grip surprisingly firm, almost frightening.

"Can we talk?"

"Now? Right now? I've got a vote to cast." He struggled in protest but felt himself being guided out of the sun, toward the shade of the building, to a rail, which he clutched.

"Listen to me, Senator, I don't have time to waste, and neither do you. I have friends with the New Hampshire state police. In twenty minutes, if I make a phone call, troopers will raid your place in Rye, grab all the pornographic material, and book your wife. I have a buddy at Channel Nine in Manchester who'll have a cameraman there."

The senator went red with pure anger. "You're a lunatic."

"I know the stuff is there, enough to charge your wife with possession with intent to distribute. You've got quite a collection. There'll also be a warrant out on you, of course." Thurston quietly cleared his throat. "By the way, I have you both on tape, not for evidence, simply for my own amusement. Lieutenant Wade gave it to me."

The senator stood firm, though one hand twitched. "Nothing will hold. Everything will be thrown out of court."

"What do I care?" said Thurston. "The damage will be done. No?"

"You bastard."

"Senator," Thurston went on smoothly, "I know Gardella washes money for you and at least a half dozen of your colleagues. I know he does it for a superior court judge, some people in the tax department, and a fair number of blue-blooded businessmen who more or less run this city. I'll tell you what else I know, Senator, they funnel the money through you, huge amounts, and you pass it to Gardella. You don't do it directly, but it gets to him. At the moment, Senator, I can't prove any of it, but it's only a matter of time."

"This is insane. I think I'd better talk to my lawyer."

"You walk away from me, Senator, and I'll make that call. When I do, don't hold me responsible for your wife's emotional stability. You know it better than I do. Also consider your own. It's your career and reputation that's going."

The senator's lips faltered, then closed. He did not crumble as Thurston thought he would, and he did not weep as Thurston had hoped. Finally, simply, he said, "It's my wife I'm thinking of."

"Naturally."

"What do you want?"

"Your cooperation."

"Who do you want?"

"Everybody." Thurston's smile was quick. "Except you of course. You walk."

"Immunity?"

"Better than that, Senator. We're going to let people think you were working for me all this time."

––––––––

On the beach Jane Gardella's bare foot accidentally touched Christopher Wade's, and she jerked hers away fast. "If you stay here much longer," she said, "I'm going to go insane."

"I need an excuse to leave."

"No, you don't."

They were sitting in low beach chairs near the surf. Anthony Gardella had left his chair and was swimming fearlessly in deep water, his stroke long and graceful, athletic. Wade said, "I'd rather stay."

"Are you doing this to be cruel?"

"You know I'm not," he said, unable to see her eyes. She was wearing a sun visor strapped to her head, and her face was lowered. She raised it to watch her husband.

"I love him," she said.

"I love you," Wade said, surprised by his own voice. "How's that for a complication?"

"I don't want you to love me. I don't even want Tony to love me. Do you know how scared I am?" She dropped her head back. "And how tired?"

"It doesn't show," Wade said. "Only when you're with me."

"I've told Thurston I can't go on, but he doesn't believe me . . . or doesn't care. Doesn't care is what it is."

"You've got to hold on."

"No, that's just it," she said. "I can't."

Gardella came out of the water tugging at his trunks, his silver hair flattened to his skull. Wade, waiting at the edge of the surf, tossed him a towel, which he caught and then almost dropped. He looked beyond Wade. "Where's Jane?"

"The sun was too much for her."

Vigorously he used the towel on his head, arms, and shoulders. Nearby a boy of thirteen or fourteen, golden-haired, was scraping a vulgarism into the wet sand and doing it deep so that the word would not soon be washed away. Gardella gave him a disappointed look and said, "Hey, kid, is that nice?"

The boy glanced up abruptly, threw away his stick, and, trotting off, said, "up your ass!"

Gardella and Wade exchanged tight smiles. Gardella's was the wryer. "Should I let him get away with that? Maybe I should put a contract out on him."

"At that age he can get away with anything."

"At that age," said Gardella, "I wouldn't have even thought of mouthing off to my elders. Everything was respect. That's the way I was brought up."

"That kid," said Wade, "will probably grow up to be a computer programmer or a junior executive or maybe a high school teacher. Look what you grew up to be."

Gardella laughed and slung the towel around his neck. "I see your point."

"For that matter," Wade said, "look what I grew up to be."

"Hey, take it easy. What I think is, there are worse than us, plenty worse. Come on. The sun's getting too much for me too."

They slipped their feet into sandals, left the beach,

and walked up the boulevard to Philbrick's store, where they sat at the fountain and smiled at the young woman working it. Gardella ordered a mocha milkshake, and Wade decided on the same. "And a hamburger," Gardella said, "if you don't mind." Wade followed suit. When their orders came, they ate greedily and took their time drinking their shakes. Gardella, who had used up one napkin and was reaching for a second, said, "Enjoying yourself?"

"Yes," said Wade.

"So am I."

When they left the store, the sun seemed hotter and brighter. They walked along sluggishly, at times on grass, other times on gravel, and crossed the boulevard when there was a break in traffic. As they neared the house, Wade noticed an extra car in the drive. Gardella said, "We've got a surprise. My sister."

————

Agent Blodgett said, "The call came in about a half hour after you left; he wouldn't give his name, said he'd only talk to you, his terms. Could be a crank."

"You didn't recognize the voice at all?" Russell Thurston asked.

"No. I can play the tape for you if you want."

"I haven't got time. I'm dropping in on Quimby at Union Bank in an hour." Thurston looked at his watch and plucked up a newspaper. "I've got to go to the john. This guy calls back, tell him I'll meet him if he makes it close by."

Thurston returned in fifteen minutes with the paper turned to the crossword puzzle, which he had completed. Blodgett said, "He called. Wants you to meet him now. He sounded anxious as hell."

Again Thurston consulted his watch. "We're playing this close. Where is he?"

"He's right down in the lobby. One other thing. He sounded like he's had a few drinks."

"Shit, maybe we ought to forget it," Thurston said and thought about it. "You come with me. You never know what kind of nut you're going to run into."

In the elevator Thurston loaded his mouth with Certs and clicked them around. Blodgett lifted his revolver from the hidden holster inside his suitcoat and inspected the chamber. Thurston, watching, said, "If he is a nut, run that up his ass and pull the trigger."

Blodgett put the weapon away as the elevator settled and stepped out first when the doors wheezed open. As they neared the foyer, he nudged Thurston. "That must be him," he whispered, nodding at a man in a powder-blue sports jacket poised behind a potted tree as if to hide himself.

Thurston peered in that direction. "I think I know him."

"Who is he?"

"His name is Tyrone O'Dea."

————

Anthony Gardella looked for Rita O'Dea in his house and found her and Sara Dillon on the patio, where his wife was pointing out places on the beach for them. Sara Dillon saw him first and lowered her eyes as he regarded her without surprise. She looked frazzled from her pregnancy and almost too old for it, especially beside the straight and sunny figure of his wife. Then his sister saw him and came at him with a bear hug that threatened to smother him. "Easy, Rita," he said, grappling with her moist flesh, "it's hot."

"Not here," she declared, releasing him gradually.

"It's beautiful. Boston's unbearable. That's why I brought Sara here. She doesn't believe me, but she can't take the heat. Look at her." Rita O'Dea, wearing a sundress that swished loosely as she moved, went to Sara Dillon and took her hand. "The drive didn't do you any good. You need a nap. Jane, show her to her room."

Gardella watched Sara Dillon leave without argument, with what was probably relief, his wife gently guiding her. With a slow turn to his sister, he said, "I don't think she wants to be here."

"I know what's best," Rita O'Dea said.

"No," he said abstractedly, "you only know what makes you feel good."

"You scolding me, Tony?"

He placed a caring hand on her. "That's something I never did enough of. Too late now."

She gazed past him. He turned to look too. Christopher Wade had come quietly onto the patio and was standing in a gauche manner, as if he felt he were intruding.

"Rita, this is—"

"I know who he is," she said. In a paradoxically dainty way, she billowed toward Wade as if to gather him up, encompass him. Her face loomed. "My parents," she said haltingly. "I never thanked you for helping us." Her voice failing, she clasped Wade's hand and kissed it.

"Rita, don't!" Gardella said sharply. To Wade, he murmured, "I'm sorry."

"It's all right," Wade said. "I understand."

In a room papered in pink, Sara Dillon loosened the front of her maternity dress, one of several Rita O'Dea had chosen, and sat on the bed's edge to force off her shoes, a task, for her feet were swollen. She rubbed them. Jane Gardella, laying out towels for her, said, "We have a sauna. You might want to use it later."

Sara said, "I don't want to be a bother."

"And the ocean will do wonders for you," Jane added.

"Do you have a cigarette?"

Jane reached into the wide pocket of her beach jacket. "Only this."

"Can we share it?"

The door was closed. The smoke tinted the air and sweetened it. Jane sat on the opposite edge of the bed, a strain in her face, alert for any approaching sound. She crossed her slim legs.

Sara said, "You're very beautiful."

The joint meandered between them. "Yes, I've been told that."

"For an hour, or even only a minute, I'd like to be beautiful, simply to know how it feels."

"Sometimes it feels like shit," Jane said and, with feelings near combustion, stretched her face into a semblance of a smile. "I don't sound beautiful, do I?"

"You're troubled. I felt it as soon as I saw you. Rita did too.

"Fuck Rita."

Sara took a slow hit on the joint and savored it. "You shouldn't discount her," she said in a vague warning that she herself did not understand. The bed began to look good to her as she viewed it out of an intense paleness and a fatigue she was fighting.

Jane, watching her, said, "How does it feel to be pregnant?"

"Crowded. Cramped. Rearranged."

"I meant mentally."

"Responsible."

"Have you asked yourself whether it's worth it?"

Sara prepared to lie back. "I'd be afraid of the answer."

———

Anthony Gardella and his sister plodded along the wet edge of the beach, their bare feet sand-caked. Rita O'Dea's hair, unloosed, flowed down the expanse of her back. At times she clung to her brother's arm, proud to be seen with him as other women looked up from under their umbrellas or over their magazines. Her voice rose. "I brought banana cake, Tony. It's on the kitchen table."

"Thank you," he said.

"And I put a pint of cream in the fridge. I told Jane to whip it up for tonight."

"Don't tell her to do things, Rita. *Ask* her."

"Don't jump all over me," she protested in a girlish tone and let go of his arm. "Jane and I get along fine. We always have. Though today . . . well, I don't know. What's the matter with her, Tony?"

He stopped in his tracks, annoyed. "Nothing's the matter with her. Don't start imagining things."

"All right, I'll shut up," she said and, hiking her sundress above her large white knees, ventured into the water. She let the tide lick her toes and swell against her shins. She looked back at him and said, "It's cold, too cold, but good."

"Rita, come here," he said, and she returned with short, splashing steps and heavy footprints. "Why didn't Ty come?"

"He didn't want to, and I didn't care. This is for Sara."

"What does she say about you taking the kid?"

"She doesn't talk about it, and I can understand why. In her heart she knows I can do more for it. Ty and me and the baby, that's the way it's going to be."

"Where does that leave Alvaro?"

"Back to handing out towels in Key Biscayne. I look at him, all I see is a leech."

"It s about time," Gardella said with a heavy sigh. "Now I've got something to tell you about the little prick."

———

Christopher Wade was waiting for her when she came out of the room, which gave her a start. "Don't do that," she said and tried to brush by him. He reached for her arm.

"You've been smoking. I can smell it in your hair and clothes."

"I'll wash. I'll change. Don't worry about me."

"I'm leaving," he said.

"Good," she said. "Have you told Tony?"

"He's on the beach with his sister. Tell him I didn't want to be in the way." He still had her arm, a gentle grip. "May I kiss you?"

"Sure, why not?"

The kiss was light, chaste, dry. He could have prolonged it, for she did not seem to care. He stepped away and said, "Things are going to work out."

"Sure," she said. "Like in the movies."

He wanted to get back to Boston fast but did not succeed. On Route 95, still in New Hampshire, the Camaro's radiator boiled over from a loose fan belt. He coasted into the breakdown lane and tried to repair the damage but merely burned his fingers and dirtied his sleeves. He flashed his shield and waved an arm, but nobody stopped. Between the time he hiked to a phone and watched a garageman replace the belt, the sun had vanished. By the time he reached Boston, it was nearly ten o'clock.

He drove through Boston and into Chestnut Hill, wasting more time looking for an address and overshooting the one he wanted. When he finally brought the Camaro to a rest, he dropped his head back, closed his eyes, and spent several minutes running things through his mind. Then he climbed out and— hungry, tired, and soiled—walked toward the apartment building where Russell Thurston lived.

24

RUSSELL THURSTON ushered Christopher Wade into the room he used as an office, shut the door sharply behind them, and turned on Wade with an angry flush. "Don't ever come here again, you hear! My privacy is sacrosanct." Wade silently looked for the chair that offered the most comfort and then simply chose the closest. Thurston stayed on his feet, his eyes burning. He was in shirt sleeves. The breast pocket bore his monogram in a staid stitch. "So what the hell do you want?"

"Out," Wade said. "Jane Gardella and I, we want out."

"*We*, is it?" Thurston said with an instant sneer. "Sweetheart and Honey. A pretty pair." He leaned a hip against the carved edge of his teak desk and crossed his arms. "The answer's no. No way."

"All right. I'll stay in, but pull her out. If you don't, she'll get herself killed. She'll let it happen, believe me."

"Excuse me for being truthful, Wade, but suicidal people bore me. Apparently they fascinate you."

"I'll get her out myself."

"You fool," Thurston said with what nearly amounted to sympathy. "I know her better than you do. It's Gardella she wants to save, not herself. I guessed that a long time ago."

"Then why are you still using her? She can't be giving you anything worthwhile."

Thurston smiled. "She tells me stuff she thinks won't hurt him that much. I use everything from everywhere, piece it all together. In the end it makes music. Beautiful music, Wade, lovely notes."

"You're proud of yourself, aren't you?"

"I should be. Everything's coming together, maybe even better than I expected. No, why be modest? I know my business." He was speaking deliberately, as if his words were lapidary. Then he pushed himself away from the desk. "You want a drink, Wade? I think you could use one."

Wade said nothing, and Thurston returned soon with a clear bottle of Arrow Peppermint Schnapps and tiny glasses. He poured with a smile, with contentment and satisfaction, and gave Wade a glass.

"Think about it," he said. "We've got no quarrel, really. We're professionals with jobs to do, and I do mine better than most."

Wade, whose eyes gave back nothing, said, "You and Gardella aren't much different in the way you do things, except I think I could trust him on some things and you on nothing."

"Well put," Thurston said with a laugh. "The wop has got to you, hasn't he? No surprise. They're a charming bunch, but let me tell you something." Thurston gestured with his schnapps. "They're a diminishing breed in what they do. They're not the power they were and never the power people thought they were. The Jews always outclassed them. The wops drew the heat, and the Jews sat in the shade skimming profits. Was there ever a wop like Meyer Lansky, a guy who lived to be Methuselah and spent most of his life under palm trees, Hallandale and Miami, wops waiting on him? Something else. Wops do hard time. Count on your fingers how many Jews do. Why are you smiling?"

"Who are you kidding? You're a hero-worshipper," Wade said softly. "Meyer Lansky isn't just a name to you. He's a deity. He still lives—right?—somewhere up in the sky. And you don't hate Italians. I think you've got a love affair with them, which is why you want Gardella so bad. You can taste him, can't you?"

"You've got a vicious mouth," Thurston said with a faint touch of respect, "but a small mind." He finished off his schnapps and poured another. "How about you?

"I'll stay with this."

"Don't try to outmaneuver me, Wade. What I've got going for me is God-given."

"You believe that?"

"Partly." Thurston looked as if he were having fun. "Let me tell you who I've got so far. I've got Deputy Superintendent Scatamacchia. You know who he is. He's mine now, I've got a ribbon around him. I've got that woman Laura. Now you know why I was asking. I've got the senator. Matchett. I'm turning that pervert into a crime-fighter, and afterward I might run him for governor. Imagine that, Wade, Commonwealth of Massachusetts could become mine."

Wade looked at him askance. "You serious?"

"Half. No, let's say three-quarters." Thurston was truly enjoying himself. "There's somebody else I've got. Didn't ask for him and didn't expect him. You ready?"

Wade made a lethargic movement. "I'm listening."

"I've got Tyrone O'Dea. He gave me things on Gardella's sister that go way back."

Wade lifted himself higher in his chair. "You're going to scoop up a lot of people, but will you get Gardella himself?"

"Come on," said Thurston with a patronizing smile. "You must know it doesn't matter. With Honey I've had him from the start. When he finds out the woman he married is a federal informer, a plant, I've destroyed him emotionally. And when the people in Providence hear about it, I've destroyed him professionally. What's left for him?"

"No choices," Wade said with a shudder.

"Exactly.".

"And where does it leave Honey?"

"Dead," said Thurston.

———

In the dim of the room Anthony Gardella rolled over in bed and shook his wife's shoulder. "Wake up," he said, and she did so with a jolt, fighting to free her arms from the covers, grimacing as if someone were restraining her. She blinked at him.

"What was I doing?"

"Talking in your sleep."

"What was I saying?"

"My name," he said. "You were shouting it. That's what woke me."

"I must have been dreaming," she said. "You were probably swimming out too far, and I was calling you back."

"A guy I knew, Chili Trignani, used to keep a tape recorder going by the bed in case his old lady said something. He thought she was seeing somebody, which she was, a shrink. Chili was driving her crazy. He also used to lift her dress when he came home, make sure she was wearing underpants."

Jane Gardella said, "I love you, Tony."

He raised an arm and let it fall over her. "I know that. I'd know if you didn't." He stroked her. "Funny thing is, Chili's wife was ugly as sin."

"Do my back, Tony."

He slid onto his side and kneaded the flesh between her shoulder blades. "How about your bum?"

"That too." She lay flat, still, legs loose. "Is it enough, Tony? The way I feel about you?"

"Have I ever asked for more?"

A curtain floated forward as salt air breezed into the room, and the sound of a sea bird cut through the night. Gardella fell back to sleep, a hand resting between her legs. She stayed awake.

———

A single light burned in Rita O'Dea's house in Hyde Park. The sole occupant was Ty O'Dea, who had been drinking heavily, which showed in his face, though he was not exactly drunk and not at all tired. Too much on edge to relax, he was sitting rigidly in a chair and watching television in what Rita O'Dea had recently started calling the family room. The solitude suited him but did not last. The sound of the front door opening jarred him. He heard lights being clicked on, the rough pitch of Alvaro's voice, and the sudden laugh of a woman. When she spoke he knew she was both Hispanic and young. He heard Alvaro direct her up the stairs. When Alvaro looked in on him he said, "You're crazy."

Alvaro grinned. "Rita's at the beach. What have I got to be worried about?"

"The chances you take, you're lucky you're alive."

"The time comes, you die. Not your time, you live. That's the way I figure things. I tried to explain that once to a guy I was going to snuff. He didn't understand either."

Ty O'Dea said, "Who's the woman?"

"A kid, real cute, just came up from Puerto Rico. In the morning I'll give her a hundred bucks, let her feel like a queen."

The woman's footsteps echoed across the ceiling. Ty O'Dea said quickly, "Not in Rita's room."

"Why not?" said Alvaro. "She knew, it would turn her on."

"You don't know Rita."

"I've screwed her a hundred times, I guess I know her."

His face full of heat, Ty O'Dea looked toward the television, an extravagant minidrama exalting mouthwash. Deep in his stomach he could feel a knot. Belching softly, he watched Alvaro advance into the room and draw near, a smirk growing, the collar of his open shirt spread over the collar of his colorful jacket.

"Got a bun on, huh?"

Ty O'Dea said nothing, his face scarlet, his soft hands twitching.

Alvaro said, "You've been acting funny lately. What've you been up to?"

"Get away from me."

Alvaro eyed him prankishly. "Maybe I oughta beat the shit out of you, find out what it is."

"You should've left when I first told you," Ty O'Dea said, blinking, a part of him numb. "You oughta go now, tonight, while she's away."

"I play everything to the end, how many times I got to tell you?"

"You're going to die," Ty O'Dea said.

"You fucking creep," said Alvaro. "Everybody dies."

———

At the door Russell Thurston said, "Be tough. And remember something, you and I, we're apart from other people. We keep society going. How we do it is our business. You got that?"

"Yes, I've got it."

"Say it so I'm convinced."

"I understand," Christopher Wade said with the barest frown.

"Good," Thurston said, "because I don't want to destroy you too.

25

THE HEAT WAVE was relentless. The midmorning sun over the city was red. Victor Scandura had bought buttered rolls at the bakery and was having them with coffee at Anthony Gardella's desk in the real estate office. The door to the room was closed to preserve the cool from the air conditioner, which was pumping to capacity. When the telephone rang he delicately wiped his fingers before answering it. The caller was Quimby from the Union Bank of Boston. "Anthony's away," Scandura said. "You want, I'll have him call you in a coupla days."

"You have him call me sooner," Quimby said in a rush. "You tell him something's going on. There are people nervous all over town. You tell him I have a federal agent breathing down my neck. You—"

"Listen to me for a minute," Scandura said stolidly. "Twice a month we have guys come in here, sweep the place electronically. But you can never be too careful. D'you know what I'm telling you?"

"Yes, I know what you're telling me. Do you know what I'm telling *you?*"

"I'll have Anthony call you.'

"You do that!"

Scandura cradled the phone and glanced at his watch. He did not want to bother Gardella too early. He finished what remained of the last roll and drained his coffee cup, craving a cigarette for the first time in years. He got up from the desk and went to the door when he heard somebody in the outer office. It was Deckler, the detective from New York.

"You got something?"

Deckler nodded. "I'll tell you something, I'm torn. After all, I used to be on the opposite side."

Scandura said, "I heard you were always on the fence, like you are now. What have you got?"

"I can't tell you. It's something Gardella's got to hear personally."

"Everything goes through me."

"Not this, believe me," said Deckler.

Scandura scrutinized the detective. "Can you tell me anything?"

"About Thurston? Yeah. The man's not normal."

———

Anthony Gardella was alone. His wife, his sister, and Sara Dillon were gone for the day, a cruise to the Isles of Shoals. He was sitting on the patio in his swim trunks, waiting. At the sound of a car in the drive, he went to the side of the house and beckoned to the man coming up the path. "Didn't take you long," he said.

"Scandura gives good directions," Deckler said and extended his hand. "Long time, Tony. I guess we've changed, huh?"

"Not really," said Gardella, "if you look hard."

"Imagine if we'd stayed in, we'd've come out generals."

"At least," said Gardella, leading him to the patio. Deckler had a large bulky envelope with him, which he rested in his lap when he sat down. Gardella poured drinks from a chilled bottle. "Cheers."

"Cheers," Deckler said and afterward smacked his lips. "Not bad. What is it?"

"An aperitif. Saint Raphael."

There was a ringing inside the house. Deckler said, "That your phone?"

"Forget it."

The envelope was offered up. "I wanted to give this to you personally. Didn't think it should go through Scandura."

"Victor's my right arm, my brother."

Deckler ignored that and said, "I also wanted to give you my bill. Look on the back of the envelope. It's written little up in the corner."

Gardella flipped the envelope over, read the pencil scratches, and lifted his hooded eyes. "I'm buying your services, not your agency."

"I think you'll pay it. You might hate me afterward, but you'll pay." Deckler gestured with his eyes. "There're pictures in there. Pull out one. One's enough."

Gardella opened the envelope and slid out a glossy eight-by-ten, which he examined carefully. He recognized the features of Russell Thurston.

"You like?"

"Yes, I like," Gardella said, pleased, "but this isn't worth what you're asking."

"There's a tape in there. Thurston had a special visitor last night. You're going to want to hear the conversation. That tape alone is worth what I'm charging, but there's more, which is the reason I didn't want to go through Scandura. It's too personal."

Gardella waited.

Deckler said, "When I was a narc I did Thurston a favor. It involved your wife."

———

Christopher Wade tried to reach Jane Gardella. He called the number in Rye with the intention of hanging up if her husband answered, but there was no answer at all. Later he tried again, with the same lack of results. He jammed the receiver down, looked around the office, and decided to leave. The place depressed him. Because he did not intend to return, he began gathering up things, his sleeping bag from the other room, his toilet gear from above the sink, his spare Beretta from the file cabinet. The thought of returning to his apartment also depressed him, but he could think of no other place to go.

The apartment was hot. The single air-conditioning unit failed to function, and he snapped on a little fan and sat in front of it, his shoes off, his shirt undone. He had had little sleep, which was the reason he couldn't keep his eyes open.

His wife woke him.

Standing over him cool and neat in a crepe shirtdress, Susan Wade said, "I was going to ring, but everything was open, even the downstairs door."

"They're not careful here," he said, surprised to see her, and rose from the chair, regretting he was not better dressed. She extracted what looked like a document from her white shoulder bag.

"The house goes on the market tomorrow," she said, "but the broker needs your signature too."

He looked at the paper, at the asking price. "That's three times what we paid for it."

"That was a million years ago, Chris."

"Yes, it was. Do you have a pen?" She produced a ballpoint bearing the logotype of Rodino Travel. He snarled his signature on the dotted line. When she started to speak, he put a finger to his lips and said, "Not here."

He led her into the bathroom.

With a confused smile, she said, "Thank you, Chris, but I don't have to tinkle."

"I'm nervous talking out there." He turned on a tap. "The place is bugged."

I'm not surprised," she said. "It's what I wanted to talk to you about. I've had dinner a couple of times with someone you know. A federal agent. Blue."

He gave her a close look. "How did you meet him?"

"That's not important. He told me what you're doing, this thing you're involved in. He told me to tell you to get out of it, right now. He said there's nobody you can trust, not even him." She touched his sleeve where it was rolled up. "I don't ever want to live with you again, Chris, but wherever I am, I want to know you're alive and well."

He smiled. "Are you saying I have a special place in your heart?"

"Yes, you do."

"Are you . . . involved with Blue?"

Now she smiled. "He's a handsome man, younger than I, excitingly black, but no, I'm not involved with him. The first time we had dinner I paid, the second time he did. And each time his wife was there. By the way, they have no secrets. They share everything, including the frustrations of their jobs. I think their marriage will work."

He watched her absently touch her hair and was moved. "You're still very attractive, Susan. You're going to find someone."

"I think so too, Chris, but it doesn't matter if I don't."

"Are you still planning to go to California?" he asked, and she nodded. "Taking your car?" Again she nodded. He opened the medicine cabinet. It was where he had stashed the spare Beretta. "Take this, please," he said. "If you're going to be driving alone across the country, you'll need some kind of protection."

"No," she said, "I wouldn't know how to use it."

"But I taught you. Remember?"

"No, Chris. You were always planning to teach me, but I was never a priority." She gently pushed his hand to one side and kissed him. "I'm on my own."

The women were back from their day at the Isles of Shoals. Jane Gardella, restless, went for a walk on the beach. She had asked her husband to accompany her, but in a quiet way he had begged off. A little later his sister went to Philbrick's to buy ice cream, which left him alone with Sara Dillon. Soundlessly he approached the door of her room and opened it. She had been in the sauna, and all she had on was a towel around her thick waist. Gardella stared at her bare back, which was marred by blemishes. Feeling his eyes, she looked over her shoulder.

"Don't I have privacy?"

"You have five minutes to get out of here," he said in a moderate tone of voice. "A taxi will be waiting. It'll take you to the Eastern terminal at Logan, and from there you take the first flight to Florida." He placed money on the dresser. "Don't ever let me see you again, even down there."

"What about Ty?" she asked, and Gardella looked at her icily.

"What about him?"

Jane Gardella came back from her walk in the diminishing sunlight and stepped onto the patio. Rita O'Dea, eating ice cream from a bowl, gave her a hard look. Her husband was standing motionless. When she started to drop into a chair, his hand shot out and gripped her for an instant.

"Let's go inside," he said. He had her lead the way. She went into the kitchen. When she turned around, he said, "Marriage, was it in the script?"

———————

Victor Scandura had a late visitor at the real estate office. He dropped his hand from the telephone, where he had been resting it, as if waiting for a ring. Looking up slowly, he said, Close the door. I'm trying to keep it cool in here."

Russell Thurston said jauntily, "You don't look surprised, just mad."

Scandura's spectacles were smudged. He took them off and wiped them. "I don't figure I deserve this. I was about to go eat."

"Must be a lot of things you can't eat," Thurston said and sat himself down. "I've got a medical report on you, and I'll tell you, that's some stomach you got. An ulcer like that can kill you."

"You've got no medical report on me."

"The hell I don't. That Negro agent of mine, you must have seen him around, his wife works at Mass. General. She sees records. She's seen yours.

Scandura put his spectacles back on. "You come here just to pull my chain or say something?"

"I came here to tell you people are talking in my ear. If I told you the names, they'd chill you. What it means is your boss is going down the tubes."

"Nice of you to tell me. I'll let him know."

"Scandura. Look at me, right in the eyes. *It's true.*"

"Excuse me. I got to wash my hands before I go eat." Scandura left his desk and went into the toilet. He bent over the sink and ran water. No paper towels were left. He blotted his hands on his pants. Thurston looked in on him with a big grin.

"You've never done hard time, Scandura. How

long do you think you'll last, you sick old thing? Do you want to deal?"

Scandura pushed the door shut.

———

Christopher Wade parked the Camaro on the boulevard. He turned off the motor and listened to it pulse down and spit heat. He had pushed it hard. The night sky over the ocean was thick with stars. There was not a single light showing from the house, which had a locked-up look. The only car in the drive was Jane Gardella's, which looked abandoned.

He tried anyway.

He catapulted out of the Camaro, loped across the boulevard, and raced up the drive to the front door. He almost expected to find a note for him tacked to the door. All he found was his ghostly reflection in the glass panel.

On the patio he stumbled over a bowl, a spoon rattling in it. On the table was a half-consumed bottle, warm to the touch, of Saint Raphael.

The terrible thought that weighed on him as he drove back to Boston was that he had no plan, no strategy, only a headache, which worsened when he sped over Mystic Tobin Bridge, lights popping at him one after the other. In the traffic in Hyde Park his foot shuddered from gas pedal to brake as he outmaneuvered a taxi discharging smoke. At Gardella's house he parked in front of the first stall of the lit garage. The loose face of Ralph Roselli loomed at him from the shadows.

"You don't have to knock," Roselli said. "Go right in."

26

CHRISTOPHER WADE stepped into the library and stood still as Ralph Roselli came up from behind and patted him down. "Look at this," Roselli said in a flat, impassive voice, "he's got two guns. Berettas. He's the fuckin' Lone Ranger."

"Let him keep one," Anthony Gardella said in a tone as stolid as Roselli's. Gardella and Victor Scandura were in leather chairs. The only light, muted, came from a single reading lamp turned to the wall.

Jane Gardella was sitting in a far corner of the room, in almost total darkness, as if her husband did not want to see her face. Wade, his eyes searching her out, said, "How are you?" She did not answer.

Gardella said, "Why do you care? She special to you?"

The silence had barbs in it.

Gardella turned in his chair and peered in the direction of his wife. "He special to you?" When there was no response Gardella looked back at Wade. "What d'you think of that? My own wife won't talk to me."

Wade said, "She'd never testify against you, you know that."

"You'd better sit down," Gardella said. "You look like you're shaking. Ralph, give him a chair."

"No, I'm fine."

297

"Forget the chair, Ralph. He says he's fine." Gardella reached down beside him, brought up the bulky envelope Deckler had given him, and withdrew a Sony cartridge, which he held up for Wade to see. "I figured you were a right guy, but now I've got to wonder." He startled Wade by snapping the cartridge in half, slivers of plastic flying up, a tape springing out. "That was you and Thurston talking."

"Then you know you're in trouble," Wade said and tried to make contact with Jane Gardella's eyes, but her face was lost in shadow. All he could see was one of her hands, the fingers spread. For a moment he wondered whether she was alive.

"You want to hurt him?" Gardella asked.

"What?"

"Thurston. You want to hurt him, I got a gift for you." He tossed the envelope at Wade, who caught it with surprising agility in one hand and stared at it. "Go ahead, open it," Gardella said. "Enjoy."

After a moment of struggle with the flap, Wade pulled out the photographs, slowly examined four or five, and then put them all back. He could feel not only Gardella's eyes on him but Scandura's as well.

Gardella said, "Now I've got a favor to ask."

"Name it," Wade said.

"No matter what happens to me, my sister walks. Nothing happens to her. I want your word."

Scandura stirred. "What d'you want to take his word for? What's it worth?"

"This is going to surprise you, Victor. But I think I know the man."

Wade said, "You've got my word."

"Good," Gardella said and looked away. "Now I've got to hurt you."

The night air was humid, and bugs swirled around their heads as they made their way from Gardella's house to his sister's. Wade and Jane Gardella were at the front of the line, with Ralph Roselli a step behind. Gardella and Scandura took up the rear. Jane Gardella had trouble with her balance, and twice Wade steadied her.

Gardella called out, "Hey, Ralph, tell them they want to hold hands, that's okay with me."

Scandura, in a whisper, said, "You're stretching this out, Anthony. We haven't got the time."

"I know what I'm doing, Victor."

Scandura also had trouble with his footing, stumbling over the grass, which was slippery. In a more urgent tone, he said, "You don't hit her, I'll have to."

"Is that the way it is?" Gardella said, unperturbed. "I guess you've been on the phone to Providence."

"What choice did I have, Anthony?"

"There are always choices," Gardella said firmly. "I'll handle this my way."

Inside his sister's house Gardella directed them to the basement door, and they descended the stairs in a single file, with Wade in the lead. The basement was carpeted and paneled and contained a game room, where Rita O'Dea was waiting for them. She looked at Wade with nothing to say, her face flat. Beneath a dart board Alvaro sat fettered to a chair, his head lolling. He was high on something.

"You know him?" Gardella asked.

"No," said Wade.

"Go close to him. Take a good look." As Wade stepped forward, Gardella held out his hand, and Roselli filled it with the spare Beretta. "All this time the little prick thinks I don't know who he is."

Wade turned around and with horror watched Gardella put the pistol to his wife's head. Jane Gardella stood frozen with her eyes wide open, staring at the dart board, the bull's-eye a cluster of feathers. Gardella said, "Do him for me, Wade. You do him, or I do her."

Wade gaped. "No."

Gardella said, "You've got your piece. Take it out."

Slowly, carefully, Wade reached inside his jacket and freed his pistol from the holster. Scandura and Ralph Roselli exchanged quick glances. Rita O'Dea's large face half smiled. "Don't force this," Wade said, and Alvaro smirked.

"Nobody's going to shoot me. It's not my time."

Gardella said, "You've got one second, Wade. And I'll tell you something. It doesn't matter to me."

Never before had Wade felt so bereft of choices, though in his heart of hearts he knew he would always wonder. The report of the Beretta was ear-shattering and the stench of cordite pervasive. The shot was on the money.

Jane Gardella clamped her hands over her eyes. Scandura lowered his. Ralph Roselli pulled a nickel-plated .32-caliber revolver from his pocket but was uncertain what to do. Rita O'Dea said, "Christ, he did it."

Gardella threw his wife at Wade. "Get out of here, both of you!"

"That ain't right," Scandura protested. "They've got to go too.

Gardella silenced him with a look and stayed Roselli with a shake of the head. "I still call the shots," he said.

27

THEY came to the real estate office to talk to him—the two men from Providence. Anthony Gardella said to one of them, "You oughta get some sun, for Christ's sake. You look like an albino."

The pale man smiled. "You said that the last time."

"Sign of age. I'm repeating myself."

The other man, wide-necked, eyes dead-looking in their pouches, said, "Shit's hittin' the fan, huh, Anthony? Lot of people gonna suffer, we hear."

"You don't need me to tell you about it. I guess Victor's taken care of that."

"He didn't have a choice. Raymond wanted to know."

"Always choices, my friend. Sometimes it's easier not to make any."

The pale man said, "We heard from Skeeter. He said the Dillon woman showed up, but your brother-in-law didn't."

"Feds have him, you know that."

"We just wanted to make sure you knew."

"Funny Skeeter called you guys," Gardella said. " 'Course he was always Raymond's eyes and ears down there, never really mine. Way it goes."

The wide-necked man said, "Never figured that about Scatamacchia. Goes to show you can never trust a cop. They don't know how to think."

With the hint of an edge, Gardella said, "You guys gonna be staying long?"

"We're leaving," said the pale man. "First we thought we'd get ourselves something to eat. Last time we saw you, we stopped off at this swell place in Amesbury. International menu. Tuesdays they give you Swiss stuff, Wednesdays it's Italian."

"You can get Italian anytime."

"Thursday is French. Friday's German. Saturday's best, they tell me. Hungarian."

Gardella looked at his hands, the manicured nails, the wedding ring he still wore. "I suppose you guys want me to go along with you."

"Our guest, Anthony."

"Who else is going?"

"Victor said he would."

Victor Scandura was already sitting in the car, which belonged to the Providence men, except it bore a Massachusetts plate, newly attached. Gardella joined him in the back seat. The Providence men climbed in front, the pale man behind the wheel. He said, "What's the best way out?"

Scandura said, "Straight ahead and take your first right."

On Route 95 the pale man drove with a light touch on the wheel at a moderately high speed. The car, a Mercury Cougar, smelled of an air-freshener. Twice Gardella twisted around to look out the rear window. The third time he said, "I think someone's following us."

"It's all right," Scandura said. "It's Ralph."

Gardella settled in the seat. Then slowly he reached over and touched Scandura's arm. "I want you to make sure Wade does right by Rita."

"If I can," Scandura said.

"What do you mean, if you can? I want you to do it."

Scandura nodded. A smile gradually grew on his face, and he said, "Thurston thinks I'm worried about an ulcer. Laugh's on him, Anthony. I got a fuckin' cancer."

Gardella let his head drop back and closed his eyes. When he wiped his brow, he felt his pulse race. Then terror touched him, swept over him. But it passed.

"Victor, you know what I read once?"

"What, Anthony?"

"Death is our ultimate revenge on those who fucking love us.

Christopher Wade's eye languished on Jane Gardella, who was asleep, charmingly so, as if posed. He woke her because he was worried. She had slept much too long, and he could not remember the last time she had eaten. She sat up and asked him the time. He told her. "Let me get you something to eat," he said, ready to pick up the phone.

"Later," she said.

"Or we could go out for something," he suggested.

"No, I don't much feel like doing that," she said and swung her legs over the side of the bed. "I think I'll take a shower."

"Yes, that's a good idea," he said at once, heartened, but he grew nervous when he watched her leg it into the bathroom and close the door. He grew more nervous when she locked it. They were in the Howard Johnson's Motor Lodge in Kenmore Square. It was where they had been living, chastely sharing a bed. He knew she had gone a little crazy since the night in Rita O'Dea's basement, but he was determined to nurse her back to normal.

Standing close to the bathroom door, he heard the flush of the john and in time the fast spray of the shower, which somewhat eased his mind. He went to the bed and tightened the sheets and straightened the blanket. When she came out of the bathroom his relief was immense.

"That was nice," she said. She had washed her hair, and he sat on the edge of the bed with her and helped her dry it with one of the towels she had carried out. He worked the towel slowly to prolong the process. "That feels good," she said. "Did Tony call?"

"No," Wade said. "Not yet."

"Turn on the TV. I like watching it."

The only thing he could tune in that was decent was a rerun of *The Rockford Files*. As he fiddled with buttons to capture the correct color he heard her climb back into bed. "When I'm home," he said, "I always watch this." When he turned around he saw that she had fallen back to sleep.

Rockford was just ending when someone rapped softly on the door. Wade got up from his chair, parted the curtain to peek through the window, and then opened the door quickly. It was Jane Gardella's mother.

"How is she today?" Mrs. Denig asked.

"Better," Wade lied.

Mrs. Denig looked beyond him and lowered her voice. "I don't want to wake her."

"You don't have to worry. You have to shake her to do that."

"If there's anything I can do . . ."

"I'll let you know."

"I'll take her back when she's well, but I can't take her this way."

"I understand. I'll look after her."

Mrs. Denig stepped toward the door and looked back at him. "Are you married, Lieutenant?"

"Yes," Wade said. "I am."

"Well, I guess there are worse things," she said and left.

———

Russell Thurston, jubilant over his success, celebrated by springing for dinner at a small and expensive French restaurant in Cambridge. Agents Blodgett and Blue arrived with him and Wade came later, soon after the waiter had uncorked the champagne. With a great smile, Thurston said, "Pour him a glass, Blue. We're going to drink to him whether he likes it or not.

Wade drew a chair and sat down. The toast was elaborate. The champagne made him a little sick. He said to Thurston, "I guess you're happy."

"You bet your ass I'm happy. There are so many indictments in the works I can't keep track of them. The U.S. Attorney's going out of his mind—with glee. Judges, pols, people from the Social Register, bankers—Christ, it's like *Who's Who in Massachusetts*. We've already alerted TV, radio, newspapers, and magazines."

"But you missed Gardella."

"Yeah, I missed him," Thurston said with a wink, "but his friends sure as hell didn't. Real professional. Single bullet in the back of the head." The waiter served soup, which included a bowl for Wade. It was onion. Thurston said, "I ordered for us all, didn't want to hold things up. *Boeuf roulade aux champignons.*" Thurston kissed his fingers. "The way they do it here is superb."

Wade looked down at his soup and poked his spoon through the lid of cheese. "What's happened with Rita O'Dea?"

"With her I couldn't wait. She's already been picked up. Tyrone O'Dea gave us enough on her to put her away for twenty years. We haven't told her yet about her brother. Afraid she might go nuts on us."

Wade glanced at Blue, who raised his linen napkin and wiped his mouth. Thurston nudged Blodgett.

"Eat your soup. Don't be bashful."

Wade said, "There's the matter of the money Gardella gave me."

"Yeah, I know. It's in Crédit Suisse in Geneva."

"It stays there. You guys can't touch it, and neither can I. Only my daughters can, in twenty long years."

Thurston picked up the wine list. "We'll talk about it later."

"Talk about it all you want," Wade said, "but that's the way it's going to be."

Thurston smiled patronizingly without looking up. Wade, who had come in with a large envelope and had propped it against his chair, now slipped it into Blue's lap.

"Take a look at what's inside," he murmured. "Then give it to your boss."

With relentless attention to the wine list, his brow furrowed, Thurston said, "I don't care for any of the reds. Do you mind if I choose a white?"

Blue, who had removed the photographs from the envelope, slowly lifted his eyes. "You sure you want to do this?" Without replying, Wade snatched up the first photo in the pile and, letting Blodgett glimpse it, dropped it beside Thurston's plate.

The reaction was delayed, the silence terrible.

Thurston would not touch the picture. He was rigid, colorless, suddenly spent. Blodgett did not know where to put his eyes, nor did Blue.

Wade said, "You're a fag. You play with young

men, boys. Doesn't bother me, but the Bureau won't like it."

"Get out of here," Thuston said, and Blodgett and Blue rose immediately and left gladly. To Wade, he said, "What do you want?"

"Rita O'Dea walks. That's the deal."

Thurston's dignity died hard. In a tone of superiority he said, "Who's calling your shots?"

"Gardella," Wade said. "From the grave."

Epilogue

Late that evening, alone in his apartment, Russell Thurston opened his door to a handsome, dark-haired youth who looked vaguely familiar. Thurston made a dispirited gesture and said, "Not tonight. I'm tired."

But the youth lingered in the doorway, eyes soulful, shoulders slightly slouched. Thurston gave him a longer look.

"Do I know you?"

"No, sir."

"But I've met you, right?"

The youth shrugged and mumbled that he was in town only for the evening and had to get back to the Cape. He had a job there. Thurston smiled.

College kid, huh? But not Harvard, I can tell. You're too neat. Too conscious of how you look. What college, kid?"

"Holy Cross."

"Wow, a Catholic." Thurston let him in and, at a portable bar, made two drinks, strong ones, stingers. For a second or so his head throbbed, images from the earlier part of the evening rushing back at him, but then he got hold of himself. Raising his glass, he said, "Win some, lose some, right, kid?"

The youth's smile seemed ungenerous, neutral at best. Thurston studied him but failed to place him, which intrigued him, the way certain sly crossword puzzles did.

"Sir, could I have another?"

Thurston took the youth's empty glass and turned his back on him "Life takes queer bounces kid. You gotta go with the bounce.

The youth opened his blazer and drew out a Beretta semiautomatic pistol, which he had found hidden in his father's library. "Yes, sir, you do," he said and fired.

About the Author

Andrew Coburn is a former crime reporter
and editor for *The Boston Globe* and the *Eagle-
Tribune* of Lawrence, Massachusetts. His previous
novels include *The Trespassers, The Babysitter,* and
Off Duty. He is married, with four children, and
lives in Andover, Massachusetts.